# BLACK ANNIS YEAR

## The Fair Folk of Mullarkey Book 1

Kim McDougall

Paperback ISBN: 978-1-990570-52-0
Hardcover ISBN: 978-1-990570-55-1
eBook ISBN: 978-1-990570-51-3

Version 2
FICTION / Fantasy / Fairy Tales
FICTION / Fantasy / Paranormal & Urban /Contemporary

# Author's Note

I took inspiration for Black Annis Year from many sources—music, art, personal experience and local flavor from my home town. Some of these sources appear in the book, such as the many references to Quebecois songs. Others were more for my reference. For instance, I created maps of Equinox Farm and the layout of Kiso House so that I knew where Elenna was going in each chapter. Finally, many of the animals you'll find in these pages are inspired by my own rescue adventures, and I have written about them in my blog over the years.

Visit The Fair Folk of Mullarkey page on my website (at KimMcDougall.com) if you're interested in book extras like the maps, playlists and animal-related articles.

Welcome to Mullarkey Mills. I hope you enjoy your stay.

For all those who have rescued an animal in need.

# Welcome to Mullarkey Mills

If you head north on Highway 148 out of Gatineau, Quebec, wind along the beautiful Outaouais River for about an hour, then turn right at the old gold mine and trek ten clicks into the forest, you'll come to a place unlike any other. Mullarkey Mills is an English speaking village nestled into a predominantly French province. It's a modern village that retains the flavor of its old Irish roots—a tight-knit community of diverse individuals.

Some might even call it quirky.

And really, Mullarkey Mills isn't much of a settlement, just a cluster of centennial farm houses with Auntie Clare's bakery and general store as its focus. Villagers can find anything from fresh pies to wine to cat food on Auntie Clare's shelves. During the short summer, a chip wagon parks beside the store and picnic tables are set up with bright umbrellas. Everyone agrees that *Frites Mullarkey* has the best poutine in all of the Pontiac Region.

The Pishogue Shop shares the same dusty parking lot and caters to those looking for more eclectic gifts than Auntie Clare provides—gem stones, dream catchers, smudge sticks and anything else a modern witch might need.

Across the street, tucked into a small park next to the bridge, two granite cenotaphs etched with the names of soldiers who perished during the great wars sit beside a decommissioned tank. In summers of old, children whose families cottaged along the Outaouais River would beg their parents to bring them to see the tank. Now, children would rather play with digital tanks and the village is much quieter for it.

If you turn right at this intersection, you'll cross a covered bridge with red peeling paint and the Bryce River. Following that road will eventually take you to Cedar Grove Inn, a hundred-year-old rambling hotel with a history of hauntings.

But if you turn left at Auntie Clare's and drive just a little ways up Mill Road, you'll find Equinox Rescue Ranch, home to three horses, one stubborn pig, two Mediterranean donkeys, three goats, four alpacas and the meanest llama this side of the Andes. Along with one retired guard dog and a clowder of barn cats.

Equinox Farm was once Jamie Nolan's pride and joy, until he drove his snowmobile into a tree. That was fourteen months and twelve days ago.

Now the farm belongs to his wife, and she has no idea how she's going to care for it.

This is the story of Elenna Kane, reluctant animal rescuer, scribbler, and wannabe spinner of tales. It is the story of the year she learned all about second chances from an old plow horse. It's also the year she discovered that fairies are real.

# SUMMER

*Sassy* is just a nice way of saying *nasty*. And Sassy the sorrel mare earned her name. She stood on the other side of the fence, hoofing the ground like a bull ready to charge and glared at Elenna, daring her to open the gate.

"Mean old horse," Elenna muttered under her breath. Sassy's ears flicked backward, never a good sign.

Elenna had a dilemma. She'd just lugged a wheelbarrow loaded with grain, hay, and jugs of water down the gravel path to the lower pasture. The wheelbarrow was heavy and the path steep. She'd nearly lost control of it twice. Now she had to wrangle the wheelbarrow into the pasture without Sassy escaping.

Of course, she could have avoided this complication if only she'd learned to drive the Honda ATV. That's how Jamie had always done it. He would open the gate and the machine would block Sassy's escape route. But Elenna had never felt the need to drive the ATV, and now she was stuck hauling a wheelbarrow. And facing off with the nasty horse—or the *sassy* horse.

She squinted into the morning sun. Sassy was still pacing along the fence. The rest of the little herd watched with placid attention. Sadie, the old Belgian draft horse, looked resigned. Shin Mei, the roan gelding hid behind her like a shy toddler. The two Mediterranean donkeys, Jude and Missy, stood in the shade of the run-in shed. From behind her, Elenna heard the alpacas bleating for their own breakfast.

Sassy ran along the fence, turned and bolted back to the gate. She let out a piercing whinny.

"Hold on!" Geez. You'd think she hadn't eaten in a week.

Elenna set down the wheelbarrow and reached for the gate. Technically, it wasn't really a gate, just a junction where she could safely unhook the electrified fence. She grabbed the plastic handles of the grounding wires, ready to unhook them, and paused.

Sassy stood five feet away. Her nostrils flared. Her tail rose.

"Don't you dare!" Elenna pointed a finger. Sassy blew out a huff.

They had this battle every morning. Somehow, Elenna had to open the gate, bring in the wheelbarrow and shut the gate, all while fending off the hungry mare. She didn't have enough arms for the job.

She unhooked the fence wires and gently laid them on the ground, then turned back to the wheelbarrow. Her body blocked the exit from the pastures and the precious food. Sassy whinnied in frustration.

Elenna hefted the handles of the wheelbarrow. Lugging hay, grain, and water built muscle and stamina. That's what she told herself. Every day. As she was trying to make herself believe it, a shadow passed over her. The wind of a hoof whooshed by, only inches from her head. She jumped backward, fell on her butt, and scrambled up to find…Sassy prancing on the grass. Outside the pasture.

"Did you just hurdle me? You bloody…horse!" The mare stood perfectly still, not impressed with Elenna's flimsy insult. "Get back into there!" Elenna pointed to the other two horses and the pair of donkeys watching from inside the pasture. Sadie munched grass with the air of a disappointed parent. Sassy pranced a few paces up the hill, toward the gravel path that led to the car park and eventually to the road.

"Sassy, get your butt back in here or you're not getting one bite of grain!"

Sassy scuttled another few feet up the path. She was proud to have pulled a fast one.

Now Elenna had another dilemma. She couldn't leave Sassy to wander around the farm. The knucklehead mare could run into the road. But she couldn't leave the buckets of grain unattended either. The donkeys would eat it all in seconds.

*Screw it.* She turned into the pasture, leaving the fence open and set the wheelbarrow down, then she started hooking grain buckets onto the fence hooks. Sadie and Shen Mei tucked into their feed.

Out in the yard, Sassy let out a nicker. She was just realizing that her act of defiance might cost her a breakfast. By the time Elenna finished setting out buckets for the donkeys, Sassy had trotted into the pasture. Elenna hid a smile.

*Gotcha at your own game, you sassy rascal.*

As Sassy stuck her nose in her bucket, Elenna dashed back to close the gate, thinking there had to be a better system to feed the beasts.

Jamie had never had a problem with Sassy. He'd been her savior and she would have followed him to the ends of the earth. Elenna didn't have any such claim on Sassy's affections or loyalty. If only she could drive the ATV. She knew she could learn, but since Jamie's death she had only barely managed to keep the animals fed. Anything else was simply too much to consider. Grief was exhausting. It sapped all her vitality and left her with the energy of a limp dishrag. For the sake of the animals and her own sanity, she'd have to do better.

Sassy finished her grain in seconds. Sadie took longer, as if she savored each bite as her last. Sassy sniffed Sadie's bucket but the old plow horse put her in her place with a swift nip on the neck.

*Good for you, old girl.* Sadie was nearing a quarter century in years, but she still had some mettle in her kettle.

Elenna patted Sadie's neck and pulled a piece of hay from her thick blond mane. Then she topped up the water trough and hauled the hay bale off the wheelbarrow.

The horses and donkeys were installed in this smaller north pasture while the main pasture recovered from a few weeks of their hooves churning up the mud. The grass was coming in nicely and the hay would soon be a second choice. Thank God. She'd been hauling the stuff all winter. Of course, if she learned to drive the ATV, this chore would be a lot easier.

*And if I sold the farm and animals, life would be even easier.*

That thought snuck up on her more frequently these days.

The horses finished their grain and went back to grazing. Elenna leaned against a fence post and took in the beauty of the farm. Buttery morning sun lit the dew, making the pastures sparkle. The air was filled with *chick-a-dee-dee-dees* and the louder squawk of blue jays, and it smelled like earth, a rich loamy scent with a hint of wildflowers. She would be sad to leave this place, but these days, sadness was as ingrained in her as the dirt under her fingernails

Sadie nudged her shoulder. She was taller than Elenna at the withers and thick across the shoulders. Her hooves were wider than dinner plates, and she could no longer hold them up to let Elenna pick out stones and dirt.

Another problem she hadn't found a solution to yet.

Most of the residents of Equinox Farm had health or temperament issues. There was Sassy, who refused to be broke under saddle, and Shin Mei, the failed racehorse with bad hips. The donkeys, Jude and Missy, both had foot issues and were prone to rain rot. Then there were the goats, the pig, the alpacas and Luther, the llama with anger issues.

Jamie had had a big heart. He'd started Equinox Farm simply to house his growing collection of castoffs—animals that nobody wanted. But last year Jamie had wrapped his snowmobile around a tree. All for the love of speed—for his need to go faster, go farther, to always go, go, go—and Elenna was left to deal with his mission.

As always, that thought hit like a spike to the chest. Her heart seized, then reluctantly beat again. She sucked in a lungful of sweet summer air and blew it out.

It would get easier. It had to.

Sadie's nose appeared over her shoulder. She hugged the sweet, blond head and kissed her cheek. Of course, she couldn't sell Sadie. Who would buy a geriatric ex-plow horse anyway?

She hoisted the wheelbarrow and snuck out the gate while Sassy was busy with the hay pile. Trundling up the hill toward the barn again, with a lighter load this time, she thought about a new feeding arrangement, one that didn't involve wheelbarrows.

"Elenna! Elenna! Elenna!"

The call came from beyond the pastures where a trail led into the woods. Elenna turned to spot Ruby, the local wild-child, sprinting up the hill. Ruby was only nine-years old, but she ran barefoot and loose in the village of Mullarkey and the forest around it from the day school let out in June until her mother somehow wrangled shoes back onto her feet in September.

And there was something a little fay about her. She was a skinny kid who seemed to be all knees and elbows, and yet she moved with the grace of a dragonfly. Her untamed red curls were usually tangled with bits of twigs and grass. And when the morning light hit her just right, Elenna could almost believe that gossamer wings trailed behind her.

"Elenna! Elenna! Elenna!" Ruby rarely said anything just once, and she always spoke loud enough for her voice to carry across a field. She careened around the barn and ran up the gravel path, not seeming to care if stones dug into her bare feet. In her exuberance, she overshot her mark, then backtracked and bounced around the wheelbarrow.

"You have to come! You have to. There's a monster! I heard it!" Her words were punctuated with gasping efforts to catch her breath.

"Come where?"

Ruby pointed across the little creek running below the pastures and into the forest that loomed beyond it.

"I can't come now, Ruby. I have chores to do." The goats stayed in the barn overnight to protect them from coyotes, and she needed to let them out.

Ruby pulled at her hand.

"But this is really important. It's hurt."

"What's hurt?"

"The monster. I could hear it crying."

Ruby knew how to push her buttons. Elenna would never turn her back on an injured animal. Not even a monstrous one.

She brought the wheelbarrow to a stop at the barn and turned to the child.

"Are you telling the truth?"

Ruby took Elenna's hand in her smaller, dirt-caked hands and pressed it to her cheek. She stared at her with an open expression, completely free of guile.

"Would I lie to you?" She batted her strawberry blond eyelashes.

Elenna had to laugh. The kid was a master manipulator.

"Oh, come on then. Show me the monster."

Ruby took off at a run toward the little bridge that forded the creek.

Elenna sighed and followed.

They headed upstream, following the creek to where it met the larger Bryce River. An old water mill sat on the farm's property at the juncture of these two streams. The mill hadn't been in operation for over a hundred years and the building was mostly taken over by foliage. Ruby raced up the path beside the mill and disappeared into the forest.

"Don't get too far ahead!" Elenna called after her. She wasn't worried about Ruby getting lost. The girl probably knew these woods better than anyone in town, but Elenna wasn't a lithe nine-year-old sprite who seemed to float across the ground. She was thirty-six. She earned every step up the hill, and by the time she passed the old stone shed behind the mill, she was panting. Sweat trickled down the small of her back.

Ruby danced back along the path to catch her hand and pull her along. She babbled as they walked, pointing out unusual rock formations and mounds of dirt where moles tunneled near the surface.

"Tig says that the Wild Hunt came right through here once. Not *the* Wild Hunt, of course. That one never leaves the old country, Tig says. But *a* Wild Hunt. Anyway wouldn't that be super fantastic to see?"

"Does your mother know you visit Tig?"

Ruby looked affronted. "Of course. She says Tig is an *essential* part of my education."

"Essential, huh?"

Ruby nodded solemnly. "Essential. She said so."

Elenna couldn't argue with that, but if she had a kid—she breathed past that little land-mine of a thought—if she had a kid, she wouldn't let her run wild in the forest and she certainly wouldn't let her visit Tig, the hedge-witch wannabe who lived in a shack that should have been condemned in 1950. Her property bordered Equinox Farm to the west and ran all the way up to the old abandoned gold mine in the north. She wasn't a social sort, and mostly kept to herself.

Elenna paused to dig at the stitch in her side. "Are we getting close to this monster of yours? I really do have chores."

"Shh!" Ruby put a finger to her lips and crouched. Her bony knees framed her face as she peered into the shadows under the trees. "There! Did you hear that?"

Elenna squatted beside her and listened. She did hear something. A bird, maybe? The gabbling sound came again. Several gabbling sounds.

Elenna rose, ignoring the creak of her knees.

"That's not a monster."

Ruby scrunched up one eye. "You sure?"

"I'm sure. Come on." She touched Ruby's shoulder to urge her forward, then left the trail and headed toward the river. Ruby slid down the bank like an otter.

Bryce River widened to a little pool here and the current was less fierce. It was only ankle deep near the shore but it deepened enough to swim in the middle. It was one of Elenna's favorite spots to bring her sketchbook. She and Jamie used to come here to cool off in the hot summers too. They'd even made love on the bank once. She felt herself blush thinking about it now, and she glanced at Ruby.

That had been at least three years ago. Ruby would have been only six. Surely the little imp hadn't been running loose at that age. Though her mother would have probably thought spying on her neighbors' debauchery was essential education.

The wind picked up and tossed branches overhead, sending dapples of sunlight through the forest's canopy. The light reflecting off the water confused her, so it took Elenna a few seconds to spot the flock of five ducks floating in the slow-moving river.

"What's wrong with them?" Ruby asked.

"They're just babies." But Ruby's concern was reasonable. The ducklings were clearly unhealthy. Their white feathers were burnished with yellow baby down that was matted with dirt. They watched the human interlopers with dull expressions. One of them peeped out a pitiful sound. Another wouldn't even swim, but sat limply in the shallow water.

"There's your monster. Or monsters." Elenna looked around for a mother duck, but didn't have high hopes of finding one. These babies were starving.

"Sh—" She cut off the curse word before finishing it and glanced at Ruby.

"It's okay. You can swear in front of me. Daniel does it all the time." Daniel was Ruby's older brother. He could add to Ruby's vocabulary all he wanted. Elenna didn't have to.

"Those ducks will die if we leave them here."

"We can't let them die!" Ruby's eyes were big enough to swallow her head.

"We won't. Can you run back and ask Gilly for a pet carrier from the barn? Better ask her to come back with you and bring a second one." Ruby was already off and running. "She'll be in the vegetable garden!" Elenna called after her, but the child had already disappeared into the trees.

She turned back to study the ducks. Could they fly? She didn't think so. They might be old enough, but their feathers were in poor shape. She backed up to the path so she didn't spook them while she waited for the girls.

The cool wind had blown in and the new leaves on the birch trees turned silver backs outward. The sky overhead was still blue, but a cloud covered the sun, plunging the forest into shadow.

The hairs on Elenna's arms lifted. She had the unpleasant feeling that someone was watching her. She glanced up the trail. It disappeared into deep shadows. Was someone up there? This was her property. No one walked these trails but her. And Ruby, of course, and sometimes Max, her neighbor, but no one she need fear.

She shivered as the wind raised goosebumps on her skin. Before she knew what she was doing, she stepped forward along the darkening trail. Another step. Her brain told her something was really wrong, but her feet kept shuffling along the dirt path.

"Hello?" The wind seemed to whisk her voice away. She took another few steps around a bend in the trail. She didn't realize how far she'd walked until she spotted a familiar landmark. An oak tree had grown around a huge mossy boulder right next to the river. At some point in its long life, the trunk had bent to keep growing around the boulder, and against all odds, the mighty oak had grown crooked but strong. The tree was old now, nearing its end. Grayish vines wrapped its trunk and were tangled in its leaves. A heavy branch had fallen from its peak. Peach-colored mushrooms bloomed along this rotting limb. Beyond the tree and boulder, the ground sloped away to the river, but it was all covered in some kind of weedy gray lichen. Her overactive imagination supplied the ominous threads of horror movie music, and she shivered.

Though she was far from home, Elenna's property continued for another ten acres or so, almost to the edge of the old gold mine.

A gust of wind rattled the oak leaves.

"Hello?" She peered at the boulder, and more specifically at the hole under the boulder. It was black and deep, and it seemed to call to her. She imagined sticking a hand into that black hole, then an arm, then climbing down into its fathomless depths. Like a waking dream, she pictured herself walking a dark path full of magic with fairy lights dancing around her head while a brighter light lured her onward—a softly diffused light, warm and brimming with the promise of comfort. The wind howled like a sad ballad heard from far away. The music grew louder and more frantic and suddenly she was running. The dark path furled by under her feet but she never seemed to close on that promising light. A cackle sounded like the boom of thunder...

The wind suddenly shifted and sunlight poured through the forest canopy again.

Elenna was startled to find herself crouched right beside the boulder, her hand reaching for the hole.

She scrambled backward and stood, obsessively wiping her hands on her jeans and feeling silly. She recognized that her writer's brain sometimes went into overdrive, and where she saw bogie men, there were only shadows. When she heard howling voices, it was only the voice of the wind. Her imagination let her sculpt intriguing stories, but it could also be unsettling.

She stared at the hole under the boulder. It was just a den for some industrious creature. A porcupine or muskrat was probably watching her right now, waiting patiently for the invader to leave their home.

An oak leaf floated down and landed on the crook of her arm. She picked it up and thought of the old wives tale: if you catch a falling leaf, it's a good luck charm from Mother Nature.

Except it was June. The leaves shouldn't be falling.

She turned the leaf over. The deep green veins were overlaid with a grungy silver and black patina. Looking around, she found more blight on a nearby alder. The rot had crawled up its trunk and covered half its leaves. She'd heard of a disease affecting birch and beech trees in the area, but not oaks or alders. Alders were indestructible. They were the first trees to grow back after a forest fire, and they grew in swampy ground no other trees could handle. And oaks? The thought of something eating her beautiful red oaks saddened her.

She dropped the leaf and brushed off her hands.

"Elenna?" Gilly's voice came from far away.

"I'm coming." She put the thought of blighted trees aside for now. There were ducks to rescue.

ELENNA CLOSED THE COMPUTER ON her lap and scratched Gado's ears. The retired Akita guard dog was flopped on the patio stones at her feet. She lifted her face to take in the afternoon sun. She'd just finished the farm's bookkeeping for the month of May. It wasn't good. The price of hay had gone up again last year, and grain rose in the spring. The farm was quite literally eating through the inheritance Jamie had left her. His intention had never been to make a profit. The farm's only income came from a few sales of fresh eggs and seasonal produce from a garden that Gilly had begged Elenna to set up. It wasn't enough.

And Jamie had never told her just how bad things were.

She sighed and closed the computer. Why had she not been more involved in the business side of things before now? She knew the answer, even though it stuck in her craw. Because she'd been off in her own world of fantasy and fairy tales, always hoping her next story would be the one that made it big.

And Jamie hadn't wanted her to worry about finances or the farm. His promise when they'd married was that he'd make a home for them, a quiet, safe place where she could finally write her masterpiece and he could pursue his many hobbies— hobbies that mostly involved driving vehicles too fast and too dangerously.

She was staring at one of his other hobbies right now as she sat in the courtyard that cozied into the crook of their ridiculous U-shaped house. *Her* ridiculous U-shaped house, she amended. The courtyard's only ornamentation were beds of gravel and sand.

Once these beds had been lovingly raked into flowing patterns that were meant to aid in meditation. Now, stubborn weeds pushed through the gravel as if trying to take back a piece of this hostile, anti-foliage world.

Jamie had been an adrenaline junkie in constant motion. If he wasn't riding Shen Mei, his off-the-track racehorse, he was buzzing down the trails on his dirt bike or hooking up the boat for fishing. Or cycling. Or running. Or, or, or.

Maybe that's why she'd put up with this zen garden for so long. To her it was nothing more than a desolation of stone and sand. But Jamie had doted on it. He'd loved to putter with his rakes, and the only time she'd ever seen him stand still was when contemplating the flowing lines in the sand beds.

But everything about this meditation garden irked her—the lack of foliage, the drab color scheme, and the austerity. One bed was laid with pea gravel of obsidian black. Another had larger white stones. And yet another held fine gray sand. That last one was even more offending since a stack of smooth round black stones sat in the middle of it like some bad motivational poster that expounded on the virtues of serenity or forgiveness—traits she was in short supply of right now.

One row of rake marks had survived the flattening snows of winter. It swelled like a wave through the gravel at her feet. In a sudden fit of pique, she reached out with her foot and smeared the gravel under her shoe, erasing the last of Jamie's meticulously worked lines.

*Take that, you bastard.*

Then she sat back feeling foolish. It was just a garden. And Jamie was dead. He deserved to be remembered with love.

She was probably redirecting sadness into rage because they'd lost two ducklings overnight. Watching the little creatures fade away had left her feeling helpless and angry. She had no idea how to care for ducks, let alone malnourished, mite-ridden ones. And Max, the local vet who made house calls, hadn't been available. She'd searched the internet for care of baby ducks, and found only the basics: keep them warm and don't feed them bread. Well, duh.

She'd tried her best, staying up most of the night, coaxing the two weakest to eat the chicken feed, which was all she'd had on hand, but they'd been too frail to survive.

Ruby had cried when they buried the little bodies this

morning. Elenna didn't have any more tears to give to ducks.

Beside her shoe, a green stalk had pushed through the gravel. It was kind of pretty with a heavy ring of leaves topped by a white flower that was only partially open. A bee landed and stuck its head deep into the flower. Only its fat little behind and legs were visible. She watched it for a while, letting her anger drain away. There was no way to stay angry while watching bumblebee butts.

*I should turn this garden into a bee haven.*

Maybe she could plant some bee balm and milk weed or purple coneflowers—turn the space into a refuge for pollinators.

She rose, stalked over to the stack of zen stones and nudged it with a toe. The top stone wobbled. A sharper kick sent the stones skittering across the gravel.

That was petty, but it made her feel better.

"That was rather aggressive," said a voice from behind her. Gado lifted his head and woofed, then saw who it was and laid his head back on his paws.

Elenna turned to greet Max, her neighbor and local animal doctor.

"More like passive-aggressive. What I should really do is pull out all these gravel beds and plant flowers. Maybe some herbs."

"So why don't you?"

"Because…" She let the thought fade with a sigh.

"Because you'd feel guilty destroying Jamie's garden, but if Mother Nature does it, you're not at fault."

She shot him with little finger guns. "Exacto-mundo." She brushed the little white flower with a toe. "But weeds can be pretty too."

"They can. And useful. That's bloodroot. It makes a terrible tea, but it's supposed to be good for getting rid of plaque on your teeth."

"I'll stick to my toothpaste, thanks."

Foraging was Max's passion, though she didn't know how he found time for it. He was the only vet in their area, and even though he was semi-retired, he still treated animals at several farms around Mullarkey.

His craggy face was framed by a mane of hair that was more silver than black. He had soft eyes, the kind that put animals and people at ease. His nose was too big for conventional standards of beauty, but it gave him an air of authority. And it went well with his full silver mustache.

"So what's this about some ducks?" he asked.

"Ruby found them in the woods. Their parents must have been killed by a fox or coyote. They're in pretty rough shape. Two died this morning, but there are three left."

"Let's take a look then. I'll get my bag and meet you in the barn."

Max walked away slowly and with deliberation, like a man used to the pace of country life.

Elenna waited for him to round the corner of the big barn, then carefully re-stacked the zen stones.

GRACIE, THE VIETNAMESE POTBELLIED PIG, grunted and waggled a foot when Elenna entered the barn.

"Good morning, Gracie." It was always a good idea to greet the pig. She was a bit of a diva and could be ornery if she thought she was being disrespected. Gracie grunted, then turned over in her bed of hay and went back to sleep.

At least the ducks weren't bothering her as they quacked and flapped in the spare stall. Elenna had heard their squabbling cacophony from out in the yard, but the noise was welcome news. It meant they were getting stronger.

She peered into the stall. Yes, three healthy little fluff balls. They definitely looked better than yesterday.

Movement in the yard caught her eye. She turned, expecting to find Max coming up from the car park, but spied Henrik instead. He was bringing back the empty muck bucket. The morning was already hot and his shirt stuck to him like a second skin.

Henrik was over-the-top gorgeous, with a body built to fight off barbarians, blond hair that was just a touch too long and the face of a fallen angel.

He stopped at the hose that was curled up on the ground outside the barn.

*Oh, no. Don't do it.*

He picked up the hose. He was definitely going to do it.

His shoulders flexed. He tucked his elbows into the hem of his t-shirt and pulled it over his head. Dear God. The stretch smoothed out the ridges on his abs. Sweat frosted his perfectly sculpted chest. He tossed the t-shirt over a fence post and raised the hose, squeezing the nozzle. Water droplets danced over his face.

The music from a romcom montage echoed in Elenna's head.

*Boom, shucka-shucka, boom.*

Time became a loose construct as Henrik slicked back his hair in slow motion. Afternoon light caught droplets of water as they shimmied down his wet torso. Wide farmer's hands wiped downward from his shoulders to his chest and stomach, thrusting water before them. He shook his head, spraying light-kissed droplets off him like he was a fae prince robed in sparkling gems.

In an instant they were up on horseback, Henrik in front, Elenna clinging to his damp torso. The music soared. Her legs clamped around the horse, her hands gripping his sweat-slicked shoulders as he urged the horse into a gallop…

"Whoa there, girl. You'll trap flies with that gaping mouth."

The music screeched to a stop like a needle scratched across old vinyl. Time and sense returned to normal and Elenna found Max grinning at her.

"Can't say as I blame you." Max nodded toward Henrik who, oblivious to the spectators, was now wheeling the muck bucket to its place behind the barn. "And you're not the only one caught in Henrik the Beautiful's vortex."

Gilly stood in the vegetable garden just past the barn. She was leaning on a hoe and had a dopey expression on her face. Elenna could only hope her own expression hadn't been so…so what? Obvious? Honest? Foolish?

"Gilly? Don't be silly. She's seventeen." Elenna snorted.

Max had a twinkle in his eye. "Don't you remember being seventeen?"

She did. There was something wild about a seventeen-year-old girl, as if the promise of all those adventures to come vibrated in her bones.

"Still, she's just a kid."

"You'd better hope Henrik sees her that way."

Great. Now she had to chaperone the farm help. At least Henrik wouldn't be around for long. He'd arrived a week ago as a work-away laborer from Austria. He had a visa to work at Equinox for the summer in exchange for room and board in the old farm cottage. It was a win-win arrangement. Elenna got farm labor she wouldn't have been able to afford otherwise, and Henrik got a summer in Canada.

Max's warm hand touched her bare arm.

"It's okay to look, you know. It's not cheating."

She swallowed a sudden lump in her throat and nodded.

"I know." But looking was as far as it would get. She wasn't ready for more, and she didn't think she ever would be.

"All right." Max clapped his hands. "So these are the little blighters you found?"

Glad for the change of subject, she turned her attention back to the ducklings.

"There were five, but two died in the night. The others seem stronger today. Poor things, who knows how long they've been without their parents. Probably been too terrified to rest."

Max's brows came together, making a deep crease between them.

"What? What's the matter?"

"Nothing," Max assured her. "They look healthy enough. But they weren't abandoned by their mama."

"What do you mean?"

"I mean, these are Pekin ducks. Not native to this area. Someone dumped them in the forest."

"You're kidding. Why would someone do that?"

People—and she used that term loosely—often dumped cats nearby because they saw the barn and assumed domesticated cats could survive just fine as barn cats. That was rarely the case. Pet cats are too pampered to survive on their own. Elenna usually sent them to the local animal aid to be re-adopted.

But ducks? Who dumped ducks?

"It's common enough." Max picked up a duckling and

checked its underside. "When was Easter?"

"I don't know." She thought back. "It was late this year. Mid-April maybe?"

"That sounds about right. Most likely, someone with more money than sense bought a bunch of eggs for their kids at Easter. The kids get all excited to watch them hatch. But then the ducks grow and the parents realize they're a lot more noise and mess than they anticipated. And of course the kids lose interest the first time they have to clean the duck cage. So they get dumped."

Elenna shook her head. "I hate people. You really think that's what happened?"

"I've seen it before. And the timing fits. These guys are about four weeks old."

"So what do I do with them?"

"Duck eggs make great omelets." Max gently replaced the last duckling onto the hay. Was his hand shaking?

"You can't be serious. I can't keep them."

He scratched the back of his head. "You could try Pontiac Animal Care, but I don't know that they take fowl. You might post them online."

Elenna ground her teeth. She didn't trust online buyers. Who knew what nefarious plans they would have for the babies.

She leaned her arms on the ledge of the stall and peered at the ducklings.

"It looks like Equinox Farm has three new residents."

Max nodded. "I'll give them something for the mites. You'll need a proper enclosure. Something with water."

Perfect. Another chore. Another expense.

Max took a wet wipe from his bag and scrubbed his hands. They were definitely shaky.

"While I'm here, there's something else I wanted to talk about."

He wasn't looking at her and his tone was much too serious for good news.

"Go on."

Max let out a sharp breath that whistled through his mustache. "You know I've been retired for a while now. I take only a few clients, you and Felix mostly." In his fifties, Felix was the maple syrup farmer down the road who kept a small flock of sheep.

"And?" she prompted when Max seemed reluctant to go on.

"And I've decided it's time to make that retirement official."

"Official?"

"No more farm visits. At least not as a doctor."

"You can't be serious?"

"As serious as a heart attack. Or in this case, Parkinson's." He lifted one hand and held his fingers flat, palm down. The tremble was obvious.

"I can't trust these old hands to give needles anymore. And it's only going to get worse."

"That's why you went into the city yesterday."

Max nodded. "Doc confirmed it."

"Oh, Max! I'm so sorry." She flung her arms around his neck. He let out a grunt and patted her back roughly.

"Now don't go getting all maudlin on me, girl. I'm not going anywhere. And if you ever need a cup of tea, you know where to find me."

Elenna sniffled back the tears that were always close to the surface these days. Max was more than an animal doctor. He was the first friend she'd made when she moved to Mullarkey.

"But you'll need a new vet." His voice was gruff, as if he was also fighting back emotions.

She wiped her eyes. "That's unlikely to happen."

There were no vets in their area. It was a problem that all local farmers had to deal with. Newly graduated vet students preferred city practices where they kept normal office hours and never had to deal with anything bigger than a Great Dane. Few wanted to come out to a rural area, and in predominantly French Quebec, even fewer wanted to live in the mainly English-speaking Pontiac Region. The provincial government compounded the issue by refusing to let vets from out of the province practice here unless they passed a French language test. The result was that Max was her only hope for veterinary care.

He took her hand. "You know I'd continue to help, if I could."

"I know. I'll figure something out." She often saw call-outs online for other farms that had spots in their horse trailers for trips to the vet in Ottawa. It was time she reached out to those farmers. She tugged on her ponytail.

"That's a bad habit." Max pointed at her fingers twined in her hair. "Good way to give yourself duck mites."

"Ew." Elenna let her hand drop. Max was right. It *was* a bad habit that left her hair dirtier than it needed to be.

Max sighed. "Don't worry. I won't leave you high and dry. I already found you a new vet."

"You what?"

"There's a practice in Orleans, near Ottawa. Two of their staff doctors passed the French test to practice across the river. Two more should have their certificates by the end of the year. They plan to have one vet doing rounds in this area every week.

"That's amazing! Thank you so much!" She threw her arms around him again and kissed his cheek.

"Oh, don't go on now," he groused. "It was nothing. I know the clinic owner. She went ahead and booked one of their doctors to visit you next week. You can get all your vaccines done."

"Thank you, thank you, thank you!" It wasn't nothing. Max had just saved her a huge amount of stress. She had a vet!

"But you know, I expect payment in pie." Max packed away his medical bag. "Not one of yours, mind you. Auntie Clare's. I hear she has a special on peach pie this week."

"Absolutely! One peach pie will be coming your way soon."

And one mite bath for the ducks. Elenna's hand instinctively went for her ponytail and she stopped it. Maybe a disinfectant bath for herself too. Oh, the life of a farmer.

"Hi, Dad."

"Elen…Ho…Can…ou hear me?" Her dad's voice came over the line in bits of truncated dialogue.

"Hold on." She stepped out of her living room and closed the paper screen behind her. This led to a long hallway that ran around the inside of the U-shaped house. The hallway was floor-to-ceiling glass to showcase the garden of stone and sand in the courtyard. She walked to the door at the end and then outside.

The sun reflected off all the glass and seemed to bake the garden. Her sunglasses had been perched on her head and she slid them on.

Gado was lazing in a bit of shade in one corner of the garden. His eyebrows twitched when she came out, but there was no reason to get excited.

"Can you hear me now?" she asked. The tin roof made her

house a dead zone for cellular connections. Outside wasn't much better. She glanced at her phone. One bar.

"I can hear you," he said. "Can you hear me?" It was the game they played every time he called. She tried to get him to FaceTime instead, but he said his thumbs were too clumsy to find the right buttons.

"I can hear you fine, Dad. You sound congested. I hope you're getting enough bed rest." Covid had blazed through his retirement community last month, proving that even though the pandemic was over, the illness was not gone. Her dad had been hit hard, though he was recovering now.

"Well, I've spent a lot of time in bed, but I can't say it's been all that restful, if you know what I mean."

She could almost hear his eyebrows waggling, and she groaned. She *did* know.

Her mother had died when she was very young. Elenna had only fleeting memories of her—the smell of her favorite hand lotion, or one verse of a song she liked to sing in the kitchen. Mom was Dad's fourth wife and he'd been forty-two when Elenna was born. Now at seventy-eight, he spent winters in Florida as a snowbird. In the summer he lived in a retirement home in Ottawa. He said there were not enough old guys, so he was in hot demand with the ladies, just the way he liked it.

"Please, Dad, spare me the details."

"Come on, Lanie, don't be a prude. People will think I didn't raise you right."

Elenna walked over to Gado's shaded nook, tucking her glasses on top of her head again so she could lean her forehead against the cool glass. It wasn't even nine o'clock and the heat was already intolerable.

"I'm not a prude. I just don't need to hear about my father's sex life. It's gross."

"Fair enough. When are you planning—" His voice cut off as a cough seized him. She waited a full minute before he had enough breath to continue.

"When do you think you'll be out this way?" he said finally.

"I was thinking, maybe you should come here for a visit. Get out of the city for a bit." She hadn't been thinking that at all, but that cough worried her.

"Maybe. Are there any hot babes in your town?"

She thought about the residents of Mullarkey. "There's Auntie Clare. I mean Clare Mullarkey. You met her last time you were here."

"Awk, Lanie, she's an old lady."

"She's the same age as you." Elenna let exasperation color her tone.

"Exactly. Old."

"Well, think about it, anyway."

"I will, gotta go, kid. My PT is here. Gotta show off my muscles for the girls."

"Bye Dad. I love you."

"Love you too."

The line went dead. She stood in the zen garden staring at her reflection in the glass wall. What had she been thinking, inviting her dad to come and stay? There was absolutely no room for him here. Her eyes roamed up the wall and followed it around the courtyard.

Their house—her house—was completely impractical for receiving guests. It was impractical for a lot of other reasons too. Shaped like a giant U, it was all glass on the inner arch. The outside was painted wood siding with narrow windows up high on the walls. When she approached the front door, she couldn't help thinking those windows looked like arrow slits and armed marksmen were waiting behind them to fend off invaders. Facing the house from the inner courtyard, the right wing of the U was one long room, separated into dining and living areas. The ceilings were vaulted and the walls serene eggshell. Their only adornments were some Japanese calligraphy and a katana hanging on the wall. The left wing housed her bedroom and a giant bathroom. Colossal. There were no words for how big this bathroom was. It had all the usual bathroom amenities, plus a separate tub room which Jamie had called the *ofuro*, though it didn't conform exactly in style to the traditional Japanese soaking tubs. Secretly, she'd always thought the *ofuro* was a little pretentious. It filled the entire room—a room bigger than most luxury bathrooms in suburban homes—with jets distributed along the tiled sides and shower heads sprouting from the walls. And it was inconvenient as a bath because her well couldn't fill it in one go.

The short wing of the U was the only section with two floors. Downstairs housed the kitchen, foyer, and storage. Upstairs, there was a library where she wrote, another storage room, and a large workout space where Jamie used to burn off excess energy in the winter months.

The house had been Jamie's vision. He even christened it Kiso House, named for a breed of Japanese horses.

After he got a degree in history that he really had no use for, Jamie had taken time off to travel and ended up in Japan for nearly a year. He fell in love with the culture and the Japanese aesthetic and when he inherited the farm, he built Kiso House in the light of those memories.

When she moved in, Elenna tried to love it. She really did. But lordy-lord, bachelors should never design houses. It was completely impractical. There were no guest rooms. And only the one shower and toilet. No pantry. No linen closet. No closets of any kind. She'd had to convince Jamie to buy a wardrobe for the bedroom just so she could hang up her dresses. And, oh, the best part? There were no walls on the inner sides of the rooms, only paper screens that slid open and closed and did nothing to dull the noise.

Even if she gave her dad her room, she'd hear him snoring while she tried to sleep on the couch in the living room.

Studying the house now, a little piece of her hated it, and then she hated herself for that pettiness.

What she really wanted to do was tear it down and build a sturdy little cottage, something that suited the brief but scorching Quebec summers and the long frigid Quebec winters.

Her finger swiped at dirt on the glass. The two-story high windows framed the entire courtyard, and they always needed cleaning. Jamie had paid a service to do them—just another extravagance she'd learned to do without.

Movement in the window's reflection caught her eye. Gado let out a quiet woof. That meant the visitor wasn't a stranger.

Elenna turned to find Nina hurrying up the drive, carrying a large box. She lost a flip-flop, stumbled, hopped on one foot for a bit, backtracked to get her shoe, and then kept coming.

Elenna sighed. She liked Nina, but she could be…a lot.

"Hey sister!" Nina waved her free hand. Nina wasn't her sister. Elenna had one somewhere, the product of her dad's first marriage, but she hadn't seen her in over ten years. Nina called every woman sister, as if having boobs meant they were all some big happy family—a united front of womanliness.

"What's in the box?" Elenna shielded her eyes against the morning sun's glare. Gado was already bored with the visit and had gone back to his busy work of sleeping on the cool gravel.

"It's a present." Nina beamed.

Elenna felt her nose wrinkle. When she wrote her stories, she never described a character as "beaming." It was a silly metaphor that made her think of aliens for some reason. But Nina really did beam. Her teeth were whiter than white. And she showed them off. A lot. She had round cheeks, as if she had never quite lost her baby fat, and they turned a brilliant shade of pink at the hint of embarrassment. Add in hair so blond it was almost white, and she seemed to glow with an inner energy that was never quenched.

Nina owned the Pishogue Shop in the village and she called herself a witch, though Elenna had never seen her perform any magic other than blinding people with her teeth. Nina assured her that modern witches were more about living united with nature than casting spells.

"For you." Nina held out the box and grinned. Elenna slid her sunglasses down over her eyes. The box held an old rotary phone. It was avocado green.

"What, is 1970 calling?"

"Don't be silly." Nina's cheeks turned pink. "It's a wind phone."

"A what now?"

"It's all the rage in Japan. I read about it on a geocaching site. People come from all over to find them. There are maps online and everything."

"I don't get it."

Nina let out an exaggerated sigh as if Elenna were seriously dimwitted.

"You don't have to get it. You just need to give me permission to set it up on your property."

"And why would I do that?"

"Because it's…" Nina searched for the word that would convince her, but all she came up with was, "it's important." She could see Elenna's skepticism and she rushed on. "You have that open gate farm tour next month, right?"

Elenna nodded.

"This will bring attention to the farm. I promise."

"I don't see how."

"That's because you know nothing about social media. Trust me on this, okay?"

She looked so earnest. "Fine, but you'll have to explain it to me."

"Of course. Let's go find the perfect spot to install it. I was thinking near the old mill. There's parking there and it's not too far from the road."

"Okay, let me put some shoes on and take care of the dog." Poor old Gado was starting to pant even in the shade.

"Come on, buddy. Enjoy the air conditioning for a bit." She coaxed him inside. He flopped down on the tiles right inside the door while she shoved her feet into sneakers.

She met Nina on the path next to the barn and they headed toward the old mill.

"Sweet mother, it's hot." Nina plucked at her tank top. Elenna followed the line of her gaze and found…yup. Henrik was spreading used straw around the pasture. He'd already lost his shirt and his sweat-slicked skin glistened in the sun. He worked the pitchfork in a steady beat, his shoulders flexing with each swing.

"That's some good forking." Nina ran her hand up her neck to catch a droplet of sweat.

Elenna tugged on her arm. "Quit ogling the help. It's bad enough that Gilly has gone all googly-eyed for him."

"Come on. You're trying to tell me," she waved a hand at the Adonis in the field, "that sight doesn't make your loins ache just a little bit?"

"Loins? Really? Who talks like that?"

"Loins is a perfectly good word."

"If you're roasting pork, maybe."

Nina huffed. "Elenna Kane, I refuse to believe that you're really that dead inside."

Elenna fell silent for a few steps, then said, "Not dead, but…I don't know. Hibernating, maybe."

Nina shuffled the box around so she could squeeze her arm.

"Aw, geez. I'm sorry. I can be such a jerk sometimes." Nina's cheeks flared red.

"It's okay. I get it." Fourteen months seemed like a lot for somebody else, someone who'd known Jamie, but didn't *know* him. To Elenna it felt like a few days, sometimes a few hours, since that QPP officer arrived at her door to give her the horrible, unalterable news.

By now they'd walked past the barn and the small pasture and into the gravel parking area. A short path through the grass at the side of the road brought them to the old mill. It had once been a working flour mill, serving farmers for miles around. The water wheel had been removed many years ago, and now Elenna used the building for storing winter stuff like the snowblower and shovels.

"So tell me about this phone."

"It's a Japanese custom, so it will fit right in here. It's called a Shiba Inu." Nina paused. "No wait, that's a manga character."

"Actually, I think that's a dog breed."

"Whatever. Something like that."

"What does it do, exactly?"

"Well, you talk into it." Nina was huffing so Elenna took the box from her.

"And does someone talk back?"

"No, silly. That's not the point."

"Okay." Clearly Elenna was missing the point entirely. The point was so far out of her sight, it wasn't even a dot on her horizon.

"This would be a perfect spot to install it." Nina indicated an old stone wall that ran behind the mill. It still had the remnants of a wooden gate. She rifled through the box and came out with a couple of nails and a hammer. She pounded a nail into the old fence post at face height, then hung the phone and gave it a tug.

"Good. Nice and secure."

"Now what?"

"Now people can come and use it to call, you know, people from their past they can't connect with. Lost loved ones…" She suddenly realized what she'd done. Her hand went to her mouth. "Oh, sister. I'm so sorry. I didn't think."

"It's okay." Elenna gave her a moment to get over her embarrassment. She picked up the receiver, but didn't put it to her ear. "So, let's say I call Jamie. Then what?"

Nina took a deep breath. She might have made a ginormous blunder bringing this thing into her grieving friend's world, but now that she had, she wasn't going to back down. Elenna had to admire her blind enthusiasm.

"Well, then you talk to him. Say all the things you didn't get a chance to say." She saw Elenna's one raised eyebrow and looked chagrined. "People say it's very therapeutic. Look." She held up her phone and scrolled to an app. "These are all comments by people who've used wind phones in other places."

Elenna eyed the hundreds of comments scrolling by with skepticism.

"So I put this phone on that app and people will come to talk on it?"

"Exactly. And look!" Nina pulled a small wooden box with a brass lock from the cardboard box. She pounded a second nail into the post and hung the box. There was a sign on it that Elenna leaned in to read.

"Sponsored by Equinox Farm. All donations go to the care and feeding of rescue animals."

"It's a donation box. See?" Nina slid a coin into the slot.

"What makes you think someone won't break that open and steal the change?"

Nina reared back like she'd been slapped. "Why would anybody do that?"

"Because that's what people do."

"Not the people *I* know." She sniffed.

Clearly, Nina had more faith in humanity than Elenna did.

"Fine. We'll give it a try. But you have to add the phone to that app. I'm not doing it." Computers made her head hurt. The only thing she used hers for was bookkeeping and writing.

"Of course!" She clicked a few buttons, took a picture of the phone, and clicked a few more times. "There, all done. Your wind phone is officially open for business."

"Great. I'm sure we'll be beating customers off with a stick soon."

Nina didn't hear her. Something on her smart phone had caught her attention and she was typing away.

Elenna turned to study the path that led past the mill and into the forest, thinking she should go get a sample of that lichen she'd found, maybe take it to the local nursery to see if the forest was at risk.

The General marched into sight at the side of the road. A car was coming fast through the village, kicking up dust. The

General lifted a hand and waved. Then he saw her and Nina and he waved again.

Elenna didn't know the General's name, no one did, except maybe Auntie Clare who'd lived in Mullarkey longer than anyone. He was called the General because every day—rain, snow or shine—he walked from his house up near the old gold mine to the village, where he'd stop at the cenotaphs and bow his head in silent prayer before giving the fallen soldiers a sharp military salute. Sometimes he would sit in the park by the bridge for a while, watching the Bryce River flow by. Then he'd walk home. But he never paused on his walks, and he waved to everyone he met.

Today, he paused. Elenna thought she might actually hear him speak, but he only squinted and pointed at the phone.

Nina waved to him. "It's a wind phone. Do you want to try it?"

The General hesitated. Another car came up the road and he turned to wave at it, seeming to forget the unexpected detour of his daily trip.

"Poor old guy," Nina said. "Auntie Clare told me he was a civil engineer in the army. Saw some pretty awful things, I guess."

"Not in World War II?" The General was old, but he couldn't be that old.

"Nah. Africa somewhere. I think she said Rwanda."

Elenna watched the General's back as he walked toward the village. He lifted his hand to wave at another car.

"It's all about sympathetic magic," Nina said.

"The war?"

"No, silly. The wind phone." She saw Elenna's screwed up expression of confusion and huffed out a laugh. "Sympathetic magic works on the principles of cause and effect. You can make something true simply by enacting it."

"So if I act out rain falling from the sky, it will rain?"

"Sort of. There's more to it, of course. Belief plays a big part, but essentially, yes. That's the basic principle behind rain dances."

"So if I pretend to talk to Jamie on the phone, I'll be able to really talk to him?"

"Don't take everything so literally!" Nina's tone was a little sharp. She didn't like having her witchy beliefs questioned. Then she softened. "It's about intent. What you get out of the wind phone is what you put in. Do you want to try it?" Nina held out the phone's receiver.

Did she want to open that can of magic? If she could talk to Jamie—really talk to him—the first words out of her mouth would be spoken in anger not love. How could that help anyone?

Elenna shook her head. "No, thanks."

Nina shrugged. "Suit yourself, but you might be surprised at how cathartic it is."

Elenna forced a smile through closed lips. Catharsis was for other people. She was glad to hold onto her rage for now. It was her only remaining tie to Jamie.

THE DUCKS WERE GETTING BIGGER. And louder. At seven weeks old, their adult feathers were starting to come in. They couldn't fly, but they flapped around the small horse stall until Elenna gave them the run of the barn and closed the big Dutch doors.

Gracie had moved to her summer quarters in a sty next to the large pasture, so she didn't have to worry about her, but the goats were a problem. She couldn't leave them out at night. There were coyotes and wolves in the area.

Bella was an Angora goat with only one horn. The other had cracked and fallen off the week that Beezle arrived on the farm. Beezle liked to head-butt anyone and everyone, and it had taken some time for Bella to put him in his place, though it had cost her a horn. Max estimated Bella's age at ten years, which was geriatric for her breed. Beezle was an American Pygmy goat who stood no higher than her knee. Newton, the Nubian, was tall, but he suffered from Cushing's disease and was rail thin. Any one of them would make a good midnight snack for a coyote. So every night, Elenna brought them up to the barn. And every morning, she let them out again. Each time, she had to fight off the increasingly curious ducks.

She returned to the barn after her morning goat wrangling session—who needed Pilates when you had goats?—and filled the kiddie pool with fresh water for the ducks, Hewie, Louie and Dewey. No, they weren't original names, but since she couldn't tell them apart anyway, she didn't bother with anything more unique.

The small side door opened and Henrik's bulky form was silhouetted against the brilliant summer light. She shot him a quick smile and continued to fill the pool.

She could feel him watching her. Why should that bother her so much? And why was it suddenly so hot in there?

"Did you need something," she asked without turning around.

"You are beautiful this morning." Henrik's English was getting better. His "th" only had a slight burr to it.

"Thank you."

The ducks were already splashing in their makeshift pond.

She shut off the hose and turned. With the light behind him, Henrik's face was nearly hidden in shadow. She waited for him to speak. It was coming. She could feel it. That moment when his comments and smoldering looks would cross the line and she would have to decide to go with it or reject him.

*Please don't let it be today.*

"You should come outside. *Ze hexe* is here. Gilly needs you."

*Hexe?* She didn't know the word, but she nodded and wiped her hands before leaving through the side door. Henrik didn't move out of the way, and her shoulder brushed against him.

Today wasn't the day, but it was coming. Soon.

She blinked in the sharp sunlight and scanned the open space between the barn and the farm cottage, looking for Gilly. She was standing next to the vegetable garden, leaning on a rake while Tig waved her walking stick and berated her.

Ah. *Hexe* was probably German for witch.

Tig was the local eccentric, or *one* of the local eccentrics. Elenna had tried to base a character in a story on Tig once and realized that she defied description. Her hair was somewhere between gray, brown and white. She wore gray and brown homespun dresses that looked like feed sacks, and a hooded cloak over that, even in the heat. The cloak looked like pressed velvet in a dizzying array of colors that seemed to shift with the light. Her face was lined, but her eyes sharp. She could be anywhere from fifty to eighty years old. Auntie Clare said she remembered Tig from her own childhood and she'd been old even then, but that couldn't be right. Auntie Clare's memory wasn't what it used to be.

People in the village called Tig a hedge witch. Nina, with witchy aspirations of her own, said Tig was a hag—in the old sense of the word, as in a wise woman. The kind that got burned at the stake a couple hundred years ago.

Tig waved her walking stick. She was clearly angry. Gilly had perfected that bored and disdainful adolescent expression. She rested both hands on her rake, and her chin on her hands while Tig's words washed over her like a summer storm.

The rant ended as Elenna arrived.

"What's going on?"

"Full of bad manners and ill humors, that one." Tig thrust out one gnarled fist that gripped the walking stick and pointed at Gilly.

Gilly rolled her eyes. "I just told her that we don't sell animals."

"You want an animal?" Elenna looked from Gilly to Tig.

"She wants a goat," Gilly said.

"Ye have goats, sure." Tig's lower jaw thrust forward.

"We do, but Gilly's right. We don't sell or adopt out animals."

Tig stamped the stick on the ground. "What kind of farm is it, then?"

"It's a rescue farm," Elenna said patiently. "We take animals in that nobody wants."

Tig took a ceramic jug from some pocket hidden inside her cloak and pulled the cork. She swallowed a gulp and jammed the cork back on.

Elenna raised one eyebrow.

"Don't ye be giving me the eye, girl. 'Tis medicine. Elderberry syrup for my allergies."

Sure it was. Elenna could smell the alcohol.

"Well, I'll be wanting a goat, and ye should be glad to be rid of it."

"No. Equinox Farm is a forever home." Elenna spoke slowly. "Some of these animals have been neglected or abused. Here, they live in peace and safety."

Tig tilted her head. She squinted one eye and glared with the other.

"A forever home? Nought but a fairy story." Tig's stick flashed out and knocked Gilly's rake aside. Gilly stumbled forward as her perch fell away.

"Hey!"

A very long and bony finger stuck out of Tig's sleeve. The last joint was bent at a painful angle, but Tig jabbed it at Gilly. "Ye be sorry, sure." She turned and stalked down the drive, her stick punctuating every step with a tap on the ground.

Gilly's eyes were wide. Her hand went to her throat. "Did she just curse me?"

"I don't think so…"

"My dad said old Tig cursed him in high school and he never got a date to the prom because of it."

Elenna had met Gilly's father. She didn't think a curse was to blame for his woman troubles. It probably had more to do with his over-bearing nature and penchant for crude jokes.

They watched Tig turn up the path toward the forest.

"Crazy old bat," Gilly muttered.

"Be nice," Elenna admonished, though her thoughts ran in the same direction. "What do you think that was all about?"

"I dunno. Goat stew, probably."

Terrific. Now she had to worry about coyotes, wolves and witches.

"I'm going into town," she said. "Do you need anything?"

"Nah. I'm almost done here."

Elenna glanced at the vegetable garden. Quebec's growing season was short and frantic. Gilly had planted bean seeds only six weeks ago, but the plants were already twining up the bamboo supports she'd put in place.

"It looks really great." She pointed to the rows of tomatoes that were in full flower. "You did better with the tomatoes than I could ever do." It was true. If there was an opposite to green thumbs, that's what Elenna had. Red thumbs, maybe.

Gilly had been volunteering at the farm since she was a kid, and two years ago she'd asked to take over the derelict garden behind the old cottage. This would be her second harvest and all the money it raised would go to animal care.

Elenna squeezed her arm. "I appreciate all your hard work."

"Aw, that's okay. Now that school's done. I've got nothing to do all day anyway."

Most kids her age wouldn't agree with that. They could spend hours on their phones, doom-scrolling and texting. Gilly was a rare treat.

"Well, thanks. I'll bring you a coffee from Auntie Clare's."

"Extra whip cream!" she called after her. Elenna waved back as she turned up the road toward the village.

Felix was chasing a loose sheep. Again. He was her closest neighbor, and his sheep got loose at least once a week. She watched him cajole the ewe up the road to his farm.

She passed the General going in the other direction. He lifted his hand. She waved back.

It was a beautiful day in Mullarkey.

Auntie Clare's bakery and general store was actually called Dépanneur Mullarkey, but everyone just referred to it as Auntie Clare's. *Dépanneur* is a Quebecois word that comes from the verb *dépanner*, which means to MacGyver something or make do in a pinch. Auntie Clare's was meant to be a convenient stop on your way home to pick up bread, milk and dog food. And beer, of course. This was Quebec, after all. But for many of the local residents who made the trip to Shawville for groceries only every couple of weeks, Auntie Clare's was a lifeline.

The empty gravel parking lot stretched along the road, past Warrick's chip truck and Nina's Pishogue shop, all the way to the covered bridge. It was Tuesday just after the big Canada Day weekend and Auntie Clare's bakery and general store was quiet. The few tourists who enjoyed out-of-the-way attractions were back at work.

Warrick leaned out the window of his chip truck and gave her a bored wave. The lunch crowd hadn't materialized yet.

She opened the door to Auntie Clare's, setting off a little bell that jangled like fairy music and stepped inside. The left side of the store was one long counter with the cash register at the nearest end, then a deli case with cold cuts and cheese. Prepared foods came next. Locals could order sandwiches or choose from a selection of hot meals. Finally, the bakery counter took up the back corner. The rest of the store was given over to groceries, beer and wine.

Ruby's brother, Daniel, lounged at the front cash, reading a comic book.

"Hey, Danny, is Hadley in?"

The teen grumbled something without looking up. It was his first summer job, and he wasn't exactly excelling at customer service. She gave him a pass and headed to the back of the store. Pushing through double doors brought her to a large kitchen. A cook whose name she didn't know was stirring a pot of soup on the stove. At another work station, Hadley was rolling out pie dough.

"Hey, those look nice." Elenna stepped up to the counter. Two questionable pies were already stuffed and ready to bake. She knew Hadley had been struggling to fill in for Auntie Clare, who usually did the baking.

Hadley grunted. She was rolling out a crust that was so cracked, it looked like the torn edges of a medieval manuscript. Hadley tried to pinch a tear together, but it only broke in another spot.

"Did you order pickles?" The querulous voice came from the storeroom at the back of the kitchen.

Hadley turned her head to holler back, "Yes, Auntie."

"What about cranberry sauce? Can't have Thanksgiving without cranberry."

"Thanksgiving isn't for another three months!" Hadley shook her head. Dark curls dusted with flour framed her face. Another smear of flour hid freckles that speckled her cheeks and nose. She was petite, a good six inches shorter than Elenna, but curvier. She had that hourglass figure and darkly-lashed eyes that would have made her an excellent starlet in the early days of Hollywood.

She pushed too hard on the rolling pin, squeezing the dough into a paper thin mess, then sighed and put it aside.

"We're out of olive oil," Auntie Clare shouted from the storeroom.

Hadley forced a smile and her voice rose to falsely happy heights. "I have some on order."

"What's she doing?" Elenna whispered.

Hadley leaned in and whispered back. "Inventory."

Auntie Clare had given up the daily running of the store over five years ago. She tried to keep up with the baking because people came from all over for her pies, but Hadley ran the day-to-day operations.

Elenna was about to comment on that when Auntie Clare came into the kitchen. She was a shorter, white-haired version of Hadley, who was actually her great-niece.

"I need to order these." Auntie laid a sheet of paper on the work table. It looked like it had been torn from a cookbook. She'd scrawled "INVENTORY" across the page in black marker. The rest of the list was illegible.

Hadley glanced at the sheet and smiled sadly. "Thank you, Auntie. I'll take care of it."

Auntie hummed "Toora Loora" and picked up the rolling pin. Within a minute, she had a new crust rolled out perfectly.

Hadley wiped her hands on her apron and nodded toward the back door. Elenna followed her out.

"Is she okay?" Elenna asked once they stepped into the bright morning.

Hadley lit a cigarette and leaned against the wall beside the door.

"Baking is about the only thing she gets right these days and even that…I can't rely on her. Sometimes she doesn't even get out of bed, or I can't get her to turn off the TV and come downstairs." Hadley and Clare lived in the apartment above the store. She flicked ash off her cigarette. "Other days she'll bake all day, making way more pies than we can sell or even freeze."

"I'm sorry you have to go through that."

"Yeah, well, she's the one going through it. I'm just here to pick up the mess afterward." She sucked in another breath of tar and nicotine, then crushed the cigarette under her shoe. "Ugh. I really need to give these up."

"You really do."

"So, what's up?"

Elenna felt bad now burdening her with more work, but she was there, so she asked. "I was hoping you could stock a table at our place for the Open Gate Farm Tour."

Equinox would be one of a dozen local farms participating.

It was a big deal in their community and she wanted to put on a good show.

"Of course! What were you thinking? Hot food or just munchies?"

"Cold stuff. Sandwiches, pre-made salads, soft drinks. That sort of thing. And pies, of course. We'll have some early produce by then and Felix will have a table for his maple syrup. I'm hoping to get Kingston Hall there with some apple cider too."

"Sounds good." Hadley took out her phone and pulled up her calendar to mark the date. "What kind of activities are you planning?"

"Activities?" She hadn't really thought about it. "I don't know. Farm tours?"

Hadley frowned at her. "You've got to give people a reason to come. What about a petting zoo for the kids?"

Yeah, right. Elenna could just see the kids trying to pet Luther, the llama with anger issues or Gracie, the pig who set her own boundaries and refused to be caged by any sort of temporary pen they might set up.

Hadley must have seen her expression.

"Pony rides?"

Elenna laughed. "We're not really that kind of farm." It was the second time that day she'd said that. It begged the question: what kind of farm were they?

"What about donkey cart rides? Don't you have that old cart in the barn?"

She did have a cart and all the tack to hook up Missy and Jude.

"No one's taken that cart out since…well, you know." Jamie used to amuse the local kids with rides at Halloween. But she didn't know how to drive a donkey cart.

Hadley saw her expression. Her hand reached out to squeeze Elenna's.

*Here it comes…*

"Oh, Elenna. I'm so sorry. I didn't think."

Ugh. She was so tired of everyone feeling sorry for her.

"I suppose Gilly could drive the cart. Jamie taught her."

Gilly had been fifteen at the time and super excited to have the responsibility of tacking and driving the donkey cart.

"You should ask her," Hadley said. "It could be a good fundraiser."

Elenna nodded but Hadley was already scrolling through the calendar on her phone. "What's the date again?"

"August eighteenth. It's a Saturday."

"Oh, good. We have more than a month to come up with something. And we will. It's going to be the best Open Gate Farm Tour ever!"

Elenna wished she had Hadley's enthusiasm and suddenly, she also wished she hadn't committed to this event. If the farm didn't need the revenue in donations, she would have canceled it.

"I gotta get back inside before Auntie burns down the kitchen, but you should come by this Friday. I invited the new girl, the one who bought the inn. Her name's Joelle. We can make it a girls' night. Play some tunes and have a glass of wine or three." Hadley made her hands dance like an ocean wave.

Elenna had forgotten that the old Cedar Grove Inn had been bought. She *should* welcome the new owner. Pay it forward, as they say. She remembered all too well what it was like to move to this very tight community and be the odd one out. Thankfully, Hadley and Nina hadn't let her wallow in isolation for long, but it had been a while since she'd joined in a girls' night at Auntie Clare's.

A while. As if. She hadn't gone anywhere since before Jamie died.

"Maybe."

Hadley scrunched up her brows. "You should make the effort to come back to the world. We miss you."

Elenna swallowed the harsh retort that stuck in her throat. Hadley meant well. They all meant well.

They said goodbye and after ordering Gilly's super-sweet coffee, Elenna headed back up Mill Road to the farm, already planning excuses to get out of joining the girls on Friday. It wasn't that she didn't want to spend time with Hadley and Nina. They were each five to ten years younger than her, but they'd always gotten along. It was a small village. If you didn't make nice with the neighbors, you were in trouble.

But going out seemed so…wrong.

She glanced at the sky as if her dead husband might be looking down on her from heaven. Would he care that she went out and had a good time without him? Would he think she was betraying his memory by letting down her mourning cloak even for an evening?

A mosquito landed on her neck and she swatted it with more ferocity than it required. She was being ridiculous. She didn't even believe in heaven and hell.

As she came up on the old mill, movement in the trees caught her eye. The General was walking up the trail. He stopped at the wind phone, picked up the receiver and put it to his ear. His shoulders hunched and he tucked his head like he was trying to make himself a smaller target.

She heard him murmuring, but couldn't make out the words, and she wondered whose number the old soldier had dialed.

ANIMALS FOLLOWED JAMIE LIKE HE was the Pied Piper. For Elenna, wrangling the goats from the barn to the far pasture was like herding cats. Bella, the one-horned Angora goat was an angel in a mohair dress. She plodded along behind Elenna with an earnestness that bordered on devotion. The other two muppets caused trouble. Newton, her Nubian, was afraid of his own shadow. He startled at a dragonfly and again at a particularly nasty dandelion. Every time he got scared, he let out a bleat like a death knell and nearly yanked his lead from her hand.

Beezle, short for Beelzebub, got his name because he was a trickster. He was short and stocky, with black and white patches and short, sharp horns—sixty pounds of pure devil. Moving him from the barn to the pasture required kitting him out in a full harness because he somehow managed to slip his collar off no matter how tightly she buckled it.

On this fine July morning, Elenna held Newton's lead in one hand and Beezle's in the other as they marched across the yard with Bella bringing up the rear of the parade. One of the barn cats was sunning her belly on the warm dirt, but she took off as soon as the goats appeared. A couple of mourning doves cooed from their roost atop the fence and Newton greeted them.

"BLAAAAH!" He tugged on the lead, but Elenna had a firm grip. Beezle took any distraction as permission to cause trouble. He parkoured the fence post and took off at a run, which jerked her off her feet. She landed with an "oof" as air thrust from her lungs. Stupidly, she let go of Newton's lead rope instead of Beezle's and was dragged ten feet before the little goat ran out of steam.

She lay on her back, staring at the blue sky. Her hand hurt where the lead rope was wrapped around it. Her back hurt. A stick was jabbing her hip.

Newton's face suddenly filled her entire vision.

"BLAAAAH!" A wave of goat breath washed over her.

"Thanks, buddy." She pushed him away and sat up. A red road-burn marked her left knee. Worse was the embarrassment that she felt creeping into her cheeks when she spied Henrik watching from the pasture.

"Goat eez good meat." He lifted a hand to his mouth and mimed eating.

Right. They weren't going to eat the goats. She dusted herself off and let Bella, Beezle and Newton free in the pasture with the horses.

It was time to make some changes. She wasn't Jamie. He had his way of doing things, but she needed to tweak her own routines. This daily goat parade wasn't working for her.

She crossed the pasture and let herself out the back gate. The stream ran below the fence line. A small wooden bridge let her ford it and she found herself in a clearing of wildflowers. She stood in the middle of the field and shielded her eyes from the sun as she did a slow turn. It wasn't quite an acre—just enough space for three goats. And an old fieldstone building perched at the edge of the field, the same one she'd passed with Ruby the day they found the ducks.

The building had once been a tool shed for the old mill. It was only about ten feet square, with one tiny window. But it was dry, and the door seemed secure. With a little fixing up, it could make a good goat shelter. She decided to get Henrik working on it right away. He'd have to fence the field too.

A cloud passed over the sun, plunging the bright day into sudden shadow. A shiver ran through her. She glanced up the path into the trees and remembered the blight she'd seen on the oak tree. It still bothered her.

She headed into the woods. The sun continued to hide and the forest was dark. The top end of a birch tree had rotted and fallen across the path like a corpse. Serial killer music played in her head, and she felt like the too-stupid-to-live girl who left the cabin at night with only a flashlight, calling out, "Is anybody there?" She jerked her thoughts back to reality. Every hair was standing up on her arms. Her morbid imagination was turning a simple walk into an episode of CSI.

Creepy thoughts hadn't left her by the time she found the crooked oak tree. The day had darkened even more. The hole under the giant boulder stared at her like an accusing eye. She looked away from it. Gray lichen covered another small cluster of alders. Were those the same alders she'd seen last month? She couldn't remember. One alder looked much like another.

Retreating to the river, she found three large rocks, then piled them beside the alders. She used the top rock to pound a dead branch into the ground beside her marker.

Standing back, she admired her handiwork. She'd return in a couple of weeks to see if the blight had spread. Not that she had any idea what to do about it.

When she turned her back on the black hole beneath the boulder, her shoulders twitched like she was in someone's sight.

She hurried down the path toward the farm. As she passed the mill, she spied Felix at the wind phone.

Apart from keeping sheep, Felix tapped his maple trees to make syrup in the spring, and profits from the liquid gold were enough to keep him all year round.

Mullarkey Mills had been established in the 1800s by Irish immigrants. The upheavals and French language debates never managed to touch the village, and Felix was one of the few francophones in town.

Elenna had paused behind a tree to watch him and now felt foolish for spying, but the serious look on Felix's face gave her pause. She couldn't hear his words, but whatever he was saying, it was deeply personal and she didn't want to intrude.

He hung up the phone, added a coin to the donation box and wandered back toward the road.

She watched him go. First the General, now Felix. Could Nina be right? Maybe there was something cathartic about talking to the wind.

The sun suddenly reappeared as if giving her permission to do the unthinkable.

She stepped out from her hiding spot and went over to face the ancient rotary phone. She remembered the green of its casing was really popular when she was a child. In the first house they'd lived in, before her mother died, all their kitchen appliances had been avocado.

She picked up the receiver and clamped it between her ear and shoulder. How many hours had she spent like this as a teenager? It was all coming back now—the feel of the coiled wire stretched across her chest, the numb ear from talking for hours. Her finger found the hole of the first number and she spun the dial. It made those comforting zing and whir sounds.

She dialed the rest of Jamie's number.

There was no click of a call going through, and yet…she pressed her ear harder against the receiver. Something echoed down the line.

She sucked in a breath.

"I just wanted to say…" The sound of her voice broke whatever reverie had a hold on her. She slammed the receiver down.

No. Just no.

She turned and marched back to the farm.

ELENNA MET JAMIE WHEN SHE was studying literature at the University of Ottawa because she had no idea what she wanted to do with her life, and books were the only things that really interested her. She took a bunch of electives in things like philosophy, intro to psychology and art history, hoping that something would stick.

Jamie was a young history professor—the hot one that the girls talked about—and his love for all things Japanese was infectious. He seemed larger than life and was always off on some adventure—a tour of Quebec City's museums or a weekend of camping rough in Algonquin Park. He was equally comfortable in the worlds of academia and nature, and eager to talk about his adventures or his views on life, literature and art. During office hours, his office was always swarmed with students.

After her semester in his class, they had a brief but passionate fling. It felt very taboo, even though he was no longer her professor, and maybe that was part of the appeal.

They slept together a few times, but she was sure he was sleeping with other girls too, and she didn't want to seem like a child by confronting him with that fact. She really cared for him, even suspected that she loved him, and she didn't want to share. So she let the relationship fizzle out. He didn't seem too upset to end things. They saw each other in the halls a few times in the following months. He was always cordial, but didn't push for anything more.

Then, in her last year of college, Jamie's grandfather died and he inherited the farm property. She only found this out years later. At the time, all she knew was that he'd left teaching, and she never expected to meet him again.

Over the next nine years, she got her BA in English Literature, and realized it was useless unless she wanted to teach, which she didn't. Instead she took on a series of retail jobs while she decided what she really wanted to do with her life. She wrote and published a few short stories, started a dozen novels and let them all lapse.

During that time, Jamie took over his family's old farm, built Kiso House and started collecting animals and motorized toys.

Then, while she was making a display of waterproof lanterns at the hunting-camping-fishing store where she worked, she heard a familiar voice say, "Do those really last for a week without charging?"

Her hands froze and she nearly dropped a lantern box. That voice pinged off her heart, hit her on some visceral level. It was both unexpected and yet, completely expected, as if she'd been waiting to hear it for nine years.

She plastered a shaky smile on her lips and turned.

Jamie. Taller than she remembered. Broader in the shoulder, but still fit. Clean shaven, his hair lightened and skin tanned from a summer spent outdoors.

"It's Elenna, right?" His lips quirked at the edges.

She nodded.

*Play it cool. Play it cool.*

"Hey, Jamie. Or should I say professor?"

He huffed out an easy laugh and dragged his hand through his blond curls.

"Not professor. Farmer. How about you. Still writing?"

That was September of 2019. They continued their little reunion over coffee. Jamie told her he was getting ready for one last hike into the wilderness around Georgian Bay before winter. She expected the coffee was just a nostalgic interlude, but two weeks later, as soon as he had cell reception again, he called her.

Their attraction was instantly rekindled, and they had five glorious months together before the world was plunged into the chaos of Covid. They spent that first lockdown apart—Jamie at the farm and Elenna in her little apartment near Ottawa. By the second lockdown, she knew she didn't want to spend it alone again.

She told him she didn't want things to end like they did in college, and—more importantly—that she didn't want to share him.

He circled his arms around her and whispered into her hair, "Baby, there hasn't been anyone but you since I saw you stacking lanterns. If I'm being honest, it's always been you."

And so she gave up her job and moved into Kiso House. They were married on a snowy day in December.

And that's how Elenna became an animal rescuer.

She admired Jamie's dedication to his rescues, even as she wondered how he managed to keep the place going. His ADHD made him jump from one project to another, often leaving things in shambles behind him. But he loved and doted on his animals. She'd thought it was an endearing paradox that an adrenaline junkie who loved horse racing rescued Shin Mei, a failed racehorse. Even his monumental failure at organization seemed cute because somehow, he still managed to keep his rescues properly fed and housed.

It also gave her an opportunity to shine. Details were her thing. Organizing was in her blood. It was what had made her good at her various retail jobs over the years.

Right away, she made three big changes to Equinox Farm. First, she trapped the barn cats that were becoming more than a little feral. With the help of Pontiac Animal Care, a non-profit group in the area, she had them all spayed or neutered. Some of the younger ones were adopted out. The rest were returned to the farm to help cull the rodent population.

The second change was to fire the housekeeper who came three times a week. Elenna didn't feel comfortable having a stranger in her house or cleaning her things. She could see how a busy single person needed help, especially since Jamie was a slob who liked a clean and clutter-free house. But they were a couple now, and she wanted them to take care of things. Together. It seemed intimate somehow. And Jamie's enthusiasm for life—for their new life—even bled over into chores. He would sing show tunes to her, using a ladle as a microphone as they washed dishes, or recite Monty Python jokes while they sorted laundry.

Years later, the memories of small moments like those were tiny treasures—gold nuggets that shored up her broken heart— and she would be forever glad that she'd fired the housekeeper.

The last drastic change she made was in the barn. It was a hoarder's dream, and another one of those paradoxes of Jamie's personality that she found endearing. He might like a neat house and a spartan zen garden, but the barn was a disaster. Boxes of supplies stood in dusty piles. Bags of feed were not easily accessible, and tack hung on every available hook without any order. She couldn't imagine how Jamie knew which halter went with which animal, but he did, and he resisted her efforts to tag and organize everything.

She ignored him.

One bright spring morning, a few months after they were married, she brought her organizational skills to the barn. While Jamie was away fishing with a buddy, she spent two full days revamping the space.

When he returned, she was excited to show him the results. She made him close his eyes at the barn door.

"Surprise!" She threw open the big Dutch doors and flicked on the light. Bandito, the old tuxedo barn cat, wound around Jamie's ankles while he frowned and took in the completely altered space.

A row of horse stalls met them, four on one side of a wide aisle and two on the other along with a tack room and wash stall.

The place gleamed.

Gracie grunted and rolled over in the first stall by the door. The next stall usually housed the three goats, but they were outside that day. The other four stalls were empty. She'd turned one into a storage room and installed shelves for all the supplies. She'd even bought an old chest freezer from a junkyard. It didn't work, but the seal was good enough to keep mice and chipmunks out of the feed. In the tack room, she'd cleaned and sorted the tack, then organized it neatly on newly installed hooks with clear labels.

She tugged on Jamie's hand, pulling him into the barn while she chattered on about the changes. The crease between his brows should have been a warning.

"See, look. All the hooks are labeled. No more mixing up goat and alpaca halters." This was a particular pet peeve for

Elenna. The alpacas were hard to catch, and more than once she'd nabbed one only to find the halter she had ready in her hand didn't fit.

"It's great." Jamie's voice was tight and held no hint of enthusiasm.

She'd been about to expound on the merits of keeping the feed in an old freezer, but the words trailed away.

"You don't like it."

He rubbed a hand over his chin where two-days of stubble grew. He didn't like beards and had been known to take a shaver camping.

"It's not that. But you should have asked before you went ahead and moved everything. You probably threw away stuff I need."

She crossed arms over her stomach and felt herself shrinking. "I didn't throw anything away. It's all here."

"Still, now I don't know where anything is."

"I can show you." She reached for his hand again, but he pulled away.

"Not now. I need a shower and a shave."

He turned and left the barn.

They didn't fight over it. They never fought. Jamie simply turned his attention to other things, leaving her to feel like she'd lost an argument that never happened and hurt his feelings in the process.

At the time, she'd had the unkind thought that his dismissal of her work was the same behavior that made him good with animals. He didn't scold or bully. He just ignored bad behavior.

Or what he perceived as bad behavior.

But she wasn't a hyperactive dog or a horse that needed training. She was his wife. Jamie sensed her vexation, and though he never apologized, he was suddenly very sweet to her, as if his conscience needed a cleansing. Over the next few days, he brought her coffee while she worked on her new manuscript. He made her laugh with silly, teasing jokes. They made love and she forgave him. Jamie was quirky and if she loved him, she had to love all his quirks.

And finally, at the end of the month, while she stood in the barn taking inventory of the horse grain, he circled his arms around her and pulled her tight against his chest.

"I really like what you did in here." He nuzzled her neck and she arched it. "Mmmm." His lips blazed a path down the line of her jaw and her bones melted. "It all makes sense now. I don't know what I'd do without you."

"You'll never have to know." She turned into his kiss.

That was as close as she'd get to an apology, and she decided to accept it.

Memories like these hit her at the oddest times, but this one shouldn't have been a surprise because she was currently standing in the alpaca enclosure that filled a quarter acre above the horse pasture. She had one arm around an angry llama's neck. In the other hand, she held a halter for an alpaca. It would never fit Luther.

*Damn.* She'd let a lot of things slide in the last few months while she catered to grief. Keeping the barn tidy had been one of them. Now, while Luther thrashed in her grip, she was paying the price.

It had taken her fifteen minutes to trap the ornery llama, but she'd have to let him go. He'd be wary for the rest of the day, and she'd never catch him again.

Luther's ears went down. He made the guttural grunting-bleating sound that meant he was really pissed off. Luckily, she had one arm firmly around his neck, so he couldn't twist to spit on her. His chocolate brown and white wool was growing in after the spring shearing and it was like hugging a thrashing teddy bear.

"Hey, I'm looking for Elenna Kane," a deep voice said from behind her.

A stranger in his territory was just one insult too many for Luther. He kicked out his back legs, missing her, but effectively dislodging her grip, and loped to the fence.

"Hey, buddy. Aren't you a handsome fella," said the stranger.

Luther growled. Llamas weren't supposed to growl, but Luther wasn't like other llamas.

The stranger didn't take the hint. He reached out a hand. "It's okay buddy. I won't hurt you."

Luther had other opinions about friendship. His head jerked back and he launched a spit missile right into the stranger's face.

"What the—" The man yelled, ducked and covered his head. Luther favored him with another loogie and took off for the back of the pen, where his alpacas were cowering like a bunch of hens around a stew pot.

"I'm so sorry!" Elenna ran to the fence. The stranger's beard and hair were spattered with green slime.

And here's the thing about llamas. Their spit isn't just spit. When angry—and Luther was always angry—they bring up stomach juices too. It stinks and it burns.

The man wiped his face with a cloth he'd taken from a bag at his side. A medical bag. *Oh, geez.* He was the new vet.

She took the cloth and dabbed at a big gob of green that dripped from his hair. "I'm really sorry. Luther has anger issues."

"I see that." The vet took the cloth back and ran it over his beard in a futile gesture to clean off the llama goo. "No worries. Hazard of the job."

"That's why he was surrendered to us. His previous owner trained him to be a guard llama for his goats, but went about it the wrong way and turned Luther into…that." She pointed to the beast that was pawing the ground in his corner.

She didn't mention that the previous owner's vet refused to treat him. That was when the goat farmer had decided to put Luther down. Jamie had intervened and brought him to Equinox Farm.

Max had a way with Luther. Elenna just hoped that this new vet could handle him too.

He was younger than she'd expected, though maybe that was because she was used to Max. And taller. He topped her five-foot-five by a good ten inches. He wasn't big though, not like Jamie who seemed to fill every space he entered. This guy was lanky. Still, he towered over her. His dark hair was just a bit too long and curled around his ears. His beard was full and neatly-trimmed, but it gave him a feral air. His brown eyes hinted at a sense of humor.

"I'm Elenna." She held her hand over the fence. He shook it with a smile.

"Milo Hanley. The new vet." His hand was big enough to swallow hers.

She pointed to his cheek. "You missed some."

He grinned and wiped his face again. "That was some spit cannon."

"He does have good aim. I guess you're here for the vaccines. We'll never get near Luther or the alpacas now. He'll be on guard duty. But we might as well get the rest of the crew done."

He stepped back as she opened the gate and left the pen.

"Lead the way." He picked up his bag and held out his other hand for her to precede him.

She brought him to the barn first, to check on the ducklings.

Ruby had been hanging around the barn all morning, hoping to meet the new vet. Inside the duck stall, she chattered away at him while he carefully lifted each duck for an examination.

"Their feathers have changed a lot," Ruby said. Only a hint of yellow peeked through the bright white feathers.

Milo nodded. "I'd guess they're about ten weeks old."

"Are they boys or girls?" Ruby asked. "My grandad says you can tell by making them vent or something."

Milo gave the child a smile. "I'm impressed you know that."

"Ruby wants to be a vet when she grows up," Elenna said. At least that was the plan for this week. It changed about as often as Ruby changed her clothes.

"Good for you." Milo ruffled the girl's hair. She put up with it for a few seconds before ducking away.

"It's called vent sexing," Milo said. "I could do that, but it's kind of invasive." When Ruby frowned, not understanding that word, he continued, "That means it's harsh on their little bodies. And since we don't have any pressing need to know if they are boys or girls yet, I say we just leave them be. What do you think?"

Ruby nodded vigorously.

Milo set down the last duck. It flapped its stubby wings and bounded over to its mates. "But I can tell you what to look for and what I would guess. See their beaks? See how those two have darker orange beaks and that one is lighter yellow? I think that's a boy. The other two are probably girls. In another few weeks, you might see the boy's tail feather curl up. That's another good indicator. And hear that?" He laid a hand next to his ear.

Ruby squatted and put both hands to her ears in imitation.

"What do you hear?" Milo asked.

"Quacking!" Ruby's smile was huge, then she cocked her head to the side. "But only two are quacking."

"That's right. Boy Pekin ducks don't really quack. This one may just be a late bloomer, but I think you have two girls and a boy."

"I'm going to watch them every day to be sure!"

"Then you'll make a great vet."

Happy with her praise, Ruby danced off as if her legs were filled with helium and she was only moments away from flying.

"Your daughter's adorable," Milo said.

The elastic around Elenna's heart squeezed and released.

"She's not mine, just the local half-feral child."

"I see."

His gaze seemed to have weight and it made her uncomfortable, not in the oh-my-god-I'm-alone-with-a-serial-killer way, but because she had the irrational feeling that he really saw her. The light in the barn was dim and his eyes were shadowed, but they seemed to penetrate the cloud of gloom she had pulled around her like a favorite blanket.

She bent to pick straw from the ducks' wading basin. "I guess I have to find better names than Hughie, Louie and Dewey."

"Probably. They'll need a bigger enclosure soon." Milo looked around the barn. "Something with fresh air and access to water."

"I know. I've been thinking about building an enclosure for them down by the stream. It doesn't freeze in the winter."

Milo smiled. "That sounds like a good plan then."

She nodded and didn't tell him that it would depend on finances. She wasn't going to burden a stranger with her problems.

Suddenly, the barn felt very confining and she pushed past him through the stall door. "Let's get those vaccines done. We'll start with the goats."

Elenna's little caprine herd had congregated at the farthest end of the newly fenced pasture where they lounged in the shade.

Beezle kicked up his heels in sheer joy as he bounded through the tall grass and heavy daisy heads. Newton worshiped Beezle and tried to mimic the dance, but his taller Nubian shape turned it into a lumber. The two goats circled Elenna and Milo, bleating and begging for pets and treats. Bella watched from a distance. She would never disgrace herself with such a rampant display of affection.

Milo examined Beezle and gave him a booster.

"He's a healthy little guy."

Bella barely flicked an ear when he gave her the shot.

Newton was more of a concern. Milo crouched and pressed his stethoscope to the goat's chest, listened for a few minutes, then stood up.

"Has he lost weight recently?"

Elenna knew Cushing's disease would eventually waste away all Newton's muscle mass, but she hadn't seen much of a change in him yet.

"He's always been thin, but I don't think he's lost any more weight since we got him."

"Good. We'll keep a close eye on him."

She wasn't sure how "we" would figure into that plan since Milo's practice was over an hour away and on the other side of the Outaouais River, but she nodded.

They moved on to the next pasture and the horses. Sassy, the little tart, flirted with Milo. She nipped at his shirt and pretended she had an itchy nose and tried to scratch it on his shoulder.

Milo laughed and gently shoved her away.

"I'm sorry. She's a bit of a bully sometimes."

"It's okay. Maybe you could hang onto her while I look at this handsome fellow's teeth though."

"Sure." She looped a lead rope around Sassy's neck and the mare immediately settled down.

Shin Mei was as placid and timid as Sassy was obnoxious. It was the reason he'd failed as a racehorse. He let Milo listen to his heart, check his teeth and jab him with a needle without even shying away.

"He looks good, but his teeth are a little rough. When was the last time they were done?"

Elenna tried not to look guilty. Jamie had tended to the horses' teeth every year. It was another chore that she'd let slide.

"It's been over two years," she admitted. "I'm sorry. Things have been…" She ran a hand through her hair and tugged on her ponytail—a bad habit, yes, but the tiny jolt of sensation across her scalp helped when her thoughts began to careen off the rails.

"Things have just been rough for a while. I'm still getting used to being the sole caretaker around here."

"Max told me about your husband. I'm very sorry for your loss."

She was looking at the tangle of summer grass and weeds growing near her feet when she nodded.

*Sorry for your loss.* Four words that said so much and yet nothing at all. Four words that, for some reason, filled her with irrational rage. But that wasn't Milo's fault. He probably *was* truly sorry. They all were. All the well wishers who'd sent condolences after the fact. And those who continued to tiptoe around her months later.

She gave her ponytail one last pull and let the tearing sensation drive her thoughts back to the present. She lifted her head and smiled.

"Thank you. Maybe we can get the horses on the schedule for their teeth this fall?"

"Absolutely. I'll have my secretary book it as soon as I return to the office."

He gave the donkeys their shots and then lingered over Sadie, patting her blond nose and neck.

"Aren't you a beauty," he cooed. Sadie half shut her eyes. She didn't lean into his touch, but she didn't pull away either. "And how old is this girl?"

"We think, that is, I think she's about twenty-seven. She came from a Mennonite farm near the Bruce Peninsula. The farmer wasn't sure of her exact age, but she plowed his fields for nearly twenty years, and she's been here for five."

"Any health issues?"

"Just some arthritis. It's getting harder to pick out her hooves because she can't hold up her feet."

Milo pulled a hoof pick from his bag, then leaned down and grabbed one of her front hooves. He expertly lifted the massive foot and held it firmly for inspection. Sadie—dear, sweet, well-trained Sadie—complied with this request. The muscles on her shoulders bunched as she tried to steady herself and not topple onto the fragile human.

Milo quickly cleaned her hoof and moved onto the next one. Her right back leg was too stiff and, despite her willingness, Sadie simply couldn't hold it up for Milo to clean.

"It should be okay as long as she's on soft grass like this. Maybe keep her off gravel as much as you can to avoid stones lodging in her hooves." Milo dusted off his hands and knees.

"Thanks." Elenna scratched Sadie's chin. "She's the heart of this farm, but we don't—I don't—have a lot of time left with her. I just want to make her as comfortable as I can for what life she has left."

"You're doing a great job so far. Let me think about this hoof issue. Maybe I can come up with a workaround."

Milo smiled and Elenna's eyes snagged on his lips, nearly hidden in the beard. She had never really liked full beards, but she had the irrational urge to stroke this one.

Sassy chose that moment to get the zoomies, and she took off at a full gallop around the pasture. The other horses shied and Milo nearly fell over onto Elenna.

"Sorry!" He grabbed her shoulder to steady himself. The feel of his fingers digging into her skin had the same effect as her ponytail tug. It sent a jolt through her, not pain exactly, but a sharp sensation that reminded her she was still alive.

She jerked away from him like she'd been stung and folded her arms over her chest.

"I'm so sorry! Did I hurt you?"

"No!" she blurted, then said a little more softly. "No. I'm fine. Really." She tried to smile to show she meant it, but his handprint on her bare skin seemed to blaze like a burn.

Milo frowned.

"Really, I'm fine."

His lips puckered under his beard. Were those bristles soft or prickly? What would they feel like on her…

She yanked her thoughts away from that dark alley.

He watched her with that little grin as they stood in the brilliant summer sun with bees buzzing around them and daisies bumping against their knees.

*Well, this isn't awkward.*

"I guess I'll be on my way then." Milo picked up his bag. "I'll have my secretary book the teeth appointment." He turned to head up the hill and stopped. "Goodbye, Elenna."

She forced her bottom lip to hold a smile without shaking and waved.

Nope, not awkward at all.

It was one of the hottest summers on record. The blazing July slipped unnoticed into a scorching August. Quebec summers are usually muggy affairs with humidity making the temperature feel doubly hot, but July had flown by with no rain. The grass was brown and crinkled under foot. Orange, sun-loving moss turned the yard behind Kiso House into an alien landscape.

Farm chores became brutal tests of endurance. Lug water out to the pasture, fill the trough, and repeat. And repeat. And repeat. There never seemed to be enough water to slake the desiccating sun—the sun that didn't set until after 8 p.m.

Elenna finally gave in and asked Henrik to teach her to drive the old Honda ATV. She straddled the cracked vinyl seat while he pointed out the brakes and the clutch. Since she'd learned to drive on an ancient manual transmission VW bug, she easily grasped the idea of shifting gears on the ATV, but getting it into reverse was a struggle.

"It needs…" Henrik held one hand wide and the other in a fist that turned as if he was cranking something. Since his English wasn't great, he was a man of few words and that suited Elenna just fine. She was already hyper-aware of him standing close enough that his hip brushed against her bare thigh.

He still struggled to find the word and said, "Fixing?"

"You mean it needs maintenance? Like a tune up?"

"Yes, toooon up." He drew out the unfamiliar word.

Elenna nodded. "I'll have someone look at it." Felix was good with engines. He might like the extra cash too.

Henrik swung his leg over the ATV's seat behind her.

"Go now." He pointed forward.

"Um…are you sure? I mean is this safe?" The heat of his body pressed against her was palpable and she was suddenly aware of the very thin t-shirts that separated them. Sexy montage music played in her head. This was the point in the romcom, when the girl usually gave into her baser instincts. *Boom, shucka-shucka, boom.*

"Go now." Henrik urged again. She struggled to shift the gear with her left toes, then squeezed the gas. The machine lurched forward and Henrik pressed against her back. They lurched out of the old barn into the afternoon sun and down the short slope. The engine whined.

"Change gear," Henrik said, his lips right next to her ear.

Despite her rigid muscles from the constant contact with a large, sweaty man, she managed to drive the ATV around the pasture and past the big barn. She made a turn in the car park. It was surprisingly easy to drive and actually fun to zoom around on four wheels, and she wondered why she'd resisted learning for so long.

When they returned to the barn, she slowed it to an idle and hopped off, putting much needed space between her and Henrik.

He favored her with a slow smile.

"Good." That was the only praise he gave her, but it held a lot of unspoken weight.

"Thanks." She flapped a hand at him, then straightened her ponytail. "I think I can manage now."

"Good."

Henrik swung his leg over the seat and headed off to the old farm cottage. He turned back to catch her gawping and she immediately found something very interesting to inspect on the

ATV. When she looked up again, he was gone.

She needed a good shag. That was the problem. Too many pent up hormones.

She put thoughts of her sex life—or the absence of her sex life—on hold to attach the wagon to the ATV and fill several buckets of water.

The horses had spent the day inside, away from the blistering sun. She let them out in the later afternoon and they would graze all night.

Sadie especially wasn't doing well in the heat. The old draft horse struggled to breathe, and Elenna had cooled her down by splashing water on her legs and underbelly several times that day. The others weren't happy about barn time. Sassy, in particular, fretted and paced in her stall.

As the sun finally dipped below the tree line, Elenna drove the ATV to the big pasture to fill the water trough before turning them out for the night. The grazing was poor, and she'd put out an extra load of hay. She walked back to the barn in the dying light and used the hose to pour water over her head and down her back. As soon as the icy well-water hit her skin, it became tepid. She drenched herself from head to toe, wiped water from her eyes and found Henrik standing in the doorway of the barn.

He leaned on the door jamb with his arms crossed, a stance that accentuated his muscled biceps, which she suspected he knew. For once she was too tired to hear the music that usually intruded her thoughts when Henrik appeared.

He watched her with a frown.

"Eez too hot."

"It is." She ran her hand down her face and then her neck, wiping away the water. Her cooled skin prickled in the heat and she tugged at her wet t-shirt, suddenly feeling very self-conscious.

Henrik didn't move, but his eyes followed the movement of her hands.

"No. I mean eez too hot to stay. I go now."

"You're leaving? When?"

"Tonight."

Elenna's heart stuttered, and she wasn't sure if it was for the loss of the man or the work hand.

"I'm really sorry to hear that. You'll be missed around here."

He pushed away from the wall, and with one long stride of those perfectly sculpted, lightly furred, tree-trunk legs, he was standing before her. His big, blunt-fingered hand reached out and pushed wet hair from her eyes.

"I too vill miss…you." His accent thickened as his eyes smoldered. "Perhaps I stay?" His thumb ran down the side of her jaw. The calluses on his work-worn hand were rough and sent a little thrill through her as she imagined them on other more tender parts of her body.

She swallowed hard. His gaze had her trapped. It had been so long since she felt the touch of a man…

…and that brought her sharply back to reality. She wanted a man, but not this one.

Her hand hovered in front of his chest. She hesitated to push him away, afraid of what the feel of his hot, damp skin might do to her. She stepped back instead and cleared her throat.

"I'm sorry, but if you feel you must go, then you should."

Henrik's lips quirked into what would have been a sneer on a less handsome man. He shrugged, as if her rejection was a trifle. And it probably was.

She watched his back as he sauntered to the old farmhouse, thinking she'd dodged…something, and wondering if she would regret not letting that bullet hit her.

THE FOLLOWING DAY THE SKY turned orange.

Elenna woke early because Gado was whining to go out, which was unusual. Normally, she had to coax the old brute outside in the mornings.

Glancing at her clock, she saw that it was only seven, but already the day was stifling hot. She'd slept in nothing but panties and a loose tank top because the air conditioner couldn't keep up with the heat. She threw on flip-flops and pushed back the paper screen that separated her bedroom from the hallway.

Gado let out a deep woof and scratched at the door to the courtyard.

"Okay, I'm coming."

Her brain was still fuzzy with sleep, and it took a moment to register the scene as she stepped into the zen garden.

She was staring at the Apocalypse.

The morning sun was an eerie orange ball lost behind a dark orange-green haze that seemed thick enough to block sound. She could taste the air in the back of her throat—a smoky tang of charcoal and something acrid.

Gado crouched and did his business, then ducked behind her legs with an uncharacteristic whine. She opened the door and he ran inside. Following him into the living room, she turned on the TV and scanned the channels until she came to Ottawa's morning show on CBC. A reporter was standing in front of a news van parked at the side of a rural highway.

"...fire officials say only ten percent of the fire is under control and they can expect more smoke to head south in coming days."

The image flicked back to the news station where the anchor woman confirmed that fires were burning great swaths of forest in northern Quebec and the combination of heat and lack of rain caused the perfect conditions for smoke to travel as far south as New York City.

"Stay inside folks. And stay safe," the anchorwoman said with a neutral frown.

Elenna turned off the sound and let the images of the raging fire play across the screen. The scene shifted to a New York skyline covered in haze. People in the streets stopped to look up and point.

The world was on fire.

She watched for another few minutes, but the reporters had nothing new to add. They all suggested that folks hunker down and stay inside.

That wasn't an option for Elenna. Her animals couldn't get out of the smoke and they needed water and food.

She fed Gado in the kitchen. He ignored his breakfast as usual, but he'd pick at it throughout the day. She left him sprawled on the cool tiles in the hallway and headed for her bedroom where she found some questionably clean shorts and a t-shirt. She pulled her hair into a loose bun and dug through the supplies in her giant bathroom until she found an N-95 mask left over from the pandemic. Fitting the mask over her face brought back a touch of panic. For two years, such masks had been the compulsory fashion accessory that no one had predicted. The pandemic had ended three years ago, but already the mask seemed alien. Her breath fogged inside it and sweat prickled around her mouth.

Her phone pinged with a message as she stepped outside.

> *Do you need help bringing in the animals?*

It was Gilly. Barely seventeen and already so responsible, Elenna could have kissed her. She texted her back.

> *No. Stay inside. I'll be fine*

She regretted the text as soon as she sent it when she realized that Henrik's car was missing from the driveway beside the farm cottage. He'd made good on his promise to leave. It was terrible timing.

She glanced at the sky. It was otherworldly and frighteningly ominous, but she decided not to text Gilly back. This was her farm. Her responsibility.

Luckily, she'd remembered to close the barn doors last night. The air inside was reasonably clear. She ignored the squabbling ducks and went right for the horse leads and halters, grabbing the biggest one for Sadie and Sassy's smaller halter. Careful to close the doors against the smoke, she ran to the big pasture at the far end of the farm.

The herd appeared like a ghostly apparition in the smog. Horses and donkeys were huddled together. From the goat shed, she heard Beezle's anxious bleating. Sassy whinnied when she saw Elenna coming, but for once she didn't charge the fence. Wild horses would instinctively flee from the smell of smoke, but with nowhere to run, Sassy pranced around her herd-mates, clearly agitated.

"It's okay. I'm here. Everything will be okay." Elenna patted her neck. Sassy wasn't convinced. The mask probably didn't help Elenna's cause, but she couldn't take it off. Even with the protection, her eyes felt hot and full of glue from the smoke.

Sadie's head was lowered, though she wasn't eating grass. It just hung there, her eyes half closed. As Elenna got closer, she could see the mare's ribs roughly expanding with each breath.

That wasn't good.

Heaves was to horses what asthma was to humans and it could be deadly to older horses. Sadie had suffered from it one summer when they got a batch of bad hay, but that had been years ago. Max had assessed her lungs and pronounced them clear, but this Armageddon weather could set her back.

Elenna slipped the halter over Sadie's head and snapped on the lead rope. Sassy decided for once to behave and let Elenna halter her with only one apple treat as a bribe. She walked them back to the barn, released them into the empty stalls and returned twice more to retrieve Shin Mei, then the donkeys.

That filled four empty stalls.

The llama and alpacas had their own mini-barn, and luckily, Henrik had completed the repairs to the goat shed. Though the pasture fence wasn't yet complete, she'd been housing the goats in their new shed for the past few nights to protect them from coyotes. Today, they needed to stay inside, and she decided to move them up to the big barn. She grabbed two more halters and lead ropes and headed down to the goat shed.

Henrik had done a good job restoring it. The window was new, and the door opened on oiled hinges. It even had a new latch. The air inside was clear and cool. Last night's hay was trampled in one corner and, as soon as she opened the door, the goats charged her, looking for their breakfast. Elenna ran a critical eye over each of them. The goats seemed unaffected by the poor air quality, but it would be easier for her to monitor everyone in one place, so she continued with the plan to move them.

Bella, the one-horned Angora, didn't need a halter. As long as Elenna wrangled Beezle and Newton into their harnesses, Bella would follow. Newton, that sweet, placid boy accepted the halter with only a gentle head butt. Beezle expressed his judgment of halters in general with a loud, "BLAAAAH!"

American pygmy goats are tiny beasts and even though his halter was the smallest of the lot, it didn't fit him well. She fussed with the latch while he tossed his head and bleated out his woes. At least she didn't take a horn in the eye, but his head butt took her in the chin and dislodged the mask.

"Ow! Quit it!"

By the time she latched the lead rope to his halter, she was sweating and she tasted charcoal in her throat.

"Come on, pest." She tugged gently on the lead.

Newton trotted beside her like an obedient puppy, but Bella hung back.

"Come on, girl. Let's go see Sadie." She had just coaxed Bella over the threshold when Beezle tugged sharply on the lead. She turned to scold him, but his halter was suddenly dangling empty at the end of the lead. The little bugger had slipped it off.

He splayed his legs, a sure sign he was about to bolt.

"Don't even think it!" She pointed a finger at him.

"BLAAAAH!" He jerked up like a released spring and took off into the forest.

*Crap and double crap.*

"You two stay here." Elenna shoved the other two back inside the shed and closed the door. Then she followed Beezle into the forest.

The leaves filtered some of the smog, but the air still seemed fuzzy, like a movie that was filmed in soft-focus. The smog let little light through the canopy and though she'd walked this forest path a hundred times, it felt foreign and menacing.

A root tripped her and she stumbled. Her breath hitched in her chest and she wished she'd brought a water bottle. Her throat felt raw.

There was no use calling out to Beezle. He wasn't a dog, and he was in flight mode now. A muffled bleating from ahead told her she was at least on his trail. The sound of the river to her right was oddly dampened too, like the smoke was dulling all her senses.

And then she heard music. Or maybe it was only the burble of the river. She shook her head. The music lingered like the tinkling bells in a dream just as you wake.

Beezle screamed. Her head jerked in that direction and her feet followed. She plunged into the dark underbrush, leaving the safety of the trail behind. Branches grabbed her hair and shirt, ran claws across bare legs and arms.

The day darkened. She was ripping her way through a nightmare, panting into the infernal mask. Beezle's cry faded and the silence only drove her on until she realized she was completely turned around. She stopped running, hung onto a tree and tried to suck air through the mask.

The music swelled. It had no melody, or at least a melody that was so foreign to her that it was almost unrecognizable as music. It jangled like dozens of wind chimes all clashing at once.

Lights burst in front of her eyes. She yanked off the mask, thinking she was hallucinating from lack of oxygen. Tiny golden flares buzzed around her head, swirling and dancing in a spectacular murmuration. She tried to focus on one light, but the creatures—if they were even creatures—wouldn't stay still and her gaze couldn't pin one down. They moved as one unit, an undulating ball of sparks that swelled and dove behind her. She felt a zing like a zap of static electricity on her back.

"Ow!"

The creatures swirled around her, urging her forward. They circled her head again and took off through a gap in the trees like an arrow of fire.

She stood dumbfounded for an instant, not sure if she should follow.

But the sky was orange. The forest was a nightmare landscape. Who was she to look a gift fairy in the mouth?

She followed.

The ball of lights paused ahead, expanding and pulsing like a breathing beast. When she reached the tree where they waited, the lights zipped away again.

The ground was spongy where a bog had dried up in the summer heat and rocky in other places. She tripped again and lumbered on, limping now on a twisted ankle.

The fairy lights—for what else could they be?—alternated between zooming onward and falling back to urge her on with little zaps of static electricity on her bare legs.

Finally, they flew ahead, past a knoll of stone and bracken and she lost sight of them.

"Wait!"

She pushed onward, and the trees fell away. She broke free of the cloying bracken and burst into an open field.

"BLAAAAH!"

Beezle was standing in the field, munching on a raspberry bush. The fairy lights had settled on his coat like dozens of tiny dancing stars. Something had chased him there, or he'd panicked in the dark forest, but he seemed all right now.

The goat let out a pitiful bleat and the fairies, their mission complete, soared upward and away. Their golden lights were soon lost against the orange sky.

Elenna threw the lead rope around Beezle's neck before he bolted.

Beyond the raspberry bush sat an old, tilting cottage. It was almost hidden by tall grass. Smoke drifted from a tin chimney, adding to the smog.

She'd chased the fairies to the end of her property. The cabin belonged to Tig, and the old woman stood in its open doorway with a shotgun in her hand. Gloom shadowed her eyes, but Elenna could feel them boring into her. She remembered Tig's demand for a goat and while keeping her eyes on the old witch-woman, she quickly slipped Beezle's halter over his head and latched it.

"BLAAAAH!"

"You be quiet. You've caused enough fuss for one day."

He looked rueful, but her pity was in short supply.

Turning to the cottage, Elenna lifted her hand in a wave, but Tig ignored the gesture. She cradled her shotgun and sipped from her flask.

Elenna turned and headed back through the trees thinking, *the world is dark and full of wonders.*

The apocalyptic smoke hung around for three days—three days that brought back memories of Covid lockdowns as everyone was forced inside. Three days during which Elenna's animals went stir crazy. Sassy nearly kicked a hole in her stall. The ducks had grown enough to fly and were wreaking havoc inside the barn. Despite the dangers of the smoke, she caved to the alpacas' pitiful pleas and let them out for a short run each afternoon.

Then on the third day, blessed rain fell from the sky. Not the little pitter-patter of a light shower, but a real summer storm with lightning and thunder and black clouds that churned around the valley for hours. The rain fell straight down like a curtain, pounding the frail summer-burned grass.

By dinner time on that third day, the clouds had passed. Elenna saw the sunset for the first time in days and it was spectacular, as if the sky had washed off its sooty clothes and donned its finest gown. Soft light filled the pasture, turning the Queen Anne's Lace golden and setting off Sadie's palomino coloring so she seemed to glow like an angel.

The herd was content to be outside again. Elenna leaned on the fence, watching them munch grass or doze. They seemed completely unaffected by the restlessness that plagued her.

Her eyes kept diverting to the path leading into the forest. The light ended at the tree line and the trail appeared to run straight into darkness.

And the things that lived in that darkness.

Elenna knew she had an overactive imagination. She'd always loved the idea of a hidden world living alongside their own. Jamie had said her best stories were the ones that were a little fay, and they'd spent many nights wrapped in sheets, wrapped in each other, telling stories of the "other world" as he liked to call it. He hadn't laughed or thought she was lying when she told him that she once woke to find her mother standing at the end of her bed, years after she'd passed, but his interest seemed more academic, as if he'd wanted to believe but wasn't quite there yet.

And despite her literary interest in ghosts and fairies and things that went bump in the night, Elenna didn't really believe either.

Fairies? Come on. That was just ridiculous.

There had to be a rational explanation for what she'd seen in the forest. Sir Arthur Conan Doyle might have been fooled by some grainy black and white images in an English country garden, but Elenna was a modern woman. She had a better chance of meeting a terrorist than a fairy.

And yet.

Something had led her to Beezle. Some *things*.

When she closed her eyes, she saw the shining bodies alight on Beezle's back as if they were claiming him, but no matter how hard she tried, she couldn't picture their faces—like they were made of flames that constantly shifted and morphed.

But even their indistinctness didn't take away from the facts. She had seen them. She'd heard them. They'd led her to Beezle.

As she leaned on the fence, real fireflies burst into a dance under the trees and music suddenly filled the evening. Not the tinkle of fairy bells, but Quebec's favorite dashing cowboys, Les Cowboys Fringants, singing about America's tears.

The bittersweet melody floated through the trees. It made

her spine straighten and her fingers tap on the fence post.

It was Jamie's favorite song, and it wasn't coming from the forest.

Hadley had lit the Friday night beacon. In ones and twos, villagers would be trickling into the parking lot outside Auntie Clare's. They'd feast on Warrick's poutine or sausages smothered in onions and peppers. Wine would be poured. Later, Hadley would bring out a tub of ice cream and left over pies, and the music would draw people up to dance.

Jamie and Elenna had been regulars at these Friday gatherings. Her legs and arms still had the muscle memory of holding him while they danced to this song, their feet kicking up dust in the gravel lot.

She thought of Hadley's words, "You should make the effort to come back to the world."

Bah. Hadley was a mother hen in training, always worrying about those around her.

But she wasn't wrong.

Jamie had been gone for nearly a year and a half. Elenna might not be ready to dance again, but she was ready to let the music fill her.

She headed back to Kiso House to find the bottle of wine that she'd been ignoring for months.

It was almost dark when she reached the village. The Decker kids were climbing on the old tank in the square, their parents watching from a nearby bench. She waved and followed the sound of Patrice Michaud singing about cherry blossoms. It was coming from the speaker mounted on Warrick's poutine truck. A line of customers already waited for his famous gooey fries, cheese and gravy confections.

Strings of white lights hung between the canteen truck and

the stores on either side. Picnic tables with umbrellas advertising soft drinks and beer dotted the grassy expanse behind the lot. Some local teens filled out one table and she waved to Gilly.

"Elenna!" Nina waved her over to a table where she was sitting with another woman Elenna didn't recognize. The woman's dusky complexion made her look sun-kissed, even in the fading light. Her dark brown hair was pulled back in a severe French braid that accentuated a wide brow and large eyes—eyes that watched Elenna approach with a guarded expression.

"Elenna, this is Joelle. She bought the old Cedar Grove Inn and she's renovating it."

"Hey." Joelle nodded and Elenna smiled back, trying to convey, a "welcome to the neighborhood" vibe when really, she was already thinking it had been a bad idea to come.

"Sit, sit." Nina patted the bench. Elenna sat, feeling dutiful and uncomfortable.

"I brought wine." She placed the bottle on the table.

"Perfect! We'll save it for later." Nina indicated another bottle that was already open. She poured some into a red plastic cup and passed it over. Elenna shot a fragile smile at Joelle, who looked just as uncomfortable.

Nina was oblivious. She sipped her drink and smacked her lips. "The perfect wine for a perfect night. Would you look at those stars?" She lifted her glass to the sky. In truth, the strings of lights blocked out most of the stars, but Elenna nodded and sipped her wine.

"You own the rescue ranch, right?" Joelle asked.

"Yes, I was actually going to come see you next week. We're doing an Open Gate Farm Tour at the end of August. I thought maybe you'd like to set up a table to advertise the inn."

Joelle smiled and shook her head at the same time. "That's

really nice, but I won't be ready to advertise by then. The renovations are going to be extensive and I'm doing them mostly by myself."

"Sounds grueling."

"A bit. But I love it."

"Well, if you change your mind all you have to do is show up."

"Thanks."

The conversation sputtered like a dying fire. Thankfully, Nina's superpower was filling dead space with chatter.

"I was just telling Joelle about the most insufferable customer I had today. She insisted on opening every bottle of lavender oil, because she said they didn't smell right. And what a snooty-snoot. She was all, 'I buy only from Aracana in Ottawa. They have the purest oils. I suppose it's too much to ask for the same quality way out here in the country.' Ugh. She acted like she'd never watched a pimple popping video in her life."

Joelle ducked her head to hide a grin while Nina rambled on. Elenna decided then that she liked their new neighbor.

"And I'm like, 'Hey sister, lavender oil won't cure hemorrhoids and if you try it, you'll burn your butt,' but she didn't believe me, and so…"

Hadley arrived. She plunked a nearly whole chocolate mint silk pie on the table and handed out forks. Hadley's pastry might look rough, but she excelled at mousses. Elenna dug out a forkful of the minty-chocolatey cloud and let it melt on her tongue. Even Nina's stream of consciousness chatter stilled long enough for pie.

"This is really good," Joelle said around a mouthful of mousse.

"Really good," agreed Nina.

A dance tune came on. Hadley groaned.

"Warrick took over the music again. I should change the wi-fi password."

"I love this song!" Nina grabbed Joelle's hand and pulled her up. "Come dance with me!" Joelle's expression said she'd rather do anything else, but she was too polite to decline. A moment later, Nina had badgered a few of the teens into joining them and the parking lot turned into a dance floor.

Hadley tucked her fork into the mousse again. Elenna set hers down. Full night had fallen. The strings of lights lit the little party cove, but left dense shadows under the trees. Movement in those shadows made Elenna jump. Then Hadley's ginger tabby, Smores, burst through to pounce on a bug.

Hadley groaned and pushed the pie away. "Ugh. If I don't have a smoke soon, I'm going to eat my weight in pie."

"Are you quitting?"

"Trying to. Auntie Clare says my pies don't work out because I smell like smoke all the time, and the pastry can smell it. I guess that's as good a reason to quit as any." She took a pack of smokes from her pocket and turned it over in her hand. "I haven't been strong enough to throw them out yet."

"Baby steps."

"Baby steps," she agreed. "So what's got you even more broody than usual?" She held up a hand. "No judgment. The gods know you have reason to brood. You just seem…jumpy." She nodded toward Smores who was now chowing down on a moth.

"Jumpy? I don't know." She stared at the napkin in her hand and started tearing it into pieces.

"I heard that Henrik left. Are you unhappy about that?"

Elenna let out a harsh laugh. "Am I unhappy that my

workload just doubled? Yeah, sure. Am I unhappy about denying him access to my bed? Not at all."

"So he finally made his play. Can't say I'm surprised. Were you?"

Elenna shook her head. "Not surprised. Maybe a bit disappointed."

"In him or yourself?" Hadley knew her too well.

"Maybe a bit of both. But that's not why…" Why what? Why she was jumping at shadows? Why her thoughts kept circling back to a few fireflies she'd seen in the woods?

Hadley didn't speak. She was waiting her out.

The song changed and one of Gilly's friends approved the new tune with a loud whoop.

Elenna leaned in and lowered her voice, even though no one could hear her over the music and rowdy dancers.

"I saw something in the woods the other day. Something I can't explain."

Hadley's face scrunched up. "What do you mean."

"During the smoke crisis, Beezle took off. I lost him in the woods, but then…something helped me. It sounds crazy, I know. But something was out there, leading me to him."

Hadley didn't look surprised. She poured more wine and said, "Tell me exactly what you saw."

So she did.

Nina and Joelle returned just as Elenna finished her tale. Before she could warn against mentioning her possible hallucinations, Hadley said, "Elenna met the fairies."

Nina's eyes widened. "No! Where?"

"In the forest during the smoke storm. They led her to a missing goat."

"Oh, wow! You're so lucky. It's really hit and miss with fairies.

They could have easily led you over a cliff instead."

"Are we really having a conversation about fairies?" Joelle said.

Nina sighed. "You can believe her or not. But I know they're real, and so does Hadley. Elenna too, now."

Joelle stared at her for a moment, then said, "Oh, I believe you." She crossed her arms and sat back. Elenna couldn't help thinking that their new friend had some secrets, but then so did they all.

"Look," Hadley said, "fairies are real. It's a thing. Auntie Clare could tell you stories that would make your hair stand on end. And we've all seen them, but the thing is, we don't talk about them."

"Nope. Talking about fairies is bad," Nina said.

"Why?" Joelle leaned in again.

"Because it gives them weight. Purpose. You won't see them unless you believe. But once you believe, you can't unsee them. And they like to remind you of that. The more we talk about them, the more power they have to meddle in our lives, so let's just change the subject. Okay?"

Joelle crossed her arms and looked grim.

"Okay," Elenna said, but her questions weren't answered, not by a long shot.

AFTER TWO DAYS OF STORMS, the morning of the Open Gate Farm Tour dawned with blue skies and sunshine. The yearly event was run by a cooperative that showcased local growers and ranchers. Seven farms were on the tour map this year. Most had produce, goods to sell, or services to promote. There was an alpaca farm with socks knitted from their herd's wool, a bee farm with honey, an herbalist and apothecary who gave wellness classes, and even a yak farm selling frozen yak patties and other yak essentials.

Equinox Farm was the only one on the list that didn't produce anything but debt. Elenna needed a good turnout and substantial donations to get them through the winter.

With that in mind, she stood in the gravel yard they normally used as a car park. All the vehicles had been moved out. Elenna and Gilly had just finished setting up tables for Mullarkey vendors. Hadley was unpacking Auntie Clare's pies on one table. She chatted with Nina who was hanging charms on a small pegboard on her table. Felix would arrive soon with his cans of maple syrup. She had a small canopy set up for a barbecue. Hot dogs and burgers were on ice in a cooler nearby. Gilly had jumped at the chance to drive the donkey cart with Ruby's dubious help, and Max would take care of the petting zoo. The alpacas were the zoo's focal point, but they were nervous creatures and Max was the only one brave enough to enter the pen to retrieve an alpaca with Luther on duty. Newton, Bella and Beezle were also penned up in the shade. Newton enjoyed chin scritches and Beezle entertained with his boundless energy. Bella endured it all with her usual aplomb.

This year, they'd added ducks to the petting zoo. Two weeks ago, Gilly had renamed them Buffy, Willow and Xander once it became clear they had two girls and a boy. She'd told Elenna the names were bussin' because vintage TV was lit right now, and Elenna had gone to lie her ancient bones down for a nap.

With everyone taking care of their part, that left Elenna to barbecue and greet visitors and run around putting out the inevitable fires that happened at any big event. Not for the first time, she wished that Henrik hadn't left.

*I can do this. I'm a bona fide farmer. I can do anything.*

She wiped sweaty hands on her shorts and glanced around the yard. The rain had washed everything clean, and because Equinox turf was mostly sand, the storm hadn't even left a puddle in its wake. The ground had been so thirsty, it had sucked up all the rain. In a few days, everything would go back to being dry and brittle, but for now the wildflowers on the edge of the pastures looked polished to a sparkle. The barn gleamed like it didn't need a fresh coat of paint, and even the gravel car park was free of dust.

They were ready for visitors.

Nina approached the barbecue tent where Elenna was setting up the popcorn machine. She wore an orange and pink muumuu and a wide-brimmed straw hat with a dozen charms dangling from it. More charm bracelets decorated her wrists. A small leather pouch hung from a cord around her neck. Nina called it her mojo bag, and it held herbs and a small crystal. She looked like the love child of Joan Collins and a hedge witch. She was also carrying a large poster that read, WIND PHONE TRAIL, with a big arrow underneath.

"I'm putting these up at the trail head, and I added a bigger donation box at the phone."

"I appreciate the optimism, but do you really think the phone will be a big draw?"

Nina winked. "You just wait and see…what the hells is that?"

Elenna turned to follow her pointing finger. Gracie Pig sauntered from the open barn wearing a purple tutu around her ample hips. Streaks of something pink were smeared across her back, ears and nose.

Gilly followed her out. She held up pink hands and waved.

Elenna grinned. "That's just Gracie. Gilly promoted her to farm mascot."

"Why is she pink?" Nina squinted as if the sight of the hundred pound pig iced in pink frosting would look better through slitted eyes.

"It's sunscreen. She has delicate skin. When the pink wears off, we know it's time to reapply. I'm not sure it's a good idea to leave her loose in the yard though."

Gracie lumbered over and tried to eat Nina's sandal. Nina laughed and shook her foot. "People so love animal ambassadors."

Gracie grunted and stuck her snout in a cluster of weeds. Nina headed over to the mill path to install her posters.

Gracie would be fine, Elenna hoped. She'd just have to keep an eye on her. And the barbecue, and the girls on the donkey cart and the petting zoo.

She could do this.

Her pulse was starting to spike when Joelle walked into the yard.

"Morning!" Nina waved at her from the trail head. Joelle waved back then approached the barbecue tent and held out a packet of flyers.

"I know you offered me a table today. The inn isn't really set up for guests yet, since I have only two rooms available, but I thought I'd leave these flyers and maybe see if you need help for the day."

Elenna could have kissed her.

"Really? You can stay all day?"

"I'm all yours. Put me to work."

With Joelle on the grill, Elenna's day suddenly became manageable. The first guests arrived around 10 a.m., and Gracie proved to be the perfect greeter. She joined Elenna at the end of the driveway to direct visitors and sashayed around in her tutu. Guests cooed at her antics and were thrilled by her grunting demands for treats. Elenna had approved treats for all the animals available to buy and handed out warnings not to feed them anything else. Gracie would be overfed today, but she reveled in the attention.

By noon, things were going well. Joelle proved to be a whiz at flipping burgers. The donkey cart rides were a big hit, and Elenna even noticed several families and couples hiking up the wind phone trail. She mingled with visitors, supplying flyers with the farm's rescue mission statement and a list of activities. She answered questions and gently reminded inquirers how much it cost to keep even one animal for a year.

She hadn't eaten all morning, so she stopped by Hadley's table to see if she had any of her amazing banana bread left. The table was almost bare and Hadley looked a little frazzled. Her dark hair stuck out from under a baseball cap and she had a smear of something that Elenna hoped was chocolate on her cheek.

"They're not people. They're locusts!" Hadley wiped a hand across her face, smearing the chocolate. "I called the store to have stuff defrosted from the freezer, just to keep us in pies." She leaned in and said in a lower tone. "The next batch won't be as pretty, since they're mostly my creations that I deemed too ugly to sell at the store, but too much waste to throw out."

"I'm sure people will love them anyway."

"Not." Hadley sighed. "Maybe I can sell my soul to the devil to become a master pastry chef. How much is a soul going for these days, anyway?"

"I hear you can get a dream job and a pot of gold for a basic soul, so make sure you haggle."

Hadley laughed. "Thanks, I'll remember that." Her eyes widened. "Who is that?"

Elenna turned to find Milo strolling up the driveway.

"That's the new vet."

"Oh, wow. I'd let him vaccinate me any time."

"You're not a cow, so I'm thinking, not his type."

Milo stopped in the middle of the yard to let the donkeys and cart pass. Ruby sat on the box seat with Gilly and waved. Milo waved back, then stuck his hand in the pocket of his jeans—jeans that fit him very well. He saw the fluorescent pink pig in a tutu rooting after a dropped paper napkin and frowned.

Uh-oh. She was about to get a lecture about pig health. But when he spotted her, a slow grin spread across his face.

It would take a much harder woman not to be a little thrilled by that sight. But Henrik's recent departure had shown her two things. One, her treacherous hormones could still be undone by attention from a handsome man. And two, she wasn't ready to act on that hormonal reaction.

So she acknowledged the little skip of her heart—acknowledged it and set it aside.

"Oh, boy. That smile is just for you, Elenna." Hadley shoved her elbow as if that would propel her right into the path of sudden romance.

Elenna snorted. "How can you even see it under that beard."

"I like the beard."

Elenna made a disgusted sound.

"Come on, it's kind of sexy."

"For a muskrat."

"If you really believed that, you wouldn't be blushing."

"I'm not blushing. I got too much sun."

"Right."

Elenna held her ground. Milo was coming straight at them. He reached the table and smiled again.

It was a nice smile.

"Looks like a great turnout," he said. "You even have a ballerina greeter. That's quite the…"

Elenna could see he was searching for words.

"Quite the surreal experience?" Hadley supplied.

"Exactly."

Elenna introduced Hadley to Milo.

"So what else is going on here," he asked.

"Oh, the usual. Food, petting zoo, more food. We even have a phone where you can talk to the universe." Elenna pointed to the wind phone trail.

Milo squinted one eye and frowned. She'd seen him make that gesture before. It either meant he was trying to find something inoffensive to say or he was amused. She chose to think it was the latter.

He leaned in. "I'd like to talk to the universe. Maybe you can show it to me sometime."

*Sure.* That was what a normal person would say, but the word lodged in her throat, and she suddenly realized how thirsty she was.

Ruby saved her from further embarrassment.

"Dr. Milo! You *have* to try a donkey cart ride." She ran over and tugged on his hand. Before he could protest, she was shooting down any arguments.

"You can't say no. It's for a good cause. Feeding animals who can't take care of themselves is *really* important. Don't you think so?" She stared up at him with those enormous brown eyes and halo of red-gold curls.

"Well, then, I guess I'd better do my part." He let the child drag him away and the next thing Elenna knew, he was crouched on the back of the tiny cart with his knees bent to his chin, bumping along while Gilly and Ruby expertly guided Missy and Jude along the gravel trail.

"Only a very hard-hearted man could turn down that plea," Hadley said. "And it looks like our new vet is anything but hard-hearted."

"I wouldn't know."

"Uh-huh."

Elenna quickly turned her gaze to organizing the pamphlets in her hand.

A loud grunt foretold the attack before it happened.

The steady flow of guests had dwindled, but Gracie Pig wasn't done with treats. Since she had no one to pay attention to her anymore, she decided to ram Hadley's table in the hopes of knocking a pie loose.

"Gracie!" Elenna tried to shoo her away. It was like shooing a hippo. Gracie might only stand as tall as Elenna's knee, but she was a hundred pounds of muscle and determination. She head butted the table again, bending one of the legs. The table teetered.

Hadley shrieked and hung onto the pie plates that were slipping off.

Gracie could smell victory and redoubled her efforts. Elenna tried to redirect her attention, but Gracie wasn't having any of it. That's the problem with potbelly pigs. They're all sweet and sunshine as long as they're doing what they want to do. Try to get them to do what you want, and they turn into Cthulhu's battle-ready pet.

Milo jumped off the donkey cart, bolted for the barbecue tent and grabbed a bag of popcorn. He tossed a few pieces on the ground and started making kissy noises.

Elenna thought Gracie was too far gone in her pie frenzy to notice, but the smell of buttered popcorn hit her piggy brain. She squealed and spun around to gobble the treats.

Milo dropped a few more, steadily leading her toward the barn. When he was within reach, he tossed the rest into her stall.

Gracie lumbered inside and threw herself onto the straw with a grunt.

Milo closed the stall door and leaned on it. Elenna did too. Gracie snuffled the straw into a comfy nest, then flopped down and closed her eyes.

"I guess that was a long day for her," Elenna said. "For all of us, really. Thanks for the save."

"Any time. But for the record, I don't prescribe salted and buttered popcorn as a suitable pig snack. It's for emergencies only. Though I'd allow plain popcorn."

"Noted." Elenna rested her arms on the stall door and watched the sleepy pig. The stress of the day was catching up to her. She needed a moment to process it all.

Milo threw his arms over the door next to her. He was close enough that she felt the heat of his shoulder against hers. They stood quietly for a moment before he broke the silence.

"There is something so soothing about a sleeping animal. Don't you think?"

It was like he had spoken her own thoughts aloud.

"Very soothing," she agreed

"I could watch sleeping animals for hours. Doesn't matter what animal. It's the calm I like." His voice rumbled from him, gruff and low.

"I like to watch them play," she said. "Dogs, cats, donkeys. It makes me happy to see them relaxed enough to get the zoomies."

"Hmm, zoomies."

Elenna chuckled softly and turned to Milo. He was already staring back at her. His eyes were a deep dark brown that sucked her in. He smiled and a shiver went down her spine.

She realized she was staring and shut her mouth. He leaned in. She swayed toward him.

What was she thinking? She couldn't be staring at his eyes. She couldn't be *swaying*! She was still grieving. She had turned Henrik down and she would turn Milo down too. She just wasn't ready for more.

She shoved away from the stall—and from Milo.

"Gracie still has her tutu on."

Milo stepped aside as she opened the stall door. His smile no longer reached his eyes.

"I'll leave you to her, then."

Elenna roughly tugged the tulle skirt off the sleeping pig. Gracie was no help. With her belly full of treats and popcorn, she wouldn't even roll over.

By the time Elenna left the barn, she was sweaty, tired and more than a little miffed. At herself.

The day was winding down and Milo was talking to Nina near the road. He turned and waved to Elenna before heading to his car.

That was it? A wave?

She wanted to kick herself across the pasture, even though she knew her hot-and-cold blustering didn't deserve more than a friendly wave.

She tucked her grief around her like a security blanket and went over to the barbecue tent to help Joelle clean up.

ON A WARM EVENING NEAR the end of summer, something drew Elenna outside. A restlessness that the walls and paper screens of Kiso House couldn't contain. She'd been sitting in the living room with a tablet on her lap, reading a book. The tablet had gone dark as her thoughts wandered. The night had gone dark too, she realized. Rising, she walked through the dim house. Gado lifted his head from his fluffy bed in the corner, a last Christmas gift from Jamie. He woofed once.

"You can stay. I'm just getting some air."

She slipped on runners and headed into the courtyard garden.

It was early September but Mother Nature hadn't flicked the switch to autumn yet and the night was hot and muggy. Her skin prickled and a thousand mosquitoes suddenly found her delicious. She almost ducked back inside, but they wouldn't have many more such nights, so she ignored the tiny blood-suckers and walked toward the pasture.

The sky was lit with spears of red and green. At first she thought it was the sunset, but the lights came from the northern, not the western sky.

Aurora Borealis. Wow.

The sun had been spitting out storms for a week, causing the northern lights to flare in this brilliant display. So far, Elenna had missed them, but tonight color rippled over the heavens like a peacock dancing to show off its splendor, and the sight filled her with awe.

Jamie had loved the northern lights.

"Imagine living a thousand years ago and you see that in the sky," he once said while they trekked through a December night on snowshoes just for a glimpse of the lights. "That's the real meaning of awe. Inspiring and terrifying in one tiny word. It's no wonder they believed in God and heaven. How could you not, looking at that?"

She watched the lights now and wondered: was Jamie living in paradise at the right hand of God, waiting for her to join him?

Unlikely. But what was the alternative? What did she believe?

She watched the glowing sky and listened to the crickets and frogs.

She believed in this. Life. In plants returning every year. In mosquitoes and frogs and grazing horses. She believed that life couldn't be undone by death, only shifted. Jamie's energy would merge with the wind and rain, grass and wildflowers, to be eaten by his beloved goats and horses. He was part of them.

And part of her.

She couldn't deny it. And her reactions to Milo and Henrik proved that she couldn't shake it. Jamie would hang over her like a shadow for the rest of her life. That thought was both comforting and sad.

Her feet kept moving down the path, her hand trailing along the wooden fence rail. Inside the pasture, Sassy lifted her head from the grass and nickered. The others stood with back legs bent in the universal horse pose of ease, as if the fire in the sky was no big deal.

She continued through the dark. Her feet knew where she was going even if her heart and brain didn't accept it yet.

A few minutes later, she stood under the pines by the old mill. The faint light reflected off the shiny phone. Now that she'd stopped moving, the mosquitoes found her again. She slapped a few and then gave up the fight. They could take their pound of flesh.

She picked up the phone's receiver and held it to her ear. The silence on the other end was so vast, so all consuming, that she hung up.

*This is stupid. It's just a phone and an empty line.*

She picked it up again.

She forced her finger into the dial and pulled the first digit of Jamie's number. The whir of the dial spurred her on. She dialed the next number and the next, in a frenzy now and impatient for each number to finish spinning.

When the whir of the last number died, she put the phone to her ear and this time, she didn't listen to the darkness.

She filled it.

"I hate you!" A dam broke inside her. "I hate you! I hate you! I hate your stupid need to drive every vehicle faster than it should go. I hate you for pushing yourself past your limits. I hate you for doing this to yourself. For doing it to me. What a useless, senseless way to die…" Her voice snagged. She sucked in a breath and exhaled.

She had so much more to say—about how she missed him. About how they'd fought the morning he died because she'd wanted him to go into Ottawa with her instead. She wanted to ask how he could be so careless with her heart.

But the words caught in her throat.

She slammed down the receiver. The clang echoed through the forest like a reproach.

She rubbed damp palms on her shorts.

A new sound broke the stillness of the night. It was low at first, like the call of a night bird, or the growl of a wolf heard in the distance. Then it started to grow, and she glanced through the tree branches overhead, expecting to see the lights of a military helicopter. They weren't far from the base and she often spotted them flying their training missions.

But no helicopters appeared. The sound grew. It was painful to hear, like metal grating on metal. Or stone smashing stone.

Her storyteller's brain went right to the worst and the most abstract of causes, and she envisioned Baba Yaga flying overhead in her great mortar, wielding her pestle like a cudgel and gnashing her metal teeth while she looked for children to feast upon.

Yep, those are the kinds of places her brain went to. It might have seemed ridiculous, but standing there with the echo of the wind phone's emptiness in her ear and the haloes of angels painting the sky, Baba Yaga didn't seem like a far stretch.

She took off at a run and was grateful when she spied the light of Kiso House welcoming her home.

# Fall

September was Elenna's favorite month. The light turned a buttery yellow. There were fewer mosquitoes, but the days remained warm. What wasn't to love?

The weather filled her with a deep contentment as she worked through her morning chores. In the afternoon, she decided to do a little pasture maintenance. She entered by the small gate, bringing only a rake. She hoped Sassy would stay calm enough for her to clean up, or she'd have to put the horses in the barn. She needn't have worried. The horses and donkeys were feeling lazy. Even Sassy seemed lulled by the soft, warm light.

Elenna started at the bottom of the pasture with a big pile of manure. Left alone, it would burn the delicate grass. She scooped it up in her rake, and with a deft swing and flick of her wrist, she flung it. The solid mass broke into crumbs and scattered across the pasture where it would regenerate the life-giving grass. Jamie had been adamant that part of Equinox's mission was to adhere to the practice of permaculture—to treat the land as kindly as they treated their rescues. That meant no chemical fertilizers. No pesticides. And no standing manure pile that attracted pests and disease.

She hefted another lump of horse apples and grinned. Ten years ago, she would have never guessed that flinging poo could be cathartic. Scoop, fling, scatter. Scoop, fling, scatter. There was just something satisfying about the way the lump of waste broke apart to become one with the earth.

She worked her way up the slope, and by the time she reached the gate again, her shoulder muscles were loose and her mood was as smooth and sweet as jelly.

Gilly was waiting for her by the upper fence. A tall teenaged boy stood beside her.

"You look like you were enjoying that way too much," Gilly said.

"What? Raking." Elenna was nearly out of breath.

"No, flinging poop." Gilly wrinkled her nose in disgust. "I'll never get why you like it so much."

"It's like arts and crafts, a gym workout and therapy all in one. That's how monkeys do it, and aren't we just better-dressed monkeys? Seriously, you should try it."

"No, thanks. I'll stick to gardening." Gilly turned to the boy. "Elenna, this is my friend Shaun. He goes to my school." She touched his arm in a possessive way. "Shaun this is my very strange boss, Elenna."

Elenna shook Shaun's hand. "Boss isn't exactly the right word. Gilly is a volunteer here at the farm. The best volunteer."

Gilly rolled her eyes. "I'm the only volunteer."

"That too." She smiled as she scrutinized the new kid and tried to ignore Gilly's nervous twitching. She obviously had a thing for Shaun and Elenna wondered if her feelings were reciprocated. Either way, it was clearly important that Elenna liked him.

Shaun was handsome like a rough-hewn log. His shoulders were square and not yet filled out. His head was square too, with a chin to match. Dark skinned, with dark hair that seemed cut for convenience rather than style. She liked him immediately, because his eyes flashed with intelligence and a little bit of mischief.

"Gilly tells me you need a project for your senior year outreach. What did you have in mind?"

Shaun's eyes locked on Gilly's. She smiled and nodded.

"Well, Gilly said you rescued some ducks, and how someone abandoned them in the woods. I'd like to educate people about the, uh…what's the word? Not risk exactly."

"The unsuitability," Gilly injected.

"Right. That's it. How animals are *unsuitable* for Easter gifts or Christmas gifts or anything like that."

Elenna rubbed a hand across the back of her neck. September was leaving them in a heat wave.

"Sounds like a big mountain to climb."

Shaun laughed. "I guess. Maybe I can't educate everyone. Just the kids at our school. And maybe hype your farm too. You know, a few solid Insta shots."

"Right." Jamie had avoided social media after a nearby sunflower farm was decimated by tourists looking for great Instagram shots. But desperate times required appealing to the cottage-life glamor seekers.

"Okay. What do you propose?"

"First, I want to build something solid for the ducks."

"A habitat," Gilly interjected.

"Yeah, a habitat. We could throw up a sign telling their rescue story and what would've gone down if they'd been left in the woods alone. And yeah, I gotta present this whole thing to the entire school once it's ready."

Elenna didn't think about it for very long. The ducks needed a new habitat before winter, and her bank account needed free labor.

"Okay, but you need to run all the costs by me before you start."

"No worries, Mrs. Nolan. We're gonna raise the cash at a car wash next weekend."

Mrs. Nolan. She hadn't taken Jamie's name when they'd married. Few women who marry in Quebec change their names, and being called Mrs. Nolan didn't sit right.

"Please, it's Ms. Kane. Or better yet, just call me Elenna." She could feel the tightness behind her smile. "And I'm very grateful for your help. I'm sure the ducks will be too. Why don't you two scout out a few potential spots for the new habitat and let me know what you find?"

As the kids walked off, talking animatedly about their duck plans, a red pickup pulled into the driveway. It had a white covered truck bed and the logo for Orleans Veterinary Services on the door.

Milo was here for teeth and sheath day. He stepped out of the truck and gave her a curt nod.

Oh, good. He was putting on his most professional manners today. He hefted his medical bag in one hand, and met her beside the barn.

"How's the grand dame of Equinox today?"

"I'm going to assume you mean Sadie and not me."

"Of course." There was the hint of that come-get-me grin again. Maybe it was the beard. Glimpsing his lips through the rough made the smile more alluring. That was all.

Sexy romcom montage music started playing in her head again, but she resolutely put an end to that.

Milo watched her as if he could almost hear the music, his head cocked to one side, then he held a hand toward the barn.

"Shall we file some teeth and clean some sheaths?"

"Sounds like a hot date." *Oh, dear God. Did I say that out loud?* In her head, she'd just tripped and face-planted right in a horse pie.

Milo was gracious enough to ignore her stumble.

AFTER A QUICK EXAM, MILO opted to file only Sassy and Shin Mei's teeth. The donkeys weren't due yet, and since the forest fires over the summer, Sadie's breathing had been erratic. She was all right now, but he decided it wasn't worth the risk of sedating her.

He stood back and studied Sadie while she munched hay in her stall.

"Is she favoring her right leg? The back one," Milo asked.

"Yes. But I don't feel any heat in the joint."

"And you still can't pick out her hooves?"

Elenna shook her head. "She can't hold up that hoof, and I'm afraid she'll fall if I force it."

Milo nodded. He crouched and ran his hands along the leg. "I'll see what I can do about that. But for now, I think we're going to just leave her be. Let me know if she seems to have any trouble eating or if she loses weight. You might add some bran mush to her grain. She's looking a bit thin." He hesitated. She knew what was coming next. Her fingers gripped the edge of the stall door as if she could brace herself for the words.

"I'm worried about that foot. We might have to make some difficult decisions in the next few months." Milo's eyes were soft, but they didn't lessen the burden of that prediction.

"I know." Her words came out a bit strangled. Sadie had

been Jamie's first rescue. She was the gentlest soul Elenna had ever met and the undisputed matriarch of the farm. She lead by quiet example and the others followed. Even Sassy's bad habits had been somewhat tamed in Sadie's shadow. Elenna couldn't imagine Equinox Farm without the old mare.

Milo saw her expression and his hand closed over hers.

"There's no point in chasing after sorrow. Sadie's just fine for now. We'll do everything we can for her."

Elenna nodded and forced a smile. He was right. Sadie was a heartache for another day.

She gave him a half-hearted salute. "All right, captain. Who's next."

Milo closed one eye and squinted with the other. Something amused him.

"Are you still hell-bent on learning how to clean Shin Mei's sheath?"

"How far did you drive to get here today?"

"An hour and a half."

"So that's a yes, then. I have to learn to take care of my animals. On my own." The more she learned, the less she'd have to rely on vets that came from the city.

"Good. Let's do Sassy's teeth first. Then Shin Mei's. And get ready to learn some real animal husbandry."

The thing about horses is that humans tamed them. Humans brought them in from the cold, put shoes on their feet and gave them easy nutrition. It all sounds great, but their bodies were made for a harsher life. Their hooves keep growing and without rocky surfaces to wear them down, they need to be trimmed. By a human. Their teeth also keep growing and produce hook like protrusions that wild horses wear down by eating coarse grasses. In tamed horses, those need to be filed by a human too. And geldings need their boy parts cleaned. By a human.

Elenna watched her gelding who had just undergone the arduous teeth filing, and was now fully sedated in his stall.

"Remind me again, why do we have to do this? I'm sure horses in the wild don't get their sheaths cleaned regularly."

Milo's beard twitched. "Actually stallions do. They have a natural cleaning mechanism. It's called sex."

Elenna's mind stumbled over that idea.

"Gross. I bet the lady horses didn't get a say on that design detail."

Milo laughed. "No, probably not. But geldings have even less say. They didn't ask to be gelded, after all. Dirty sheaths are a completely man-made problem."

"So we gotta take care of them."

"We do."

She heaved a sigh and hiked up her imaginary big girl farmer pants.

Shin Mei's head hung low, a sure sign that the sedatives were working.

"All right. He's good and relaxed," Milo said. "See how he's letting it all hang out."

And was he ever. Shin Mei, the gentleman who didn't strut his stuff for anyone, was now swaying on his feet and displaying a good eight inches of his goods.

"So what do I do?"

Milo handed her the bucket of warm water treated with a mild, horse-safe soap and a soft cloth.

"See that pouch his penis is hanging from?"

She swallowed hard and nodded.

"You're going to have to get in there eventually to clean it out, but since he's being so forthcoming, you can start with the shaft."

"The shaft. Right."

She took the bucket and stepped into the stall. Milo handed her latex gloves. She put them on thinking they weren't nearly thick enough or long enough. Right about now, she wanted to encase herself in latex.

"Okay. Grab it below the head, just like Little Rabbit Foo Foo picking up the field mice." He mimed scooping up a mouse in his fist.

She gaped at him. "You just ruined a piece of my childhood."

"Just don't bop him on the head." A light danced in his eyes. Milo was enjoying her discomfort.

She reached for the big red dangling appendage and hesitated.

"What if I hurt him?"

"You won't."

She grabbed the shaft right below the head like Milo suggested. Shin Mei tensed, but the drugs were doing their magic, and he only shuffled sideways. She wiped his shaft, dunked the rag in the warm water and continued the awkward bath.

Behind her, Milo started humming *Little Rabbit Foo Foo*, and she squeezed her eyes tight as if that would keep her from laughing, then realized her mistake. Now her eyes were watering and she couldn't wipe them.

Milo leaned over her shoulder to get a better look. His beard tickled her ear. "Now see that lip around the tip of the penis? Get your finger in there and fish out the bean."

Ugh. She'd been expecting this. She'd even done some research online, but the videos didn't do justice to the actual stomach-churning event.

*Big girl pants. Big girl pants.*

She slipped a finger into the gap and scooped. A bead of skin and debris popped out.

"I got it!" She felt inordinately pleased as she dumped the hard bean into the bucket. The rest of the cleaning was easier. Unbelievably gross, awkward and strenuous, but easier. She stuck her arm into Shin Mei's sheath up to her elbow and washed out the muck. The gelding swayed. He tried to kick her once, but it was a halfhearted punt.

"Easy fella." Milo patted him on the withers.

Finally, when she felt no more dirt inside his sheath, she pulled off the gloves and held her arms out from her sides. She couldn't bear to have them touch her. Not until she showered with a bucket of bleach.

Milo was grinning. He looked too damn sexy in the fading afternoon light. Dust motes floated around his face, adding to his rugged appeal. She grinned right back. For once, she felt strong, capable. In control of her life.

"You've got a bit of smegma on your face." He pointed to her left cheek.

Why couldn't a sink hole open up and swallow her when she really needed it?

"Gosh, I don't think anyone has ever said that to me before."

Milo grinned. "Come on. I'll hose you off in the yard."

"Yes, please." She walked out of the barn, holding her arms out like a zombie. Milo turned on the water and lifted the hose. He sprayed her from fingertips to shoulders and back again.

She grimaced. "There's not enough water in the world to wash off the yuck."

"Oh, really. Not even this much?" He flicked the nozzle upward. Cold water hit her straight in the chest. She let out a squawk, then pretended to be angry. Milo believed it. His hand dropped.

"Psych!"

She grabbed the hose, lifted his shirt and let loose with the nozzle, soaking him from waist to chin.

He barely flinched, but gave her a martyred look. She almost felt bad. Almost.

"Is that how it is? Right." He turned the hose on her again. She jumped in the air, her feet did a high step that would be the envy of any highland dancer as cold water rained on her.

And then she heard an odd sound. Her own laughter. It was so foreign to her ears that she stopped in mid-dance. Water streamed from her face and hair. Instinctively, she stepped away and immediately tripped over a forgotten bucket someone (Elenna) had left in the way.

She saw the next few seconds flash through her mind. A nose dive into a manure-laced mud puddle, followed by an embarrassing moment that would take care of any steam growing between them.

Instead, a rough hand caught her waist and pulled her

upright. Out of the frying pan and straight into those brown eyes.

He was close. So close. His hand gripped her at the waist, and she could feel his rough calluses through her t-shirt. She wondered for a moment how many critters he had to wrangle to get those calluses and how he would look doing it. She didn't want him to let go. Not yet. So, she rested her hands lightly on his chest.

He wasn't like Henrik. He had less flashy muscles and more functional ones. Muscles he used to pull her even closer.

"Have I ever told you how much I love ponytails?" His gaze strayed from her eyes to her hairline. "Especially on a hot day, when your hair curls in the humidity." She blushed furiously as he brushed the dandelion fuzz back from her hairline.

And then kissed her. It was a soft kiss, a butterfly's touch on her forehead.

His beard was so close she could reach out to bite it.

His gaze tipped down to hers again, searching for permission. *Don't think about kissing. Don't think about kissing.*

But, of course, she did. Her lips parted and her tongue wet them. His gaze snagged on the motion and he made a strangled sound.

He kissed her, softly at first, then deeper. She felt herself opening to him, then the tingle of his beard on her chin jolted her back to reality. It was such a foreign sensation. Not unpleasant, but wholly new.

She sucked in a ragged breath and pushed him away. Turning, she stumbled over the damned bucket again. This time, he didn't save her.

He let her go, stepped back and cleared his throat.

"I must've gotten the wrong idea. I'm sorry if…" He stuttered and wouldn't look her in the eye.

Damn, she had made it awkward.

"No, no, it's not you. It's just…" She paused. How could she explain? How did she make him understand when she didn't understand the hot and cold feelings running through her?

She *needed* her grief. It was her only link to Jamie. And though she might rage at him for leaving her so suddenly, she loved him. And her aching heart told her she always would. She tried to put that feeling into words and failed. She held up her hand and waved him away as she sat on a bench beside the barn. Her breath came in gulps.

He crouched beside her, close enough to peer into her face, but not close enough to touch her. "I'm sorry. That was really… wrong." He ran a hand over his beard and gripped the back of his neck. "So sorry."

She shook her head, looking at her hands so she didn't have to see the hurt and concern in his eyes.

"I lost my husband." She ripped off the band-aid. "To everyone else, it was over a year ago. To me, it was yesterday. I'm not ready for anything… emotional yet."

He smiled at her. "You don't owe me any explanation."

"Thank you. And I'm sorry."

His hand reached for her shoulder, but she sidled away.

"I think I should check on the horses." She stood up and walked into the barn.

The familiar warm smell of hay, manure and leather soothed her. Sassy was already coming out of her sedation and Shin Mei wasn't far behind. Elenna reached into his stall and patted his nose. Sadie nickered quietly and leaned over the half door of the next stall to nuzzle her arm. Elenna leaned her forehead against Sadie's big velvety nose and felt a sob bubble up in her chest.

*No more tears!*

She wanted desperately to be done with grief. Sadie licked water and sweat off her arm, while Elenna leaned into her, letting the warm smell of horse soothe her like a balm.

"I…um, should be going." Milo's voice came from the barn entrance. "Shin Mei looks like he's doing okay. Sassy too."

She nodded without turning around.

"Are you? Okay, I mean."

She nodded again. After a minute, she decided that Milo deserved better. He at least deserved an explanation, but when she turned around, he was already gone.

She heard his truck tires rolling over gravel as he drove off, and thought, *it's for the better.*

THE AIR WAS DEAD. ELENNA had been holding the phone receiver long enough for her ear to go numb. And still, nothing but dead air. She could hear the vastness of that void. It was a long black tunnel to forever.

She shifted her grip. Her fingers were slick on the receiver. A chickadee landed on the branch next to her and seemed unconcerned by her motionless presence. She was just another rock in the forest. Moss would soon grow over her feet.

And still she couldn't speak into the phone. The endless oblivion seemed to mock her.

She finally slammed the receiver back into the cradle.

*This is ridiculous.*

Why did she want to talk to Jamie anyway? So she could tell

him that another man had kissed her? To assuage her guilt for leading Milo on? To what purpose?

She yanked on her ponytail until her scalp hurt, and the sensation brought sanity.

The little bird fluttered off with a chirp, as if she'd broken a spell.

This was a waste of time. She'd come out here to draw—the first time she'd had the urge in months—and been sidetracked by the wind phone. But really, she should be mucking out stalls. She sighed and was about to head home when she spied Max coming along the path from the forest, carrying a large basket full of bright orange chanterelles.

"What are you doing here?" Her tone was a bit too sharp. The adrenaline rush from her agitation hadn't faded yet.

Max frowned. "I thought you didn't mind me foraging in your forest. Was I wrong?"

"No, of course not. You're always welcome. You know that. But you shouldn't be out here alone."

"Aw, don't be a worry wart. My legs still work. And the day's too pretty to spend it inside. Besides, I needed to come talk to Beth." He pointed toward the wind phone.

"Don't tell me you use that ridiculous thing too."

"What's ridiculous is an old man talking to his dead wife in the kitchen. At least here, I can imagine her on the other end of the line."

Beth had succumbed to ovarian cancer nearly twenty years ago. Elenna hugged her arms over her belly. Did it take that long to get over someone? She couldn't imagine spending the next twenty years feeling like she carried a rock around in her chest.

"Sometimes I just feel the need to talk to her, you know?" Max watched her closely.

She made a noncommittal noise. She didn't want to tell him that she'd tried the wind phone and failed at it each time.

He gripped her arm. "It gets easier. I promise. The sadness doesn't pinch so much anymore. But I miss talking to her. She used to get nearly as excited as me when we found chanterelles." He held up his basket. "I just want to share the good stuff with her. That old phone helps."

Elenna felt about two inches tall. She let out a sigh. "I'm sorry. I don't have a monopoly on grief. That's really selfish of me."

"The one time we are truly alone is inside our grief. You've nothing to be ashamed about." Max patted her arm.

A sudden wind gust turned the yellow leaves on their backs. That grating sound of stone on stone followed. It raked along her nerves and made her want to duck and run.

Max shivered. "Brrr. That's a winter wind, for sure."

She glanced down the dark path that led into the forest. "Did you hear that?"

"Hear what?" Max's gaze followed hers. His brows lowered.

"Nothing. I just thought I heard…It's nothing. Enjoy your chanterelle feast. I have to go. Barn stalls to muck out." She waved and ignored his concerned expression as she hurried down the trail, away from the shadows that seemed to reach from the forest to ensnare her.

Two weeks later, the weather turned. Saturday morning dawned bright and clear, but with a definite chill in the air. Summer had finally lost its grip on Mullarkey.

Elenna rose late and dragged Gado out the door for a quick walk before breakfast. He let out a bored woof at Shaun and Gilly who were already busy on the duck enclosure. Shaun had been diligently working on it every day after school, and they were nearly finished. From on top of the pen, he waved to her, then continued hammering on the metal roof.

Elenna whistled for Gado and the old dog plodded behind her as they headed back to the house.

After breakfast, she fed the horses, goats, donkeys, pig, alpacas and llama. Then she cleaned stalls. She filled the spreader that ran behind the ATV with dirty stall bedding, again wondering why she had resisted learning to drive it for so long. Scattering hay and manure with the spreader was so much easier than lugging a wheelbarrow.

A rumble of tires had her turning to watch a truck pull into the drive. She recognized Milo's truck, but he was pulling a trailer with a massive wooden construction strapped to it.

She left the muck bucket beside the ATV and headed over to greet him.

Milo rolled down the window and leaned out.

"Howdy, pretty lady. Where can I park my stocks?"

"Stocks?"

"Just trust me. This is going to help Sadie, but I need a solid piece of flat ground out of the way to install it."

She had no idea what he was up to, but she waved him over to the far pasture where the gravel road ran out. "You can park it there, I guess. Next to the old barn."

He tipped an imaginary hat and drove on. She followed on foot.

By the time she arrived at the pasture, Shaun and Gilly had stopped their work to come see Milo's new toy.

"Mennonite farmers use these all the time for their draft horses," he explained. "Look. Sadie goes in there and this pulley system lifts her foot to rest it on that platform. The stocks hold her in place so she can't fall and you can pick out her feet while she stands comfortably."

"Too bad," Gilly said. "I thought it was some medieval thingy. Like those war re-enactors use."

Shaun nodded. "A catapult."

"Nope, just a horse stock," Milo said.

Elenna touched the wooden cross beam. "It's amazing. But I can't accept this." And there was no way she could pay for it.

"Don't worry. I got it free from a homesteader who was closing up shop. All it cost me was the trip to go get it."

Elenna pinched her lips before asking him how far that trip had been. Sadie really needed this help, and if she was going to run a not-for-profit sanctuary, she had to learn how to graciously accept donations.

"Thank you. This means a lot to me. And to Sadie."

Milo's face lit up. "Let's get it unloaded and give it a try."

It took all four of them to lug the contraption off Milo's trailer. Once settled on the ground, it stood a good six feet high and eight feet long. It consisted of a wooden platform and four tall, sturdy posts with bracers. Small platforms covered in something that looked like hemp were fixed to each post at a level that would comfortably hold a lifted hoof. The whole thing looked old and well worn.

Milo tugged one of the posts to make sure the stock was level and pronounced it ready.

"I'll go park the truck if you want to bring Sadie," he said.

Gilly offered to run up to the barn and get her halter and lead rope. Shaun and Elenna waited for the others to return.

"Seems like a big day," he said.

"Is it?" She leaned her arms on a fence post. Shaun wasn't much of a talker, so she let him take the lead.

"Yeah. I'm finished with the duck pen. Another hour to put in some gravel and we're done."

"That's great. Did it turn out as you expected?"

Shaun's face lit with a shy grin. "With help from my dad. I wouldn't have figured out the roof on my own. But, yeah. I like it."

"I'm sure the ducks will too. Give me a shout when you're ready to bring them down. I want to film their grand entrance." She'd been dipping her toe in social media lately, and the duck video would look great on Instagram.

Shaun nodded and headed off.

She called after him. "And Shaun? Thank you!" He waved back. She was getting good at this gracious acceptance thing. The ducks would be cared for and Shaun had learned how to build a roof, a skill that might come in handy one day. She had to start thinking in those terms. Even Gilly, who'd been volunteering at Equinox since she was twelve would take skills she'd learned here into her future life, whatever that might be.

Gilly returned with Sadie's kit.

"You're not unhappy that you spend so much time here, are you?" Elenna asked.

Gilly handed her the halter with a laugh. "Is that some passive-aggressive way of asking me if I like working at the farm?"

"No. I mean, yes. I guess." How were kids so smart these days? She sighed. "At your age, I didn't even know the meaning of passive-aggressive. I blame social media."

Gilly waggled her fingers like she was casting a spell. "Oooh, the evil social media. Instagram gonna steal my soul!" She laughed. "Come on, Elenna. You know I love working here. I'm going to miss it next year."

"Next year? Why? Where are you going?"

"CEGEP, dummy. Remember that place you went to eons ago?"

"Right."

Quebec was the only province to adopt the CEGEP system, which stood for *Collège d'enseignement général et professionnel* or College of General and Professional Teaching. CEGEP was a sort of two-year junior college for those going on to university. For others who chose trades, they could finish their schooling in the many technical programs. Elenna had studied at John Abbott College CEGEP near Montreal before going on to the University of Ottawa, where she met Jamie.

She grumbled something about CEGEP being not so long ago. Gilly laughed and headed down the path to help Shaun put the finishing touches on the duck enclosure while Elenna went to catch Sadie.

Catching Sadie was like catching a rock. She didn't run very fast, or at all. But Sassy, sensing that something was different, took off at a gallop around the pasture. She bucked and let out a whopping fart for emphasis.

"Such a lady," Milo said as he reached the fence.

"She's got pizzazz, you gotta give her that." Elenna ignored the younger mare and tugged on Sadie's lead. Sadie dutifully followed her out the gate, and they stopped by the stocks. Elenna let her get a good sniff of the wooden contraption.

"What if she won't get into it?"

"Then we'll have to coax her with treats, but I think you might be surprised. If she really is an old plow horse, she's probably familiar with stocks."

He took the lead rope and led Sadie behind the stocks. Elenna held her breath as Sadie seemed to pull away, but she was just getting some momentum to step forward onto the platform, which she did with ease. Milo clipped a chain closed behind her.

"Such a good girl." Elenna cooed and patted her neck. Sadie let out a long-suffering sigh. Milo lifted her right back foot and let the hoof rest on the low platform. He pulled a hoof pick from his pocket and deftly scooped out dirt, grass and debris.

"The bad news is that she's overdue for a clipping, but your farrier should be able to do the job easily now. And hopefully we'll see an improvement in this hoof."

He cleaned out her other feet, and then they backed her out of the stocks.

Sadie accepted all the fussing with her signature poise.

"She's a rock star," Milo said as they let her loose in the pasture.

"She really is."

Sassy galloped over to make sure they hadn't turned her friend into a cow or something equally heinous. Sadie told her to chill her beans with a flick of her golden tail.

"It's days like these that I love being a farmer," Elenna said. "Thank you for the stocks. They are the best gift we've ever received. After Shaun's amazing duck pen, of course."

"Of course." Milo cleared his throat. "But the stocks are more of a peace offering. I felt like I had to do something to apologize after last time. I was way out of line. Very unprofessional. It won't happen again."

"Oh, don't go harshing my mellow with your self pity. You didn't do anything wrong. But I've thought a lot about our little water fight and what happened…after. I have something to say."

He turned and leaned on the fence post.

She rushed on before she changed her mind. "This is hard for me to say, and I could be totally off base. I probably *am* off base, in which case, I apologize. And now I'm babbling." She sucked in a breath. Milo was grinning at her.

Why, oh why did his mouth look so cute tucked into that beard like a wild animal poking from its den? She dragged her thoughts back to the problem at hand.

"The thing is, I think you like me." He opened his mouth to either agree or disagree, but she held up a hand to forestall him. "And I like you. It's just that I'm not ready to like you. Or anybody. I'm not ready to have fun and laugh and leave…leave Jamie behind." She ran a hand over her eyes. "Geez, the sound of my own laughter freaked me out. How pathetic is that?"

"Not pathetic at all."

"And when you kissed me, it felt like betrayal."

"I understand. I can't say I'm not disappointed, but I understand. No more kissing."

"None."

They stood in silence for a full minute, side by side, watching the horses in the pasture, until he finally spoke.

"For what it's worth. I do like you."

Elenna smiled and he bumped her with his elbow.

A sharp whistle came from below the pasture where Shaun and Gilly were ready to let the ducks into their new home.

Elenna and Milo met them at the pen. Shaun had outdone himself. The duck enclosure was a ten by fifteen foot structure that straddled the small creek running between the horse pasture and the new goat pasture. Shaun had dug out part of the creek to make a pool and lined that with clay. A small dam regulated the flow and kept the water fresh. It wouldn't freeze in the winter. The frame was enclosed with metal mesh that was dug six inches into the ground to baffle predators. Smooth round stones lined most of the pen, so delicate duck feet wouldn't get cut on sharp gravel. A small duck coop filled one corner. Solar-powered heat lamps would keep Buffy, Willow and Xander snug all winter.

"Shaun, it's amazing!" Elenna didn't need to feign her delight. Shaun grinned and lowered his gaze. He was too shy to expound on the pen's many merits, but not Gilly.

"And look, the gate slides open here. You can let them run in the pasture eating bugs all day. Then train them to come in at night. And the ground slopes, so it'll be super easy to clean— even for you when I'm away next year."

Elenna felt her eyes growing warm. She squeezed Gilly's hand, then wiped her sniffly nose.

"Well, let's see if they like it."

The ducks were waiting impatiently in three separate cages, squawking and babbling their displeasure at being confined. One by one, Shaun and Milo lugged the cages into the new pen and released them.

The girls—Buffy and Willow—flapped their wings and immediately splashed in the water. Xander was more shy and he took his time waddling up and down the pebbles.

Gilly filmed the whole thing. Shaun added the last detail. He hung a laminated poster on the side of the pen. It told the story of the Easter ducks who had been abandoned in the woods.

She glanced over at Milo who was listening to Shaun describe his building process and smiled.

Shaun and the ducks had become part of the lore of Equinox Farm. New memories, Elenna realized. Time didn't stop just because her heart wanted it to. And maybe, just maybe, that was a good thing.

During the cool fall weather, Luther and the alpacas were more active. Their wool was growing thick and Elenna felt no need to close them in their little barn even when the temperatures dropped to near freezing. They had the run of their entire enclosure. That meant they had a lot of room to mess up. Luther liked to toss hay out of the run-in shed and trample it into the mud. The smell of five animals in one pen could be enough to peel paint and Elenna made sure to clean up after them every day.

She entered the pen cautiously with a rake laid across her wheelbarrow and a broom in her hand as a shield. As she latched the gate behind her, Luther thundered up, showing what a big tough dude he was by getting in her face. She propped the broom between them.

"I'm not in the mood for your crap today, buddy. Stand back or your tuchus will feel the wrath of a straw lashing."

Luther made his signature growl-grunt and retreated to hover in front of his herd. The alpacas sensed his stress and gabbled like a pack of frightened lemmings.

At least the alpacas had the decency to do their business in the same spot everyday. That made cleaning easier. She parked the wheelbarrow at their designated pooping site and kept it between her and the herd as she scooped up their droppings. Luther lunged a couple of times, but his bluster was all show. As she cleaned, she made up recipes for llama stew and llama pot pie in her head.

To be fair to Luther, most of her annoyance was directed elsewhere—at Milo. She was angry at him for kissing her outside the barn, and angry at him for not kissing her beside the horse stocks. She didn't care that it wasn't rational. Since when did rational have a place in love?

Love. Oof.

She leaned on the rake and sucked in a breath like she'd been punched. Was that what this thing with Milo was? What if she wasn't ready for love? Did that mean she'd sabotaged a possibly great thing and might never have another chance?

She dug the rake into the muddy ground a little too vigorously and the tines stuck. When she pulled them free, alpaca pellets sprayed across the yard. Luther took that as a sign of aggression on her part and bolted forward with a bleating growl.

She held the rake like a broadsword. She'd left the broom by the gate.

"Don't try me, mister."

Battle drums played in her head—low, ominous and mounting in tension. A cool wind blew through the yard, threatening winter. The alpacas lined up like troops behind their champion. Luther's only weapon was his spit, but it had a longer reach than her rake-sword.

She glared at him. He glared right back. The music swelled to an epic frenzy. Luther's lips curled. She raised the rake as a spray of green struck her chest, neck and arms.

"Gah!" She covered her face with her elbow and decided a quick retreat was in order. Luther harried her like a conquering general as she trundled the wheelbarrow all the way to the gate.

She slammed it behind her and heard the tell-tale *pffft* of llama spit again.

She jumped out of spit-shot and turned on him. Her fingers were clenched around the rake handle so hard they ached. She'd lost the broom in the battle. Luther would claim it as spoils of war.

In that moment, if she'd had the opportunity, she would have given the rat-bastard llama away. Then Jamie's words came back to her.

"I had to take him in. No one else wanted him." She'd never seen Jamie cry, but talking about the abuse some of his rescues had endured made him come close. "Luther is the way he is because some human groomed him to aggression. It's not his fault."

"But aren't you afraid he'll hurt someone?" she'd asked.

Jamie shrugged. "He can hurt me, but I won't hurt him."

And that right there, was the mantra of animal rescue in general.

Luther paced along the fence, guarding his flock against a repeat intrusion.

She sighed. "All right! I'm going! But I'll be back tomorrow and the day after that."

And the day after that. Not for the first time, she wondered if ranch life was for her.

She left the victors twittering about their triumph and

wheeled the full barrow into the goat pasture, intending to spread the rich poopy goodness over a bare spot.

Bella looked up from grazing, her one horn making her look like a small unicorn. Beezle kicked up his feet and bolted up the hill, just for the joy of being alive. Newton hobbled over to her. His dangling Nubian ears swayed with each step.

"BLAAAAH!" He ducked his head and she patted him. His long tongue lashed his lips and caught her hand too. "You're just a big puppy, aren't you?" She rubbed his ears some more, letting her anger at Luther—and Milo—drain away. Newton's affection was the balm her heart needed today.

She ran her hand down his shoulder and felt his ribs. He was losing weight, as Milo had warned he would. The Cushing's would take him from her at some point, but until then, she'd love him as fiercely as he deserved.

"That's all I can do, isn't it?" She rubbed his furry snout.

"BLAAAAH!"

"Love you and maybe keep you warm." That cool wind flooded the little valley again. Newton would need a blanket. She was pretty sure she had a miniature pony-sized blanket that would fit him.

She wanted to take a short walk in the woods, but Beezle would destroy anything left in the pasture, so she wheeled the empty barrow and rake out the gate and parked it on the path.

Leaving the goats to graze, she checked in on the ducks, who quacked and flapped as she peered into the pen. They were still mostly feral. She made a mental note to spend more time handling them. If they became tame enough, they would make great ambassadors for the farm.

And just like that, she realized that despite her battles with Luther, and her worries for Newton, she was a rescue rancher, and she didn't want to do anything else with her life.

The battle tune in her head lightened to a bittersweet instrumental that spoke of October's nostalgia. It was a comforting song that harmonized with the crinkle of leaves under foot and the chittering of a red squirrel busy storing pine cones for the winter. She hummed it as she headed up the path, and before she realized where her feet had taken her, she was standing in front of the wind phone.

She clamped the receiver between her shoulder and ear and dialed. The whir of the last number faded away to oppressive silence. She refused to let the void bully her this time.

"Hey, Jamie." Her voice cracked and she tried again. "Hey. I just thought you'd like an update. The ducks have settled into their new enclosure. You'd be really impressed by Shaun's work. He's Gilly's friend. Just a kid, but has a good head on his shoulders and a generous heart. You'd like him. Luther and the alpacas are up to their old tricks. Their wool is growing in thick. Probably means a cold winter coming."

She thought about other changes. "Max finally retired for good. We have a new vet, his name is Milo and he's been a big help with Sadie. He says the old girl has a few good years ahead of her still. He brought us some horse stocks so I can pick out her feet safely."

She paused. She wasn't ready to talk about the kiss.

"Newton has lost weight again. I'm going to dig out the pony blanket for him tonight. The goats love their new goat hut. I wish you could see it." Would Jamie approve of the changes she'd made? She had to hope he'd be proud of her efforts at least, and told him so. She continued with a story of Gracie Pig stubbornly refusing to go into the barn at bedtime until she bribed her with popcorn.

As she spoke, something loosened in her chest, like a fish bone had been lodged there and her words magicked it away.

"And oh! The most amazing news is there are fairies in the woods! Don't laugh. I'm not crazy. Hadley confirmed it. So far, they've been nothing but helpful."

Her words died out, but the silence on the other end of the line no longer felt harsh. It felt expectant, as if her words had opened a world—a whole universe—of possibilities.

"Goodbye, my love. I miss you." She hung up the receiver. Her last goodbye to Jamie had been said while standing over his coffin before it was lowered into the ground. This goodbye had none of that all-encompassing, breath-stopping sadness. It felt like she'd been holding her breath and could finally exhale.

She headed back to the goat pasture, humming the song she now dubbed October Nostalgia, and for the first time in months, she didn't feel like an anchor was hung over her shoulders.

HALLOWEEN WAS A BIG DEAL in Mullarkey Mills. Auntie Clare had founded the Mullarkey Halloween Parade sometime in the 1980s and it had been a yearly tradition ever since. She insisted that it was a big event because, "After all, the Irish invented Halloween. It's our duty to see it done right." And she did. People came from all over the Pontiac Region and even as far as Ottawa for the parade and market afterward.

Auntie Clare retired several years ago, but a town committee now started planning the event every April. Even the pandemic hadn't abolished it, though social distancing had meant that the after-parade market had been curtailed.

This year, they didn't have to worry about such things and the Halloween parade was ready to launch. It started at Equinox Farm since they had the parking to accommodate a gathered crowd. Parade floats would make their way down Mill Road toward Auntie Clare's store. They'd hang a right before the bridge and pass by the WWII tank that was festooned in cobwebs, then continue down the road to the community center, where hot chocolate and hot dogs would be waiting and vendors would be set up to sell their wares. Much candy would be consumed and the kids would work off their sugar rushes with games and other entertainment.

The parade floats were a mix of advertising from local businesses and displays put on by schools and church groups. The volunteer firemen dressed as devils and rode the firetruck with its siren blaring and lights flashing. The marching band from Pontiac High School did their best to be heard over the sirens.

Elenna had missed last year's parade, as she'd been deep under a shadow of grief. She was a little nervous about rejoining the fun and was thankful that no one mentioned her gap year.

Gilly and Shaun were dressed like a zombie bride and groom and they drove the donkey cart with a bloody sign on the back that said "Just Married" except that "Married" had been crossed out and "Dead" was scrawled above it. Even Jude and Missy wore white paint like skeleton bones.

"You can handle them in all this noise?" Elenna asked Gilly, even though she already knew the answer. The donkeys were unflappable creatures.

"No problem. I've got it." Gilly adjusted the bridal veil and tiara on her head. "We'll see you at the other end!" She waved as the firemen honked their horn to signal the start of the parade.

Elenna waited until all the floats had left her parking lot before following them up the road. The parade went off with only minor hitches. A toddler got away from his parents and there was some panic before he was caught climbing onto the McDowell Insurance brontosaurus float. And Felix's sheep had gotten loose again. They merged with the marching band, bleating and milling around and almost tripping the drummer. The spectators whistled and applauded, thinking the sheep were part of the procession. The General stood by the cenotaph and saluted each parade float as they passed him by.

Elenna brought up the rear of the procession, wearing a black witch hat and waving the Equinox Farm flag—a red horse head against a white background. Jamie had designed it to mimic the Japanese rising sun flag.

She'd brought Gracie Pig, Beezle, Bella, Newton and the ducks over to the community center earlier in the afternoon. They would make up a mini petting zoo, and Max had volunteered to babysit them until she arrived.

She got there just as the three-legged races were beginning. In another section of the parking lot, kids were climbing into the fire truck's cab and trying on fire gear. Tables were set up outside, since the weather was holding, and vendors sold everything from home baked goods to antique toys.

She waved to Joelle who had a small kiosk to promote Cedar Grove Inn, which was officially open for business. Joelle waved back, but then her attention was taken by a young couple who stopped by her table.

Max was on the far side of the recreation center, where they'd set up a temporary pen for the goats. Gracie Pig was also inside the pen, but that was only because she hadn't decided to bulldoze her way out of it yet. Elenna had dressed her in a black onesie with bat wings, and she was delighting a group of kids with their fathers. One little girl squealed as Gracie snuffled her fingers. Her father turned to say something to Max and Elenna's heart did a little flip.

It was Milo.

He saw her and his expression softened.

"Elenna!" He waved. With her heart doing an annoying little jig in her chest, she headed over to them.

"This is my brother, Ben." Milo indicated the man standing beside him. "And his kids, Julia, Graham and Josh. I thought they might enjoy Halloween in Mullarkey. Guys, this is Elenna. She's the one who runs the rescue farm."

The kids barely glanced at her, but Ben gave her the once over. She suspected that she'd been the topic of conversation between brothers.

Ben wore a pirate hat and had a stuffed parrot on his shoulder. He was a bit shorter than Milo, but broader in the shoulder and clean shaven with a few more creases around his eyes. Other than that, the brothers were nearly identical, and seeing Ben gave her a good idea what Milo looked like under all that fur.

She decided she liked the fur. Not that she would admit it to him.

"Milo told me all about your farm," Ben said.

"You're welcome to bring the kids for a visit. They could see the horses."

"I'm sure they'd love that."

Julia, the youngest child who was dressed as a bumblebee, pulled on his hand. *"Papa, viens voir les moutons!"* She spoke in a perfect Quebecois accent.

"They're goats, not sheep, dummy," said her older brother in flawless English.

Elenna felt a sudden rush of love for her quirky town where languages were interchangeable and a simple community parade brought everyone together.

Ben apologized as the kids pulled his attention away.

She turned to Milo.

"You didn't dress up."

"Did too." He pointed to his red, green and brown flannel shirt and held up a cardboard axe that Elenna hadn't noticed before. "I'm a lumberjack. Julia always jokes that I look like one anyway."

"She's not wrong. It's the beard."

He gave her an exaggerated affronted look. "You don't like the beard? It's classic."

"It's feral."

He leaned in so his head ducked under the brim of her witch hat. "Isn't that your job, looking after feral animals in need?"

He was close enough to kiss. She swallowed and lifted her chin. "My rescues aren't feral."

"Mmm. Too bad." He stood back. She felt an irrational moment of pique.

"I thought we weren't doing this."

"Doing what?"

She waved a hand between them. "This flirting thing."

"Ah, no. I promised not to kiss you. We never said anything about flirting."

"So you're honoring the letter of our agreement, but not the spirit."

His lips opened for a rebuttal, but she never got the chance to hear it because a child's scream tore through the crowd.

"A monster! There's a monster in the woods!"

All eyes turned to find Ruby, dressed as a wolf, standing on a pile of hay bales with her arms extended and her fingers bent into claws. She let out a roar that seemed impossibly loud to have come from her small chest, then she bellowed, "I'm the monster in the woods. Beware to all who enter my domain! ROAR!"

In the silence that followed a few people clapped. These were Mullarkey residents who were used to Ruby's antics. She didn't need a formal stage to put on a play. Those who had come to town just for the festivities looked confused, but then Ruby bowed like a diva and they all clapped.

The child leaped off the bales with the grace of a cat and the murmur of small conversations filled the afternoon again.

"What's the matter? You look like you've seen a ghost." Milo smiled and nodded toward a tot in a white sheet with cutout eyes.

"It's nothing," she said with a wide smile.

But the incident left her unsettled because for a fleeting, breathless moment when she first heard Ruby scream about monsters, she had believed her.

ELENNA HUNG UP THE WIND phone's receiver after giving Jamie an update on the Halloween parade and petting zoo.

The donation box beside the phone held four toonies and three loonies—eleven bucks total. It was enough for some cat treats for the barn cats. Luckily they'd received enough donations from the Halloween fair to keep them in feed and hay through to the end of the year. She didn't know what she'd do after that, but she'd promised Jamie she'd find a way to keep the lights on.

She had a vague idea about publishing her collection of short stories and making millions off a best-seller. In reality, she didn't have enough polished stories to make a full volume, and all her research indicated that collections didn't sell anyway.

Whatever.

She wasn't going to let that get her down on this fine November morning when the sun was snubbing its nose at winter.

She clutched her sketchbook as she headed up the forest path. With all her chores done, she wanted to sketch the old oak tree at the center of the forest. She paused as she spied the General coming up from the road.

"Good morning." She smiled and he waved. She paused on the trail to watch him stop and deposit a coin in the donation box before picking up the wind phone.

How many of the coins in her pocket were his? She turned around and marched back to the phone.

"You don't need to donate."

The General paused with one finger in the rotary dial. His white mustache worked upward in a smile.

"Really, that's just for tourists. I want Mullarkey residents to feel free to use it."

He nodded and mumbled something unintelligible. She smiled again and left him to his privacy. No one came out to the wind phone to make a public call.

With that resolved, she mounted the small hill that led to the forest trail. Autumn dulled the landscape. The brilliant greens and yellows of summer had turned to dun. Gone was the constant chatter of birds, and damp leaves muted footsteps. Only the smells were heightened. The air had a loamy tang made up of new rot and the promise of snow. She inhaled deeply, letting the scent fill her soul. This scent, right here, was the reason she lived in the boonies away from most modern conveniences.

Deeper down the tunnel of trees, bright patches of winterberries added a splash of color to the otherwise barren forest decor. As she approached the river, a brief but sharp gust of wind stirred the few leaves that still clung to branches. She zipped her jacket and stared at the bits of sky she could see through the canopy. The day had been gray but bright when she left. Now, dark clouds churned overhead.

She hurried up the path.

At the bend in the trail, she paused to study the oak tree growing around the boulder. It still seemed like an impossible thing. The crooked trunk cradled the rock, and where the roots met stone, that black hole glared like an eye.

She opened her sketchbook and quickly scribbled a rough outline of tree and boulder.

Bells tinkled an alien melody in the distance.

Elenna wasn't crazy. She realized that the average person didn't have movie soundtracks playing in the background of their lives. She knew the musical interludes were a figment of her imagination.

But not this time.

The melody was faint and kind of hazy, as if she heard it through a dream, and a rougher sound overlapped it like a discordant melody—that strident stone-on-stone sound that she'd heard before.

She shivered but couldn't shake off the dream music. Tucking the sketchbook into her pocket, she bent to examine the gray lichen that spread outward from the boulder. She looked around for the stake she'd driven into the ground to mark the progress of the blight. The border of the blight's growth was now a good three feet past her marking post. She skirted the rock and tree. The lichen grew right to the river in the other direction.

On the riverbank, her toe turned over a leaf to reveal a white shard of bone. She bent down to study it. A leg bone from a squirrel or rabbit. She kicked away a few leaves and found more bones, including a half rotten fish head. The ground was littered with them, far too many to be the work of a passing fox or coyote.

"Yer just daft enough to be out here alone, aren't ye?"

Elenna nearly jumped out of her skin. With the burble of the river in her ear, she hadn't heard anyone approach. She turned to find Tig's bent figure, clinging to a crooked walking stick and peering up at her through lanky hair.

The dreamy music had faded and the forest seemed to be holding its breath.

"If I'm daft, so are you," she pointed out.

Tig spat on the ground at her feet.

"So, ye say." Tig turned her back and hobbled up the trail, sweeping her stick in front of her as if testing for land mines. Neither her stick nor her feet ever crossed the boundary into the lichen.

She paused at the top of the rise to study the black hole beneath the rock.

Elenna pointed to the gray infestation. "Do you know what that is?" Her voice was quiet, but it seemed to ruffle something in the air, as if a flock of invisible starlings had just taken off from the trees.

"I do. 'Tis a blight." The wrinkles around Tig's mouth became more pronounced as she pursed her lips.

"I get that. But do you know how to treat it? If we don't do something about it soon, it'll take over the forest."

Tig shook her head.

After a moment, Elenna tried again. "There's an arborist in Quyon. I can get him to come out for a consult."

Tig shook her head again. "He won't help none. Ye must kill the root to stop the blight."

"The root of the tree?"

The poor oak had defied the odds to grow around the rock. Killing it on the off chance it might stop the blight didn't seem fair.

"Not the tree. The fae. The root of the blight…'tis a dark fae now, isn't it. Though I cannot guess at the kind. Not yet." She turned lightning fast, and gripped Elenna's arm with more force than her old muscles should have been able to achieve.

"Have ye seen anything odd, here abouts? Heard anything?" Her eyes were bright and wide.

"N…no." Elenna yanked her arm away and rubbed it.

Tig scoffed. "Yer a terrible liar." She poked her arm with one bent finger. "There are fae in these woods, sure. I know ye saw 'em."

"I…don't believe in fae…in fairies."

"Ye don't need to. They believe." Tig pulled the cork on her flask and took a deep swig. Elenna was mesmerized by the wrinkled skin of her throat as it worked to swallow.

Hadley and Nina had said something similar about fairies. Why was she resisting the idea? She'd seen…something that day of the forest fires. Something had drawn her onward to find Beezle. But whatever those lights had been, they were the antithesis of this gray, killing blight.

"I heard something. Maybe." She rubbed a hand through her

hair, noting its slight tremble. Tig cocked her head and watched her. "Just now I thought I heard music, like bells and a harsher sound. I've heard that one before."

"Harsh how? Be specific, now. 'Tis important."

Elenna thought of the echoing noise and how it had seemed to rake her nerve endings. "It was metallic or like stone. Like rusty blades rubbing against each other. That can't be fairies."

"Probably not a fae of the Seelie Court, sure. A hag, maybe or a witch. Baba Yaga or mayhaps Black Annis." She bent forward, getting as close to the hole under the rock as she could without stepping on the blight. "Expelled from Underhill herself. Oh, sure as night, Black Annis would be taking up home and hearth in such a hole."

"I've never heard of…Annis." This all seemed surreal. Was she having a conversation about witches and fairies and Underhill?

"Black Annis," Tig corrected. "Older than the mountains and as cruel as time. Likes the taste o' human flesh, but her teeth be chipped away long ago now. And didn't she replace 'em with bone spikes. Poor lass, the new teeth don't fit her so well, and now she can only dine on the tender bones o' babes."

Poor lass?

"That sound ye heard, 'tis ol' Black Annis grinding her teeth in frustration for the lack o' meat on her plate. T'will only get louder 'til she feeds."

Tig stood taller and nodded her head.

"And the blight?" Elenna asked.

"'Tis the snare she sets. Any beast, fowl or fish that steps within her domain be fair game." Tig pointed toward the river and the scattering of bones. "She feeds and grows stronger. And the blight grows."

"So how do we stop her?" Elenna's mind raced down

alleyways it had never considered before. "Nina has all kinds of charms against such things in her shop. Maybe burn some sage?" She was grasping at smudge sticks here and way out of her depth.

Tig scoffed. "Black Annis is no sprite to be banished by a bit o' smoke." She jabbed her walking stick at the blight. "'Tis dark magic, the kind that prospers in blood. And only in blood can it be quelled."

Elenna returned home wondering who was more crazy, Tig or herself for half-believing the old woman's words.

Elenna had been filling the *ofuro* all day. From the doorway, she walked down three steps into the massive tiled bathtub. One corner had benches to sit on and jets for the rare times she actually filled it. Today, she'd emptied the well in order to fill it twelve inches above the bench level. Luckily, Jamie had considered that problem and installed a heater, so the water was blissfully hot. She didn't bother with the jets, but sank down beside the bench so the water covered her to the chin.

The room was silent as if the water absorbed all sound and drowned it. The walls were tiled in a blue mosaic that mimicked waves and ocean spray. The serenity was almost suffocating.

In the opposite corner from the bench, a rain shower head jutted from the ceiling. It could soak her like a waterfall. Six more shower heads dotted the two walls at different heights. These could be set to sprays that were gentle as a kiss or rough as a deep-tissue massage. When the tub was empty she could stand in that corner to be soaked, pummeled and massaged from head to toe. Between the shower and the bath benches, the upper portion of the outside wall was filled with three panels of frosted glass—one large window in the center flanked by two smaller panels. She'd propped open one of these smaller windows to let out the steam.

A lone white orchid was perched on the window ledge, silhouetted by the last of the day's light.

She eyed the orchid. Its pale face seemed to mock her.

Elenna loved plants, flowers, and even fungi. She liked them growing in wild abandon. Spring dandelions that lined the mown trails in a river of yellow. Or a field of Queen Anne's Lace bobbing with heavy heads in the fall. But a single orchid seemed self-important, and like the house, it was a beast out of its natural habitat. It even needed a tiny stake to prop up its spindly stem. How could such a thing survive in the wild? It didn't, of course. It was a product of human manipulation, bred for beauty, not resilience. Like Shin Mei's dirty sheath, it was a human-made problem that now needed human hands to care for it.

She'd taken to staring at the orchid while she showered, as if it were a symbol of her general malaise. She couldn't get rid of it. Jamie had loved orchids. He'd loved this house. He'd loved her. Somehow she had tangled his love for her with these other things, and changing even one felt like cutting away a piece of him.

She sank into the steaming water until it covered her chin and thought of all the times their love-making had begun or ended in this tub. She closed her eyes and ran a slippery hand up her leg, pretending it was Jamie's…and stopped.

The thump of a deep bass beat pulsed in the air. At first she thought it was her internal montage, but then the music changed and Mylene Farmer began singing about the disenchanted generation.

Warrick had started the Friday night party at Auntie Clare's.

Elenna's hands froze on her inner thigh. The music had intruded on her solitude and now she felt as if the entire town stood at the window peering in.

And so what? A girl had needs. Self-love was the only kind of love available to her these days.

A stray breeze made the orchid bob. It looked smug.

"Shut up."

She waved her hand and drenched the offending flower with a splash.

The music lilted, reminding her of the fairy bells she'd heard in the woods, and she decided that a bit of girl time was exactly what she needed. She rose and turned off the water heater, but left the water in case she wanted another soak before bed.

Then she dressed in fuzzy-lined leggings, a thick sweater, jacket, scarf, and tuque.

Gado raised his head at the back door.

"Stay," she said, though the old dog had no intention of leaving his warm bed at this time of night. He let out a half-whine, half-sigh and laid his head on his paws.

Outside, she followed the music through the dark to Auntie Clare's. Felix came out of the dépanneur and stopped to light a cigarette.

"Salut." He waved to her as she passed, then took a pull on the cigarette. The tip burned orange, lighting his craggy face.

"Salut, Felix." She walked through the haze of smoke to find Hadley, Nina, and Joelle sitting at a single picnic table. A propane patio heater kept them warm.

"Let me smell you," Hadley said as Elenna sat.

"Really? I just had a bath. I promise I don't smell like goat."

"It's not that. I'm hoping for a whiff of nicotine from Felix's ciggy." Her hands were clenched in front of her.

"I thought you quit."

"She did," Nina said. "Last week and the week before. And the week before that too."

Hadley tipped her neck side-to-side, like a boxer getting ready to fight.

"Quitting cold turkey is hard, okay?"

"How long since you had one?" Elenna asked.

"Three days, four hours and," Hadley looked at the time on her phone, "thirteen minutes."

"That bad, huh?"

She sighed. "I live vicariously through people who smoke outside the store. They probably think I'm some kind of stalker. But Auntie Clare swears my baking will improve once I get the smell of nicotine out of my nose."

"She's exactly right," Nina said. "I've got some herbal remedies that might help you quit. Some ginseng tea every day will curb those cravings."

Hadley sighed. "Only if I roll it and smoke it."

The conversation moved on. Nina congratulated Joelle on her first month of paying customers at the inn. "So how did it go? Any good Yelp reviews yet?"

Joelle smiled. Elenna didn't know her well yet, but her expressions were becoming familiar. She had an endearing way of smiling with a touch of sadness in her eyes that made Elenna feel like they could be kindred spirits.

"No reviews yet, but no complaints either. We did have a bit of an upset with one guest. He misplaced his glasses and insisted they were stolen. It was all a little weird."

The music picked up its beat and Blue Jeans Bleu started singing about eating too many *patates frites*. At the same moment, Warrick burst out of his canteen truck, brandishing a huge platter of French fries with all the garnishings—gravy, squeaky cheese, chili, and sautéed peppers and onions.

Hadley actually squealed when the scent of greasy fries hit her.

"*J'ai mangé trop de patates frites!*" She sang along with the band.

She pointed at Warrick. "Since when do you synchronize the music and food?"

Like his cousin Hadley, Warrick was dark-haired, on the short side but muscular, and he wore a lace-edged apron with style. "Since today." He brandished a wooden spoon like a fairy godmother wielding a wand. "It's dark and it's cold and we all need more fries and music in our lives. Voilà!" He tapped the platter of fries.

"Agreed." Hadley and Nina were already digging into the steaming hot potato goodness.

"And I brought you extra gravy, madame." Warrick tapped a bowl of his signature sauce. He knew Elenna adored it. She stuck her finger in the sauce and licked it.

"Mmmm. So good."

Warrick dipped his finger and dotted her nose with gravy, then grinned. "It looks good on you."

Warrick was a terrible flirt. And he was gay, so flirting with him didn't bring up all the angst it did when she flirted with Henrik or Milo.

"Thank you, sir, but I prefer not to wear my food."

"Shame. I have some whipped cream that's going to waste." He waggled his eyebrows like an old-time vaudevillian.

"Well, you'll have to find another food model. I look terrible in white."

Warrick gave an exaggerated sigh. "Story of my life." New customers appeared at his truck and he dashed off to serve them.

Around the table, there was a few minutes of quiet as plates were loaded and glasses were poured. Then Nina asked Joelle about her customer and his missing glasses.

"Why was it weird?"

"I don't know. He insisted that he hadn't taken his glasses out of his room, but I found them in the library. And other things have gone missing only to show up in odd places."

Nina and Hadley shared a look.

"Brownies," Nina said and Hadley nodded.

"Brownies?" Joelle looked confused.

"Not the chocolate kind. The mischievous gnome kind."

"Yeah, right." Joelle smiled and Nina shrugged.

"Tig says we have a Black Annis in the woods," Elenna blurted.

Nina stopped with a handful of fries halfway to her mouth.

"You're not serious. Did she say *a* Black Annis or *the* Black Annis?"

"Does it matter?"

"It sure does. It's the difference between meeting a demon or the devil himself. Black Annis has spawned many copycats in the fairy realm, but the original?" She shuddered. "The original Black Annis was one mean chick."

Elenna felt a cold wind worm under her jacket and she pulled her scarf tighter.

Hadley leaned toward Nina. "Tell us."

Nina finished a mouthful of fries before continuing.

"She was a hag, and not in the derogatory sense that we

know the word. She had power that only comes to old women, women who have lived through the changes in life." She lowered her voice and leaned in. "The kind of women that old white men feared.

"The kind that were burned at the stake," Joelle said quietly.

"Exactly."

"I thought those witches were mostly kindly wise women," Elenna said.

"Mostly, yeah, but there are always a few bad apples, if you know what I mean. There were hags with true dark power. The healers and midwives just got caught up in the frenzy of the witch hunters."

"So Black Annis was a witch?" Elenna asked. "Tig seemed to think she was some kind of fairy creature."

"She could be both. I believe that true witches are descendants of fairies that got stuck in our world."

"Stuck? Why do you say that?"

Nina made an exaggerated frown. "If you could live in Underhill among the fairies with all their beauty, music and art, wouldn't you? I mean, come on. Any fairy in our realm was either banished or lost."

"In Black Annis's case, I would say banished. At least Tig implied as much."

Nina nodded. "That would make sense. She caused a lot of trouble. She was known to creep through windows to snatch babies from their cribs. After she ate them, she'd add their tanned skins to her patchwork cloak." Nina was never more animated than when she told stories of magic and fairies. She seemed to grow with confidence as she spoke.

"Old Annis lived in a cave that she carved out of a hill with nothing but the stone claws on her gnarled hands." Nina held her fingers bent like claws. "Her teeth were made of stone too, all the better to break the bones of children in her stew." She lunged outward with her hands. Hadley squeaked and jumped back.

"In the old country, people said they could hear the gnashing of Old Annis's teeth from five miles away, and that's when you knew to bring the sheep inside and bolt the doors."

Warrick's playlist had run out as Nina spoke and her last words fell into silence. They all stared at her.

"Well, that's not creepy at all," Joelle said, breaking the spell.

Nina laughed. "Actually I feel kinda sorry for the old girl."

"Sorry?" Elenna couldn't hide her surprise.

"Yeah, how would you like to be tossed out of the only home you ever knew and restricted by human laws you don't understand? She's probably pretty lonely."

"But she eats children," Elenna said.

"Well, so the stories say. But the stories also tell about evil witches who turned out to be midwives. How are we to know which category the Black Annis falls under?"

Hadley looked like the fries were curdling in her gut. "I thought we weren't supposed to talk about the fae."

Nina sat back with a satisfied look on her face. "We're not, but if Elenna is facing Black Annis, she needs all the ammunition she can get."

"Any idea how to get rid of her?" Elenna asked. "Tig says it must be a blood ritual."

Nina waved a hand like she smelled something foul. "Tig would use blood magic to cure a hangnail. I don't remember the specifics, but there was something about a cat and aniseed that would drive her off. You want me to look into it?"

Elenna bit her bottom lip. "I think it's best to just ignore Tig. She seems a bit...volatile."

"I'll say. She came into the store the other day and made a fuss because I don't sell authentic grave dirt. Like, who does that? Real spell craft doesn't use grave dirt or blood or…"

Nina continued to rant about harmful stereotypes for witches and the real benefits of a good sage smudging until Warrick restarted the music. Soon the deep voice of the lead singer for Les Trois Accords sang his lament about losing his wife to Saskatchewan. The slow tune settled over them and the mood of the party turned gray around the edges. Hadley picked at the fries while Elenna hunkered down in her jacket, trying to stay warm.

"So brownies, eh?" Joelle said, and they all nodded.

# WINTER

THE MULLARKEY CHRISTMAS MARKET WAS in full swing. Thirty vendors were crammed into the community center. The market boasted local farmers, vendors with home-made preserves, pies and cookies; plus jewelry makers, crocheters, woodworkers and three booths dedicated to Christmas ornaments.

The doors had just opened and a crowd was already filling the room, making the large community center feel much smaller. Elenna had left the petting zoo at home for this one and her booth was mostly informational, with pictures and bios of all her rescues, volunteer opportunities, plus some maps of nearby hiking trails that included a geocaching route and the wind phone. She also had a couple of baskets up for raffle. She'd put a lot of thought into planning her booth and had high hopes that it would generate some much needed revenue to get the farm through to the spring.

As the first hour went by with buyers filing into the hall and making their rounds, her hopes began to flag. The raffle jar had only two tickets, and she'd given out one informational brochure. Her booth was on the third leg of the hall, tucked into a corner. She wondered if it was too easily overlooked. But the truth was, people didn't come to Christmas markets to donate money to animal rescues. They came to buy jams and ornaments.

She tried to keep a smile on her face. If she'd had Gracie Pig as her mascot, people would be flocking to her table, but city bylaws didn't allow animals inside the community center. Maybe she could get Gracie certified as a therapy pig. She could just see her barreling down the corridor at a seniors' center, creating chaos and joy in equal proportions.

Elenna was smiling at her own private joke when she saw a commotion near the door.

A large man in a tuque and puffy jacket was carrying a box and pushing his way through the hall. She saw only his profile, but she recognized that beard.

Milo dumped the box on the empty table directly opposite hers. It was on the far side of the hall next to the empty throne that awaited a visit from Santa. He began unloading materials from the box. Like Elenna's, his booth would be informational, and she suspected the brochures were for his vet clinic.

He finished arranging his display, then removed his jacket and hat and laid them on a chair behind the table. Then he turned his mischievous smile on her and winked. He pulled up his phone and tapped something into it. Her phone chimed and she looked down to find his text.

*I'm late. Got caught up with a colicky horse in Quyon*

*You didn't miss much*

*That slow?*

Not if you're selling pie. But I had only two raffle takers so far.

She pointed to her raffle jar. Milo frowned and typed.

*I should have made pie.*

*Can you bake?*

*I have many secret talents*

He looked up from his phone and quirked one eyebrow.

Elenna laughed. This was fun. The phone was an artificial barrier that made flirting safe.

A big crowd came through the door and things picked up. The morning drove on with more activity at her table than she expected. The slow moments were punctuated with texts from Milo as he poked fun at visitors with overlarge tuques and red noses.

> *Looks like the eggnog has been flowing early with that one.*

And,

> *That woman had 14 dogs and wanted to know what I thought about spaying some of them! Sheesh. I wouldn't want to be in her kitchen at feeding time.*

Elenna enjoyed the irreverent comments. There was something freeing about voicing a gripe, even if only by text. She added her own observations.

> *Someone just asked me if I sold frozen goat meat. I told her that the only goat available was Newton but since he had Cushing's there wouldn't be much meat on him.*

Several minutes went by without an answer and she thought she'd taken things too far, then she got a laughing emoji. More visitors arrived at her table. She put down her phone to give them the whole Equinox Farm spiel. When she looked up again, Milo was busy helping a group of children set up their music stands next to Santa's chair—right in front of his booth. The four children looked no older than ten. Two little girls wearing red velvet Christmas dresses pulled violins from their cases. An older boy wearing a dress shirt with suspenders, bow tie, and a very serious expression took out a clarinet. A younger boy of about six, stood grinning with shakers in each hand.

Her phone chimed.

> *They promised a full hour of musical entertainment.*

Milo stood behind his table, completely boxed in by the impromptu orchestra and a pinched expression on his face. She tapped off a quick text.

> *Got earplugs?*

> *Maybe they'll be good?*

He added a shrugging emoji.

The musicians—and Elenna thought that was a generous use of the term—started playing a shaky version of *Here Comes Santa Claus*. The clarinet squeaked on every D note and the violins weren't synchronized. Milo's smile was frozen in place.

A red-suited man came through the front door and hollered, "Ho ho ho!" Elenna expected him to salute because she recognized the General under the white beard and padded suit. He paused at several tables to greet the vendors with a "Ho ho ho!" that was barely audible over the screaming clarinet.

Milo sent another text.

Elenna held a hand to her lips to hold in a disrespectful giggle. Poor Milo. The quartet was loud from across the room but they were practically standing on his table. She resisted the urge to cover her ears. The song ended as Santa took his seat on his throne decorated with paper snowflakes and ribbons. The line of children waiting for their chance to sit on Santa's knee already snaked up the aisle toward her table.

The clarinetist switched his instrument for a simple recorder, and the band struck up a new tune. She recognized the opening squeaks of *Patapan*, a French carol about a little boy and his drum. An overly cheery woman who was either a mom or a music teacher handed the younger boy a tambourine. The child stood on a chair and crashed the drum over his head with no semblance of rhythm but a smile as big as the North Star.

Elenna felt her phone vibrate, its beep lost in the reverberating noise of the hall.



She snorted back a giggle. Milo couldn't stand it any longer. She watched him wedge through the crowd of impatient children, trying not to trample any of the little ankle biters. He reached her and held a hand toward the door at the front of the hall.

"I think this would be a good time to get lunch. You?"

"Absolutely."

He took her hand. She had a moment of involuntary flinching, but then she relaxed into it. The place was crowded and he only wanted to make sure they weren't separated.

Outside, the temperature was well above freezing and the day bright, with a sky so blue you felt like you could dive into its depths. She let go of his hand and pretended that her fingers didn't tingle where they'd touched.

"Lucked out with the weather," Milo said.

Oh, good. They were talking about weather. She could do that.

"Yep, we won't get many more days like this." That was cool and noncommittal.

Milo smiled. Was it her imagination or was he just a little bit nervous too?

Warrick had brought over his poutine truck and set it up in the park beside the recreation center. In the small park between the community center and the old United Church, a bonfire blazed and benches made from tree stumps circled it. *The Huron Carole* rang from Warrick's speakers, and Tom Jackson's soothing baritone was a welcome comfort after the raucous noise inside the hall.

They stood in line for their *frites* without speaking. When they finally reached the front of the line, Warrick looked at Milo, then winked at her.

"The Valentine Special? Poutine for two?"

"Uh, sure. I mean if that's okay with you?" she said to Milo.

"Sure. I haven't had my cholesterol for the day."

They took their food and sat beside the fire. She balanced the carton of steamy fries, cheese and gravy on her knee within Milo's reach.

"Are we bad people for making fun of those kids?" She

scooped a French fry with her fork and slopped gravy on her leg.

Milo wiped it with a paper napkin. "You know, I like my niece and nephews, but other people's kids? Meh."

"You've got gravy on your beard too."

He grinned. "I'm keeping that for a snack later."

"Ew! What else have you got hiding in there?"

"Oh, just a family of mice and a few coins in case I forget my wallet." He shrugged. "And some bacon. The usual stuff."

She laughed. "You can never have too much bacon."

"That's what this poutine is missing! Bacon!"

"Right, because the cheese curds and gravy aren't doing enough to clog our arteries."

Milo's smile turned down at the corners. "I like this. It's easy being with you."

"I like this too." And she was surprised that she meant it. She was also surprised that for the first time in nearly two years, she didn't feel guilty for being happy.

He stabbed a gravy-covered cheese curd and she watched him eat it. Her eyes were drawn to his beard. She couldn't help being fascinated by the way his lips—half hidden in the fur—bunched as he chewed.

"I see you looking at me," he drawled. She yanked her gaze back to the poutine.

"You like the beard. Admit it."

That put her back up.

"It looks like a squirrel is mugging your face."

He laughed. It was an unselfconscious sound and it thrilled her. Making Jamie laugh had been the best thing about their relationship…

Scratch that. No more comparing bears to squirrels.

"Is it soft?" Did she just say that out loud?

"I dunno. Why don't you touch it and see." When she hesitated, he added, "It doesn't bite."

Her hand reached up without permission from her brain. When it was inches from his face, he turned and snapped his jaws at her fingers. She yanked them back with a gasp and he grinned.

"Just kidding. Go on."

"Bastard." But her fingers roamed along the side of his chin, all the way to his ear.

He closed his eyes and a small, deep noise rumbled from him.

She pulled her hand away and he opened his eyes.

"So?"

"So it's more like a beaver than a squirrel. Or maybe a muskrat."

Milo let out a pained sigh. "You are a hard woman to please, Elenna Kane."

Milo's phone chimed. He looked at the message and started to rise.

"That colicky horse has taken a turn for the worse, I have to go." He glanced at the community center and at his watch. Quyon was a good twenty minutes away.

"You go," Elenna urged. "I'll pack up your table and bring the stuff home. You can pick it up…later."

He nodded. "Later." There was a lot of meaning packed into that one word.

He wiped his mouth on the napkin one more time and left. Elenna watched him walk to his car. He had a certain grace, a quiet strength that came from tall men who knew they didn't need to take up more space in the world.

She sat alone before the bonfire long enough that the poutine congealed on her knee.

IT WAS THE SATURDAY BEFORE Christmas and Elenna couldn't get out of bed. Balled up tissues were mounded on the bedside table and spilling onto the floor. Under the covers, she hugged the squashed tissue box to her chest and sniffled. She'd blown her nose so many times, it felt like her brains were leaking from her eyes and nose.

She still had days like these, but they were rarer. It was the thought of Christmas that drove her under the covers—the thought of spending another Christmas Eve alone in a dark house, another Christmas morning without Jamie's child-like exuberance for presents and coffee with Bailey's and homemade baked beans that had been simmering in the oven all night.

She stretched her arm across the mattress to the cold spot that never warmed, then pulled a pillow over her face. Her stomach churned like it held a nest of eels.

Gado whined. She peeked at him from beneath the pillow. He sat on the floor beside her with his big head on the mattress. His fuzzy eyebrows twitched as he watched for any movement on her part.

"Poor guy." A dog's bladder didn't wait for sorrow to pass. "Come on."

She sniffled, rose, tucked her feet into slippers and pulled a robe around her. Her phone lay on the mattress beside the pillow. A touch to the screen told her it was nearly noon. Sleep had eluded her, and she'd spent most of the night huddled on the couch, weeping over sappy holiday movies. Then she'd fallen into bed around dawn, only to wake to more tears.

She tucked the phone into the pocket of her robe.

The house was cold and dark. The high windows usually let in a good amount of light, but the morning was shrouded in fog. She let Gado into the garden and shuffled to the kitchen to put coffee on. The clock above the stove was blinking, which meant the electricity had gone off sometime in the early morning hours. No wonder the house was so cold.

As she poured coffee, she heard Gado let out a single woof, a deep rumbling sound that signaled greeting rather than alert. She made her way back down the long glassed-in corridor to the garden door.

Gado was sitting at the edge of the zen garden, ears perked forward. She stepped outside, pulling her robe around her. Cold air swirled around her bare legs, but it wasn't as cold as it could be for December. A light sprinkling of snow had blown in overnight, but the ground wasn't frozen yet and it wouldn't stick around. Fog bloomed in the pasture like flocks of ghosts. Clouds blocked the sun, and the day was dark enough that the light was still on over the barn door.

She put a hand on Gado's neck. "What do you see?" He let out a soft woof. Laughter and the jingle of bells whispered through the fog.

God help her, her first thought was fairies.

Then she spied Gilly and Shaun lugging boxes from the barn. Shaun was shaking a horseshoe-shaped frame covered in sleigh bells. Gilly laughed and threw a garland over his shoulders.

She recognized the horseshoe. Jamie had made it their first Christmas together, and every year since, he wove fresh spruce boughs around it and hung it on the barn door. It had been in storage for two years.

The kids didn't see her standing in the corner of the frozen zen garden. She watched them with mixed feelings as they pulled out more familiar decorations. Gilly hung a string of lights along the fence in the car park. Shaun wrapped the fence posts in red garland.

Elenna closed her eyes. This was all wrong. Those were Jamie's decorations. He was the one who loved Christmas as much as one of Santa's elves. He was the one who wrapped garland and strung lights, turning their little farm into a winter wonderland.

Her fists clenched around the coffee mug.

Gilly squealed in mock protest and Elenna opened her eyes. Shaun scooped up a bit of wet snow and packed it into a ball. He didn't have the chance to toss it at Gilly because she used her mittened hands to scoop snow like a shovel and thrust it forward. He laughed and dropped his snow missile, then grabbed her in a hug.

Elenna turned away as their lips met under the glow of Christmas lights.

They could have their decorations. Christmas was for those with someone to share it, and she wasn't enough of a Scrooge to deny them that joy. And if she was being honest, the lights on the paddock fence looked pretty in the fog.

Her phone vibrated in her pocket and she answered it as she stepped inside. Her father's face filled the screen from the nose up. He was finally learning to use FaceTime.

"Hi Dad. How're things in sunny Florida?"

"Perfect. As always. The sky is blue and the ladies are bronze."

She rolled her eyes.

"You're using protection, right?" He'd had an awful scare last year when one of his past liaisons had contracted chlamydia and suggested he get tested. Her dad had been too embarrassed to see the doctor about it. She'd cajoled, bribed and threatened until he relented, but only with the promise that she go with him. She didn't need to hear that conversation with his doctor ever again. At least he had learned that seniors weren't immune to STDs.

"Of course. You can buy condoms in bulk at the pharmacy here."

"Perfect." She resisted another eye roll. It would be wasted on him anyway. His eyesight was failing and small screens were a particular problem.

She could tell that he was walking because the camera lurched in a steady rhythm. His bald, pink dome filled half the screen. The rest was blue sky.

"Dad, I can only see your forehead."

"Oh. How's this?" He adjusted the camera's view so that she was looking up his nose from chest level.

"That's fine. What's up?"

"I'm just checking up on you." He frowned. "I know how this time of year gets you down."

"I'm fine."

He scrunched his eyebrows, then one eye filled the screen as he tried to get a better look at her.

"You're wearing your robe. You just getting up?"

"I had the girls over. We watched movies all night." That was only half a lie.

"Oh, good. Good. I'm glad you're making an effort to…you know."

"I know."

Her dad, the extrovert, could never understand how he'd produced such an introverted daughter. "Look I'm up late and the herd needs feeding. Can I call you later?"

"No good. Big party at the pool this afternoon. I'll call you on Christmas morning, okay?"

"Okay. I love you, Dad."

"Love you too, Lanie."

She disconnected and stood at the edge of the garden, watching the fog roll over the pasture.

There was one good thing about having animals. Even on your worst days, when you wanted to crawl back into bed and never come out, they still needed to be fed.

She went inside to get dressed.

AUNTIE CLARE WAS THE LAST village elder with the Mullarkey surname. Hadley and Warrick's mothers were her nieces and Mullarkeys by birth. Warrick still lived in the Mullarkey heritage home that was only a short distance from the community center and their extended family descended on the village every year to celebrate Christmas. Hadley usually pulled Elenna and Jamie into the festivities, but Elenna had refused the invitation for the last two years. She couldn't stand the idea of all that forced merriness. She was content to hunker down and watch cheesy holiday movies, eat popcorn and drink hot chocolate.

She avoided the village for the last week of December, and her Christmas and New Year's Eve passed with little fanfare.

The first day of January dawned gray and bleak like it was hungover from New Year's Eve. Despite the fog clinging to the windows, Elenna jumped out of bed, eager to get to work. It was a relief that she no longer had to skulk around to avoid the holiday cheer.

She completed her morning chores under the blanket of fog. The whole world was reduced to a dozen feet of visibility and all sounds were hushed.

Just before lunch, she made one last tour of the goat pastures to be sure Beezle hadn't dumped the water bucket again, and found that Newton had pulled off his pony blanket. It lay trampled in the mud near the stone hut.

Elenna hung the wet blanket across the fence. At least it was small enough to fit in her washing machine—unlike the larger horse blankets—but she didn't have another one that would fit him in the meantime.

"BLAAAAH!" His cry seemed over-loud in the utter silence of the day.

She pointed a finger at him. "It's not my fault you're cold, mister. Now you're going to have to spend the day inside until I clean up your blanket."

"BLAAAAH!"

"What am I going to do with you?"

She draped his long ears through her fingers. Then she ran her hand along his ribs, which stuck out prominently, and kissed his damp muzzle.

"I think it's time to make you some pajamas." She ruffled his ears. "What do you think about that?"

"BLAAAAH!"

"A fair point, well made."

She had a plan to sew fleece pajamas that he could wear under the pony blanket to keep his legs warm, but she hadn't had time to make them yet, mainly because her sewing machine was in storage. Setting it up would mean cleaning out Jamie's old workout room, something she'd been putting off for much too long.

Newton shivered.

"It's okay, buddy. Let's get you inside and warmed up. I'll figure out something."

Goats don't blink much, which gives them either a perpetually startled look or a mischievous air. Newton was the startled kind and Beezle, the mischievous kind. He bounded up and blustered right between them before she could get a good handle on Newton's collar. Newton balked and trotted away. Beezle thought it was a game and lowered his head to butt his friend. Bella watched the antics of the younger goats with her usual stoic disdain.

It took Elenna another fifteen minutes to round up all three and get them settled inside their hut with a good load of hay and some fresh water.

She was just locking the door behind her when Ruby came bounding out of the forest.

"Elenna! Elenna! It's a monster!" She pointed back the way she'd come. The child was dressed well for the cold, but her pants were smeared with mud and sopping wet mittens drooped off her hands. Her cheeks were bright pink and a drop of snot hung from her nose. Damp curls clung to her face under a saggy tuque. How did she get so wet and dirty so early in the morning?

"Ruby! Does your mother know you're out here like that?"

Ruby nodded vigorously, then wiped her nose on the back of her mitten. "She sent me outside to get dirty and learn something."

"Uh-huh. And what did you learn?"

Her eyes widened and she pointed up the dark forest trail. "That there's a monster in the woods!"

"Remember last time you thought there was a monster? It was just the ducks."

"Not this time. I swear! I saw it." She held her hands as wide as her slender arms would allow. "Big, big horns! And a horrible black face with teeth like this." She pulled off a mitt and waggled her fingers under her chin. "Huge teeth. And it roared!"

Elenna considered the child. How many times had Ruby called wolf? But she actually looked scared. If nothing else, Ruby didn't scare easily.

Elenna sighed. "All right. I'll check it out. But promise me that you'll head right home and get out of those wet clothes before you catch a cold."

Ruby hesitated, but Elenna pointed toward the road. "Go! No more playing until you get dry."

"Okay. Take this." She pulled a small slingshot made from a forked stick and a thick rubber band from her pocket and thrust it into Elenna's hand. Then she dashed through the goat pasture, skidded on a wet patch, and climbed over the gate like a monkey.

Elenna tucked the slingshot into her pocket and headed into the forest. As soon as the canopy closed around her, the temperature dropped and the day grew significantly darker. The trees creaked as bark scraped against bark. It was an unsettling sound.

She jammed her hands into her pockets and trudged on. Her right hand closed around the slingshot. Ruby's intentions were good, but it wouldn't fire anything bigger than a pebble. Elenna was irrationally glad that she had her utility knife with her too. She fished it out of her pants pocket and gripped it in her hand.

A stuttering wail crept through the shadows—a sort of *ca-ca-ca* like a broken automaton might make. That couldn't be the trees creaking. As if to confirm her thought, the sound faded into a dreadful moan.

*What am I doing out here alone on this cold and dreary morning?*

It was a good question and one she had no answer to, other than hoping—and worrying—that Ruby's imagination was as good as her own and the "monster" would turn out to be another abandoned animal.

Fog swirled thickly around her legs, ghostly white tendrils grabbing at her as she walked through them. At eye level the mist thinned, but not by much. She could see only a dozen yards ahead. The river's burble echoed hollowly from her right. Her feet knew this path well, but old root systems made it treacherous, and she kept her eyes on the ground so she didn't trip.

Finally, she recognized a swell in the path. They'd found the ducklings just over that rise. Around one more bend in the trail she'd find the old oak tree and boulder that was—according to Tig—the residence of Black Annis.

She stopped on the trail. A stake had been pounded into the earth. For one disorienting moment, she thought it was the stake she'd used to mark the boundary of the blight, but no, she could see that one a few steps further along. This stake was just outside the reach of the blight. She picked up a piece of hemp cord that hung from it. The end was torn and frayed as if something had been tied to it and had yanked itself free. She let the cord drop and looked around.

The fog dissipated a little, giving her a clear view of the boulder with the black hole underneath. That *ca-ca-ca-mooooan* sound wailed through the shadows again. She tucked her arms tight around her chest like a shield.

Two eyes blinked open in the hole, bilious green irises that seemed to glow.

Had she found Ruby's monster or the Black Annis? Maybe both.

"You think you're very scary, frightening a child. But I'm not afraid of you." Her voice sounded flat in the dampening fog.

*Ca-ca-ca…*

She thought of Tig's words and Nina's description of the hag with stone jaws, good for breaking soft bones. Was that what she heard? Was she clacking her rock teeth like an old coot with badly fitting dentures?

A hand reached from the hole, long spidery fingers tinged in blue and tipped with broken and blackened nails.

Elenna's breath caught in her throat.

The hand grew and reached as if it could cross the distance and strike at her throat.

A flurry of yellow lights whooshed between her and Black Annis, pushing her backward, until she stumbled clumsily onto the trail—out of the blighted territory.

The hag clacked her teeth and a low, menacing laugh followed.

Elenna had only a second to process what she'd heard, what she'd seen, then a goat bleated. She whirled, trying to see where it came from. When she turned back, the hole under the boulder was dark and still again.

She let out a little laugh as if that could bolster her courage. The shadows and fog were enough to make anyone jumpy. There was no Black Annis, just her imagination conjuring boogie men. She was no better than Ruby.

The bleating sounded again. The fog made it hard to determine its origin. Her goats were all shut away in their hut. Maybe she was hearing Felix's sheep? They were far away, past the north end of the forest, but sound traveled oddly in the fog.

Again the bleating echoed through the trees. It was definitely coming from ahead. Felix's sheep must have gotten loose again, and Ruby had run into one of them.

She turned for home. Felix was an old hand at rounding up

his lost ewes. And stumbling around in this fog wasn't her best idea yet.

The sheep cried out again, this time with an edge of desperation.

There were coyotes in these woods. Or what if the sheep was trapped or hurt? She couldn't leave it to die out here alone. She looked both ways, up and down the trail. South led to a hot cup of coffee and dry clothes. North led to cold, wet uncertainty.

A light blinked on the northern path. Then another. And another. The fairies were diffused in the fog, but they bobbed with urgency.

Decision made. She headed up the northern path.

The lights zipped on ahead. She followed until they turned off the trail, and then she hesitated. The fog thickened between the trees. She would be plunging in blind.

The fairies rushed back and swirled around her head. Their brightness was nearly blinding, and made it difficult to look at them. She caught only a glimpse of a vaguely humanoid shape with the double wings of a dragonfly and long legs that fluttered like a tail. The head was bald and oddly faceless as if an inner light washed away its features.

The faint tinkle of bells accompanied the beating wings. They flew behind her and swooped forward, leaving her with a zap of static electricity.

She stepped off the path.

Something moved in the fog ahead.

"BAAAAH!"

She was close.

She stumbled through the underbrush. The fairies alighted on the struggling beast, then flew off leaving them in near darkness.

It was a ram. The poor creature was stuck in a bramble bush. A long hemp lead rope was tangled in the branches. The other end was wrapped around his throat and his struggles had tightened it to the point of strangulation.

She tried to make sense of what she was seeing. The sheep was all black and he blended with the shadows. And he seemed to have too many horns. Two long black horns shot backward from his forehead. One of these was caught in the brambles. Two more horns curved downward from his temples to frame his chin.

He turned desperate eyes on her.

"BAAAAH!"

She jumped back and nearly fell on her butt. Something was very wrong with his face. Instead of a snout, his nose was flat and strangely human. An underbite pushed his chin forward and crooked teeth jutted from the lower jaw.

Ruby's monster.

"BAAAAH!"

The ram's cries were weakening. He thrashed again, sides heaving with the effort.

Monster or not, he was suffering.

"It's okay, buddy." She used her soothing voice, the one that got Newton through the worst of his shakes. She tugged on the rope tangled in the branches. The sheep thrashed. One horn came free, but the roped pulled even tighter around his neck.

She held out her hands and let him sniff them.

"You're all right. I'm just gonna cut that rope, okay?" She pulled out her knife, flicked it open and sawed at the rope as close to the branch as possible. It came away with a snapping of twigs.

The ram reared back. She grabbed the rope and hung on,

wishing she'd had the brains to put on her gloves as the rope burned across her palms. The poor beast was tired of being strangled and he slowed his struggles. She let up on the rope.

He panted and froth flecked his lips.

She grabbed the rope firmly in one hand and reached for her belt pouch that was full of Newton's favorite pellet treats.

"Are you hungry?" She held out a pellet. "I bet you are."

The ram sniffed it. His lips curled around the cookie and he sucked it in.

"Good boy." She fed him another. By the time they'd emptied half of the treat pouch, he was calm enough for her to stroke him.

His coat was long and kinked like Bella's Angora coat, but it was black, leaching to copper at the tips. His horns were also black and glossy. Despite his odd face, she thought he was beautiful.

She grasped the rope at his collar so he wasn't strangled again and they emptied the rest of the treat bag as they headed home to safer pastures.

THAT EVENING, AFTER SHE SETTLED her new rescue in the barn, she put on her favorite fluffy socks and curled up on the couch with her laptop and a glass of wine. A wood stove would have been a great addition to the room. It would disrupt the clean aesthetic that Jamie had so loved, but the dry heat would help to dispel the dampness that never seemed to leave her bones these days.

She piled a blanket over her legs and did a quick internet search for the costs of installing a wood-burning stove, then just as quickly decided it was out of her budget. Next, she turned her attention to the rescued ram, but her search didn't reveal a definitive breed for her new charge. The closest she could find was a Hebridean sheep. The long black and bronze coat and double set of horns matched, but not that face, which suggested that its odd features might be a deformity.

Mutations happened often in goat and sheep stock. Breeders would cull the "defective" offspring so it wouldn't pass along its genes. Or worse, they'd sell them to someone who would revere the animal for its disfigurements. There was a goat in India being worshiped as a god because of its human-like face. Such arrangements rarely turned out well for the critter. Either way, it made no sense that someone would stake out a Hebridean sheep in her woods, mutant or not.

She tapped her fingers on the keyboard, then sent a quick text to Felix.

> *Are you missing any sheep?*

She waited a full minute for his response.

> *Mes dames sont toutes là.*

*My ladies are all here.* So Felix wasn't branching out into exotic livestock. Pekin ducks in the spring and now a mutant sheep all the way from the Scottish Highlands for the New Year.

Who ever said life on a farm was boring? By the time she went to bed, cold and tired, she was no closer to unraveling the mystery of the lost ram.

The temperature dropped overnight and she woke to a world of white. Snow covered all the pastures and sat like fluffy caps on fence posts. This time, it would stick.

But cold and snow never stopped a farmer. She needed to set up a temporary fence within the goat pasture so Beezle, Newton and Bella could get used to the new addition to their flock. So, after a cup of coffee, she added a second pair of socks before slipping her feet into work boots. She pulled on her trapper's hat, the one with the fuzzy ear flaps. It wasn't her sexiest look, but the goats (and now sheep) wouldn't care.

Gado slept in his bed near the back door as usual. He lifted his great black head and gave her a woof to let her know he would join her outside if she really felt the need.

"It's okay. No point in both of us getting cold."

Gado agreed and dropped his head back onto his paws with a sigh.

Her phone rang just as she stepped into the zen garden. She looked at the caller ID, then stepped back inside and shut the door.

"Ms. Kane? This is Gregory Dawkins."

He paused for a moment, perhaps deciding if he needed to clarify his identity further. But she remembered Mr. Dawkins, even if the memory came to her through the black fog of grief that shrouded all her memories of the months after Jamie's death. Dawkins was Jamie's lawyer. He'd walked her through the estate arrangements after the funeral.

"Yes, Mr. Dawkins. What can I do for you?" She placed her head against the cool glass of the door. Calls from lawyers were never good.

He cleared his throat. "There's been an inquiry into the Equinox Farm property from the Nolan family, specifically from Robert and Leah Nolan."

She closed her eyes. Robert and Leah were Jamie's older brother and sister. She'd met them only a handful of times—the last had been at the funeral.

"What sort of inquiry?"

"They want to know if you are still residing at the farm and if you retain all the rescue animals that Mr. Nolan had acquired while he was alive."

"Yes. I still live here and the animals are all here, mostly."

"Mostly? Could you qualify that, please Ms. Kane?"

"Well two of the barn cats disappeared, but barn cats do that. And we…that is, I lost a goat shortly after Jamie passed. But she was sick." That had been Jolly, Beezle's sister. They'd come together from a farm that went bankrupt.

"And all the other animals remain? The horses?"

"Yes, of course. I wouldn't get rid of them." She tried to keep the irritation from her tone, but apparently she failed.

"There's no need for alarm." A ticking sound came over the line as if Mr. Dawkins were tapping a pen against his desk.

Elenna grew impatient. "What's this about? Is the Nolan family contesting the will? Jamie left the farm to me." Equinox had been in the Nolan family for generations, forgotten and falling into ruin, but maybe still coveted.

"Please don't jump to conclusions, Ms. Kane. There is no recourse for them to get the farm. Mr. Nolan's will was ironclad."

"But they could try."

The pause on the other end of the line wasn't encouraging. "Yes, they could try, but it won't amount to anything, especially at this late date. As I said, don't jump to conclusions. I'll report back to Ms. Nolan and try to find out more information. I'll get back to you."

"Thank you." She disconnected. Her heart was hammering. Dawkins was probably right. Robert and Leah had had their chance to contest the will in the months after the funeral, and she'd never heard from them. But if for some reason, they'd changed their minds, she'd have to fight. She didn't have the funds for even a short court battle.

There was nothing she could do about it now, but she headed outside into the icy wind with her stomach churning. Luckily for her, manual labor is a great stress reliever and by the time she'd hauled hay and water to the pastures, cleaned the duck pen and mucked out Gracie's stall, her muscles were humming with exertion and her worries had been put on a back burner. Farm labor was the best therapy.

The new ram was restless. He didn't like to be alone in the barn and he paced in the small enclosure. With her arms over the half door of the stall, she watched him dash ten feet in one direction, pause and dash back. She stepped inside and he immediately came over to accept rubs behind the ear.

"Well, you are clearly used to people."

"BAAAAH!" He nuzzled her hand.

"You'll make a good animal ambassador for the farm, won't you. But you need a name then. How about Dasher? Since you're so good at the zoomies. Yes, you are." She babbled more nonsense and fed him some hay, pleased when he took it right from her hand. Yes, Dasher would fit right in at Equinox.

She left Dasher sprinting around his stall and headed to the old barn to pull out the metal pen so she could set it up inside the goat pasture.

And that was when she spotted Tig, storming down the trail

from the forest with an expression like thunderclouds.

Elenna's snow removal service had cleared the car park, but the trails around the farm were left for her to deal with and she hadn't cleared this one yet.

Tig's walking stick skidded across a patch of ice. The old woman lurched and her arms pinwheeled.

"Tig!" Elenna ran but didn't get far before she was also skidding on ice. They collided like two wrecking balls, but Tig didn't go down. Gnarled fingers grasped Elenna's jacket as she steadied herself. Finally she straightened and planted her stick firmly on the ground.

"Are ye trying to kill an ol' woman?"

"I'm sorry. I guess we both slipped." Elenna tried for diplomacy when dealing with Tig.

"*Ye* slipped. I caught ye. Have ye never heard of throwin' down a bit o' sand for the ice? It's not feckin' rocket science!"

"Of course, I was about to do that," she lied. "What can I help you with?"

Tig harrumphed. Her nose was red from the cold. She didn't drive and Elenna wondered if she'd walked all the way from her little shack.

"Ye have my sheep."

It took Elenna a moment to understand.

"Your sheep?"

Tig's nod was sharp enough to cut. "Ye found a ram in the woods didn't ye?"

"That was you!" Her thoughts whirled. "You left it tied to a stake beside the blight. Why?"

"Ye know the answer, girlie."

"The Black Annis."

"The *hag*." Tig drew out the word, making it unnecessarily

aggressive. She leaned forward and frowned. The wrinkles on her forehead melted into a deep groove between her brows. "A payment in flesh is the only coin she be acceptin'."

"A sacrifice? You left that poor sheep tied up there to die?"

"Stupid girl! If not that sheep, then who? Ol' Annis will come after yours. Or a child next. Is that what ye want?"

Tig stomped her walking stick on Elenna's boot. They were steel toed, so she didn't feel it, but she jerked her foot back anyway.

"N…no, of course not, but…" But what? But did she believe that a dark fairy was camped in her woods? She thought of those eyes and that pale blue hand reaching for her throat. It wasn't just her overactive imagination.

With sudden and sharp certainty, she realized that yes, she *did* believe in fairies or fae or whatever they were called.

That didn't mean she'd let Tig sacrifice an innocent animal.

She crossed her arms over her chest. The damp and cold was starting to seep through her jacket and she shivered.

"You can't have the sheep. I named him already. He's now Dasher and an official resident of Equinox Farm." She paused. "Where did you get him anyway?"

Tig took out her flask, gulped down her "medicine," and wiped her mouth on the back of her hand. "The internet. Ye can get near anything online if ye look hard enough."

Elenna blinked. The incongruity of this ancient woman using the Internet was jarring. Her shack didn't even have electricity or running water.

Tig saw her surprise and cackled. A bony finger poked her chest. "Youngens are all alike, sure. Am I too old to learn new things? Or do ye believe that because I choose to live in simplicity and peace, I don't grasp the new world." She waved a hand as if to encompass this greater world. "If only ye knew. Haven't I seen innovations? I have. Industries, technologies, ideologies. Don't they come and go? Do ye know what is forever?"

Elenna shook her head. Tig's words had woven a web and her thoughts were as frozen as her fingers. Tig poked her again.

"Evil. Evil is forever, and isn't it living only a stone's throw from yer home? Keep yer sheep, but remember that old Tig warned ye."

She turned and shuffled up the path. Within moments, the forest swallowed her.

DASHER SETTLED IN WITH THE goats, but some of the other animals weren't doing so well. Sadie looked thin. They had a couple of bad storms in January and Elenna started bringing the horses into the barn overnight. She gave Sadie extra bran mush with applesauce each morning since animals burned extra calories keeping warm. She would have preferred that the herd stayed in the barn, but horses, being horses, didn't like to be cooped up. So after breakfast, she led them back to the pasture where they huddled in their run-in shed under the falling snow.

It was much the same with the goats, only their little barn was set inside their pasture and she left its door open during the day so they could seek shelter.

Newton had also lost weight. The pony blanket wasn't sufficient to keep him warm anymore. And so, on a cold January morning, she decided it was time to set up her sewing machine, and now she stood in Jamie's workout room with hands on hips as she scanned the space.

It was a big room, even bigger than her enormous bedroom. It took up more than half of the upstairs shorter section of the U, and was flanked by a small office where she wrote and paid the bills, and a storage room on the other end. The inside wall was all glass and looked down on the courtyard with the zen garden. The outside wall had long, high windows with a collection of Japanese katanas hanging below them.

Half the space was taken up with equipment—treadmill, bike, and weight machine. Free weights and a bench sat next to the outer wall, but the rest of the room was empty with thin mats set out for yoga or tai chi practice.

Light from the high windows filtered in, making dust motes sparkle. Suddenly, her inner montage started playing the sweet strands of a koto. It plucked out a melody as a ghost appeared in the ray of sunlight. He moved with effortless grace.

Raise leg, pause. Raise opposite arm. Pause. Rotate. Lower leg and arm. Repeat on the other side.

How many times had she sat in her little office, pretending to write but secretly watching Jamie practice tai chi through the open door?

He'd probably known she watched him, and both voyeur and voyee were aroused enough that tai chi often turned into love-making right there on the gym mats.

The sun went behind a cloud and the ghost faded.

She found herself clutching the handlebar on the stationary bike with white knuckles.

These ghostly intrusions happened less frequently than they had in the first months after Jamie's death, but they still had the power of a sucker punch right to the gut.

She sighed and looked over the room with a critical and more objective eye.

Jamie had enjoyed jogging on a treadmill and pulling weights. Personally, she got enough exercise hauling water buckets and hay. She didn't feel the need to add extra training. So for two years this room had been dormant.

With the large storage room at the far end and natural light from the floor-to-ceiling window, it would make a terrific craft room.

She took pictures of all the gym equipment so that she could list it for sale, then moved the treadmill and stationary bike out of the way and piled the mats in one corner to make room for her work space. She'd pack up the free weights and other equipment later.

In her teens, she'd gone through a crafty phase when she'd learned to make her own clothes, jewelry and even soap. The sewing machine was the last gift her grandmother had bought Elenna before she died. It had been stored for the last four years because she'd had no place to set it up.

Now she did.

She found it in the back of the storage room along with a folding table. She set both up under the outer windows. The swords would have to go if she wanted to make room for craft supplies but…baby steps. For now she was satisfied with her workspace.

She'd already found a pattern for goat pajamas online, and made a trip into Ottawa to find fleece. The stacks of material were neatly folded in a pile on her desk in the office. She brought them into her new craft room and unpacked them.

The first fleece was blue with little white sheep jumping over a fence. If you had to put pajamas on your goat, you might as well make them adorable.

As she cut and stitched fabric, something shifted inside her. Ideas about how to transform the room from a gym to an artist's hub came to her. A few shelves for craft items. Some stackable storage bins. Maybe she'd take up scrapbooking or install a pottery wheel. The possibilities were endless and they filled her with a buzzing contentment. Why hadn't she thought of this before?

The answer came like a cold splash. Because this had always been Jamie's house and she'd only been a guest. It would have seemed rude to ask him to move his gym equipment, even if the room was big enough for both a gym and a sewing machine.

But somewhere in the last two years, Kiso House had started to feel like home. She had a sudden urge to buy paint in vibrant colors and paint each room for a different flower. Her bedroom would be the blue of forget-me-nots. This room, the yellow of black-eyed Susans. She would fill the house with color. She would tear down the minimalist Japanese decor and put up paintings from local artists, collages made from river pebbles and pressed leaves. She could make her own art and fill the walls with it.

By the time she zipped through the last seam on the pajamas, she felt a little breathless just considering all the possibilities.

Then she looked at the exercise equipment, sitting forlornly in the corner.

*Get a grip, Elenna. It's just metal and plastic. It can't be forlorn.*

And yet, it was soaked in Jamie's sweat and determination. Could she really get rid of it? Could she take down the delicate Japanese calligraphy that he'd so loved? Or the katanas that still held the indentation of his fingers on their grips?

She crossed her eyes a little, imagining an orderly wall of shelves, stacked with craft paper, paints, glues and other trinkets.

Setting the finished pajamas aside, she headed into her office. The huge leather chair creaked as she settled on it. How long had it been since she'd sat here to write? She thought back and was startled to realize it had been months since she'd even attempted to put down words.

On a shelf above the desk a dozen notebooks were filled with her scribblings. She pulled one down and flipped through the pages. Some of the scribblings were sparks for future stories. Some were sketches of characters. There were bits of dialogue that amused her and even a poem or two. She stopped at a poem that was dated February 2021, not long after they'd been married. She read the words through tear-blurred eyes.

> If I had my way
> my walls would be covered with pictures
> of yetis playing in the snow.
> And dragons.
> A thunder on the wing against a full moon.
> One whole wall
> beside the fieldstone hearth
> would be painted like a dark forest
> with fireflies
> so life-like I might walk into it one day.
> I'd have throw pillows shaped like unicorns
> and bumblebees
> and a purple lava lamp in the corner.
> There would be no knickknacks because, ugh.
> Who wants to dust those?
> But I might keep a shelf for a teapot
> and a mortar and pestle
> in case Baba Yaga comes to visit.

The ceiling would be covered with glow-in-the-
dark stars
of constellations only I can see
like the exploding pineapple
or the hairy windmill.
And sometimes the doorbell will ring
with a chime like laughter heard from far away.
And when I open it
the fairies will come in.

Her eyes blurred with tears as she read the last lines.

There were daisies and vines scribbled around the margins. She didn't even remember drawing them or writing the poem, but clearly that first winter at Equinox Farm she'd been a little overwhelmed. She felt sorry for the woman who'd written those lines. Sorry and a little envious. Where had she been for the last five years—this woman who loved color and wildflowers and dragons?

Lost, she realized. Lost under the blinding glare of love.

Jamie had been a force of nature and she'd been caught up in the whirlwind of his passions, his hobbies, his tastes. She couldn't truly resent that. Love transforms people, and Jamie's love had brought her so many new experiences.

She'd learned to love hiking in the woods. Discovered sketching mushrooms and spelunking nearby caves. She learned to farm and found a deep fulfillment in treating animals with love and respect, something that wouldn't have even been on her radar if not for Jamie.

She'd learned that two people could happily live in a cocoon, filling each other's needs and weaving the threads of their lives around them.

But she'd also lost part of herself in the process. It was time to find that part, to find wonder, and whimsy and color again.

It was time to welcome fairies back into her life.

At first, Newton wasn't sure about his new jammies. Elenna slipped his stiff legs into the sleeves one at a time and did up the snaps that ran in a seam along his stomach. She'd used snaps because Beezle would chew off buttons and Velcro got matted with grass.

She finished the last snap and stood back. Newton froze like one of those fainting goats right before they toppled. He lifted one front leg and stuck it straight out, then a back leg. He let out a pitiful bleat. Elenna ruffled his ears and ran her hands up and down his back in a brisk rub.

"You'll get used to them. I promise."

The day was cold, so she buckled the pony blanket over the pajamas. That seemed to comfort Newton and he bucked out his back legs before heading back to his herd mates at the bottom of the pasture.

Elenna sighed and glanced at her phone—about the hundredth time she'd checked in the past hour. It was almost noon. She needed to head back to the house to get ready.

At eight o'clock last night, Jamie's brother, Robert, had called asking—no, *stating*—that he would be coming to see her today at 1:00 p.m.

As Elenna shucked off her work clothes and jumped under

the steaming shower in her *ofuro* room, she wondered again what he could want. She'd been agonizing over the visit for the last fourteen hours. Even her dreams had been vaguely distressing—nothing she could pinpoint exactly, just menacing shadows and an unstoppable desire to run.

After the shower she dug out dark gray wool pants that hadn't been worn in years and paired them with a pale peach sweater with a cowl neck. She adjusted the sweater and the waistband of her pants. She felt over-dressed. Once, she had dressed like this all the time, but now she longed for her jeans and t-shirt. She glanced at her muddy running shoes and groaned. Those wouldn't do. She was sweaty and even more nervous by the time she found a pair of squashed loafers at the back of her closet.

Elenna hadn't been this anxious about a meeting since her first job interview. She set the coffee to brew and had water ready to boil in case her guest preferred tea. She'd made a quick trip to Auntie Clare's that morning for scones and mini-muffins, and she set them on the dining table along with plates, cups and spoons. Gado whined when he smelled the baked goods. He had a terrible sweet tooth.

She pointed a finger at the dog. "Don't touch them." He groused and flopped down on the floor beside the table. She studied the place settings, ran a finger along the sideboard looking for dust and sighed. It was the best she could do.

She washed her hands in the bathroom and brushed her hair for the fifth time, pausing with the brush halfway through a swipe. The reflection in the mirror looked a little lost. She hadn't seen Robert since the funeral. Would he find her changed? Her normally olive-toned skin was pale. That could just be January blues, but she was thinner too. Her brown eyes looked sunken. She turned her head to the side and traced a few fine lines creeping up from the edge of her eye. Those were new. She pulled her hand through her thick, dark brown hair that fell with a loose curl to her shoulders. Jamie had once said it was the first part of her he'd fallen in love with. There were a few streaks of gray in it now.

But so what? Robert wasn't coming to talk about her appearance. That, of course, begged the question: why was Robert coming?

A faint knock at the door set Gado barking. She quickly tied her hair into a ponytail and went to meet her brother-in-law.

No one ever came in the front door of Kiso House. Everyone used the back door that led to the courtyard. The front entrance was so unused that she sometimes forgot about it and left boxes, boots and other junk cluttering the space.

She knocked a pair of old snow boots out of the way and opened the door. Gado pushed his way between her and this intruder who didn't have the sense to use the right entrance. A low growl rumbled in his chest. He might have been a retired guard dog, but she was still his flock and he wouldn't let anyone hurt her.

"Hello, Gado, old boy." Not worried about the growl, Robert bent down to let Gado sniff his closed fist. Gado's curled tail wagged frantically. He pranced and whined as he recognized a friend. Robert patted his head and smiled.

Elenna's heart lurched. The brothers didn't look much alike. Robert was leaner than Jamie, with darker hair and a longer face. But that smile...it was pure Jamie.

She cleared her throat that was suddenly aching and stepped back with a wobbly smile. "Come in."

The front entrance was on the short side of the U, tucked between the kitchen and a utility room that held her electrical panel, water heater and much needed storage for a house without a basement. The gym (now turned into a craft room) was above it, giving the foyer a cramped feel.

She led Robert to the dining room and left the paper screen open to let in light from the courtyard. He stopped at the table to admire the delicate watercolors of cherry trees in blossom on the long wall below the windows. Other than a ceremonial knife in its sheath on the sideboard, they were the only ornamentation in the room. That and the six strokes of color painted across the wall—two shades of green, a deep rose, dusky rose and two yellows. She was determined to find the right color for the light in the room, but now she wished she'd waited a few days to test the samples.

Robert smiled and shook his head. "He needed this place."

"I'm sorry?"

"Jamie. He was such a bundle of energy. Mother called him our wild child."

Elenna felt a little ripple go through her. That's how she thought of Ruby.

"He could never sit still, jumping from one project or passion to another," Robert continued. "And mother indulged them all. He was her surprise baby. She was over forty when he was born. Leah and I were almost grown. By the time Jamie entered kindergarten, we were already off to university. So, of course, she treasured him. And spoiled him."

His smile faded, but a sparkle remained in his eye. Elenna couldn't tell if it was humor or the threat of tears.

"Please sit," she said. "Can I get you coffee or tea?"

"Coffee would be perfect." He sat at the dining table and placed a black folder beside his plate.

In the kitchen Elenna filled the coffee urn and placed mugs, sugar and cream on a tray, marveling at how steady her hands were. She returned to set the tray on the dining table.

"Thank you," Robert said. He took a muffin, then stirred cream into his coffee. "Yes. I can see how Jamie would have been happy here. I believe his love of all things Japanese stemmed from his need to calm a restless soul. This room is definitely calming."

"Calming, yes." That was a perfectly non-judgmental thing to say, but Robert's eyes narrowed and he studied her with a small, tight smile. She suspected Robert Nolan didn't miss much, and he confirmed that when he nodded toward the paint swatches on the wall.

"You don't like the house." It wasn't really a question.

"Oh, it's beautiful. Just…um…not very practical."

Robert laughed. "You could say the same about Jamie."

She nodded and smiled. She desperately wanted to ask him why he was here. Robert was in no hurry to enlighten her. He sipped his coffee and seemed to contemplate its flavors.

"I saw Sadie in the pasture as I arrived. I can't believe that old plow horse is still kicking."

"She's a tough old bird." Elenna sipped her coffee and watched him.

"I loved your story about her being retired from farm work, what was it called? The Old Path? It was a poignant reminder that the road of life has many forks."

She nearly choked on her coffee, sputtered and set the mug down.

"You read my story?" How was that even possible? It had never been published.

"Of course. Jamie sent me many of your stories. He once told me that you were going to be famous because your stories often revealed a hidden truth. He was very proud of you."

She stared at him, dumbfounded. Robert smiled and broke his muffin in half. He took a bite and held the other bit out for Gado, who'd been making a puddle of drool between his paws since they'd sat down.

"May I?"

She nodded. Her thoughts were still too flustered to allow for speech.

Robert tossed the muffin to Gado.

"I see I've surprised you."

She nodded.

"In any case, it makes me happy to see Jamie's pride and joy being so well cared for. And in a round about way, that old horse and your stories are why I'm here."

Finally.

She felt herself leaning toward him and sat straighter in her seat.

"My uncle Linford died less than a week before Jamie did. I'm not sure if you remember that."

"Uh, yes. Of course. I was very sorry to hear it."

She vaguely remembered Jamie's sorrow when he'd heard about Linford Nolan's passing. He'd bought a plane ticket to Calgary for the memorial service. She found it among his things weeks later.

"He was your great-uncle, I believe?"

"Yes, my grandfather's youngest brother. A twilight baby like Jamie. Maybe that's why they always got along so well."

She made a noncommittal noise of agreement. His gaze kept going back to the black folder. Wherever this train was heading, she hoped it would arrive at the station soon.

"This farm actually belonged to Linford's father, my great-grandfather. He was raised here, though Linford left home when he was only a teen. He heard the call of oil out west and never looked back."

Was that it? Did they want their family farm back? She'd always wondered if Jamie's siblings were resentful about the inheritance. Maybe old Linford had been resentful too. Resentful that someone he barely knew was living on his family farm. Could he be reaching out from the grave to make it right?

"Is there something wrong with the farm title," she blurted. Robert looked startled and she felt her face heat with a flush. "I mean it is your family farm. I would understand if you wanted me to leave it."

Robert laid his big hand over hers. It was warm against her chilled skin. His eyes softened and the sudden resemblance to Jamie was uncanny.

"Lord no, Elenna. I'm sorry you would think that. This farm is yours. Jamie wanted it so, and I agree. Neither Leah nor I could take care of it the way you do, or love it like you do. And that is the best way we can honor his memory."

She felt her bristles lower.

Robert took a deep breath and continued. "No, the reason I'm here is because Linford left his fortune to us."

"Us?"

"Me, Jamie and Leah. The exact wording is," he finally opened the folder and read from the top page, "I leave the proceeds of the sale of…wait, that's just some legal mumbo jumbo." He skimmed a finger down the page. "Here it is. I leave it to my great niece Leah Nolan and great nephews Robert Nolan and James Nolan. In the event that these heirs predecease me, their portion will carry over to their families."

Robert put the folder down and stared at her with a pleased grin. "It's sort of odd wording, leaves a lot of gaps to argue in court." He pulled another sheet from the folder and held it between two fingers. This one was slightly thicker and folded in the middle. He seemed to be considering it, but she couldn't see what was written on the page.

"I have to admit that Leah wanted to drive through those gaps with a bull dozer. She argued that 'family' means descendants, of which, Jamie had none."

Elenna felt her hackles go up again. They had made a conscious decision not to have children of their own, though in the last few months of Jamie's life they'd discussed fostering. And now they were going to be punished for that?

Robert held up a hand as if to ward off her argument.

"But in my mind, Linford's wishes are clear. He wanted his money to benefit us and our families. And you, Elenna, are Jamie's only family. Well, you and those horses, donkeys, goats and alpacas. And even this old mutt." He ruffled Gado's ears.

"And the pig."

"Sorry?"

"There's a pig. Gracie," she said faintly.

"Of course. Gracie is family too. So this is for you." He held out the sheet of paper, which she now saw was a check. A check with her name typed on it and a sum with a whole lot of zeros attached.

"Wha…?" Her mouth went dry and the numbers swam on the page. She set it down on the table. "This can't be right."

"I assure you it is. But I also want you to consider something." Robert's expression turned serious. "This house, this farm, they were Jamie's dream. This money is not conditional on that."

"What do you mean?"

"I mean that if you wanted to sell the farm and this… *impractical* house," he arched an eyebrow toward the paper screen that divided the dining room from the hallway, "and go live on a warm island somewhere, I wouldn't blame you. And I wouldn't stop you."

"Leah might not agree."

He patted her hand. "You leave Leah to me. She's just an old wind bag who needs to let out her bluster sometimes."

She couldn't help laughing. That wasn't at all how she remembered Jamie's tall, elegant sister.

Robert closed the folder and tapped it on the table. He rose and paused at the paint samples spread across the wall like a rainbow.

"Anyway, I'll leave this with you. Whatever you decide, you will have my support."

"Thank you." She accepted the folder.

He pointed toward the paint samples and smiled. "And for what it's worth, I like the sage green."

FEBRUARY WAS THE COLDEST ELENNA remembered on the farm. One Friday morning, it was too cold even to walk the short distance to Auntie Clare's, so Elenna drove her old truck.

You don't know real cold until you have to drive on square tires. When the temperature drops well below freezing, the air compresses, leaving a softer tire that freezes flat where it presses against the ground. The result is a bumpy ride until the rubber heats up enough to even out. Elenna's truck made an appalling *kathunk-kathunk* noise the whole way to Auntie Clare's. She left it idling in the parking lot to keep it warm and dashed into the store.

Hadley was tapping a pen against a clipboard while she studied inventory on the shelves. Elenna stamped snow off her boots and rubbed her mittened hands together, trying to get blood flowing to her fingers.

"Slow day?"

Hadley smiled and tucked the pen behind her ear.

"Glacially slow. But that's okay. I need to do an inventory overhaul."

"How's Auntie?"

Everybody knew that Auntie Clare despised the cold. She wrapped herself in scarves and shawls from September to April.

Hadley glanced upward, to the apartment above the store. "She's tucked in bed with a hot water bottle and a cup of tea. At least she'll stay out of my hair today. Did you need something?"

"It's a long shot, but Milo suggested bran mush for Sadie and I'm all out. My feed delivery doesn't come for another two days, and she could really use the energy boost in this cold. Would you have any bran flakes?"

"Of course. Let me see what's in the storeroom."

Elenna waited only a minute before Hadley returned with a big paper bag.

"Auntie's bran muffins haven't been selling well anyway. Seems no one cares about staying regular these days."

She rang her up and Elenna thanked her.

"Are you still on for girls' night tonight?" Hadley raised an eyebrow.

Elenna groaned inwardly. She liked the *idea* of girls' night out, and she even enjoyed her time with Nina, Hadley and Joelle, but her introverted side always resisted leaving her nest.

Hadley saw her expression. "You have to go. It's the first time Joelle has invited us to the inn. Aren't you curious about the renovations? I know I am. And if we're lucky, we'll spot the ghost of that girl who died there in the fifties. They say she haunts the upper hallway."

"Yay?" Elenna filled her tone with as much skepticism as she could muster. "Who doesn't look forward to a night of hauntings?

"Aw, come on. It'll be fun."

She grudgingly let Hadley convince her to join them, then took her bag of bran and left.

The rest of the day was labor intensive, which was the best way to keep warm. While she mucked out stalls, her thoughts kept returning to the check that was tucked away in a drawer in her office. She hadn't dared look at it since Robert left. The idea of bringing it to the bank was even more daunting. She could just imagine the look on the teller's face when she presented it. Mullarkey was a small village, minuscule, really. Even in the larger Shawville, where her bank was located, everyone knew everyone else's business. Did she want them knowing she'd inherited a small fortune? Maybe she'd take the check into Ottawa to deposit it.

Bandito, leader of the barn cats, twined around her ankles looking for handouts. Cougar and Puma watched from atop a cabinet.

"You'll get fed when everyone else does." She used her stern voice but they were undaunted, so she tossed them each a few catnip treats, then bundled the scarf around her head and put on gloves to take the muck bucket outside.

Snow devils swirled across the open pasture like wraiths caught in an elaborate dance. The ground was too frozen to spread manure, so she dumped it on the muck pile.

Back inside, she surveyed her work, satisfied that the barn was clean enough. The weather app warned that the temperature would drop to a startling and dangerous -35 degrees Celsius tonight. Quebecers usually spent a few days every winter in those subarctic temperatures. It didn't last long, but it could be deadly if you weren't prepared. She was. This wasn't her first winter rodeo.

She didn't worry about Luther and the alpacas so much. They were bred for the Andes and had thick coats to protect them. She would just make sure they were tucked into their little hut for the night where they could huddle together for warmth.

Everyone else needed to be moved inside the big barn, including the goats. Newton suffered terribly in the extreme cold. She brought him in first, along with Dasher. Gilly and Shaun showed up after school, just as she was leading Beezle and Bella up the path. The kids were so bundled up, she could see only their eyes, and she was eternally grateful to them for braving the elements.

"How can we help," Gilly asked.

"Make sure the ducks have water and close them inside their duck house?"

Gilly saluted and they hurried off.

Elenna continued on to the barn and saw Bella and Beezle safely tucked into the first stall with Newton and Dasher. She was just latching the stall door when the lights went out. With the big Dutch doors closed against the cold, the only light came from dirty windows in the stalls.

Quebec was blessed with an abundance of hydro-electricity and an electrical grid that had the stability of a toddler hyped up on sugar. It went offline regularly, often for only a few minutes, but sometimes for hours or even days at a time.

She stood still in the dim barn, waiting. A minute passed and the barn remained dark. Her eyes adjusted to the low light, and still the electricity remained off. It looked like they weren't going to be lucky today.

She headed outside to bring in the horses. By the time she got back, Gilly and Shaun had settled the ducks and they headed out to bring in Jude and Missy. Gracie was disgruntled by all the activity in her barn. Elenna dumped extra straw in her stall and threw some treats into it to give her something to do.

Luckily, Elenna had heated water for Sadie's bran mash before the lights went out, and Gilly helped her feed the others, including the impatient barn cats.

The animals were subdued in the dim barn. The only sounds were the grinding of teeth on grain and Gracie's pawing at the straw in her nest.

"Thanks for the help," Elenna told the kids.

Gilly shivered. "What if the electricity is off all night?" The barn was warmish now, but it wouldn't last.

"I'm going to start the boiler. Don't worry. You go home and get warm."

She said goodbye to the kids and went to start the boiler.

When Jamie took over the farm, the old barn had been falling down. He replaced it with this bigger, modern barn with heating tubes under the concrete floor. There were also a couple of electric baseboard heaters, and he'd thought ahead for the tough Quebec winters, by installing a secondary heat source—an outdoor, wood-burning boiler.

Burning wood inside a barn was never a good idea. Too much dry straw and straw dust that could ignite in an instant. The outdoor boiler was a small shed between the house and barn.

Beside it, a lean-to was stocked with dry, split wood. She hadn't used the boiler last winter. She'd been too worn out by grief to even worry about it, but she was glad that she'd bought a couple of cords of wood this past fall.

She channeled her inner Girl Guide to start the fire and set the boiler to heat the barn and the house. The old farm cottage wasn't on the system, but no one was living in it at the moment. She'd already decided to spend the evening in the barn to be sure the animals weren't too restive. The horses in particular didn't like being cooped up for too long, and it was hard to convince them that the weather could kill them.

She went back to the house to feed Gado and make herself a thermos of coffee. While she waited for the coffee to brew, she texted Hadley.

> *Electricity out. Have to stay in tonight to take care of the horses.*

It was a good excuse, but she still felt guilty for bowing out. Hadley texted her back a thumbs-up.

Half an hour later, the sun went down and the barn was swallowed in darkness. She was ready for it. She'd taken a camp chair out of storage along with an LED lantern that filled the barn with cool white light. She had a book, plus a new journal and pencils, her thermos of coffee and a sandwich. She was happy.

Happy enough.

Sadie leaned her head out of her stall and nickered. Elenna hummed *You Are My Sunshine* and patted her velvety nose. The old mare was the light that shone on all of Equinox Farm, and Elenna had always thought of the old tune as Sadie's song.

Her singing did nothing for Sassy who was already pacing in her stall, so Elenna turned on the Bluetooth speaker and played an old country playlist from her phone. A little bit of the Salebarbes praying to the good Lord always soothed Sassy.

Twice, she left the comfy warmth of the barn to stoke the boiler. The second time, she turned when she heard voices on the drive. The night was bitterly cold and she couldn't imagine who would be out in it.

Then she recognized Nina's laugh, and the shadows on the drive resolved into three forms.

Nina waved. Hadley held up a bottle of wine. Even Joelle was there.

"You couldn't come to us, so we came to you," Hadley said.

"You're crazy! Did you walk?"

"Just from the store. Now let's get inside before I freeze my nippers off," Nina said.

Elenna pulled out more camp chairs and set them up in the aisle between the stalls. A second LED lantern brightened the place. Nina had brought wine and red plastic cups. Hadley supplied a tray of butter tarts and Nanaimo bars.

"Those are so much better than my turkey and cheese sandwich," Elenna said.

She made sure to keep her chair closest to Sadie's stall. The old mare still had her mischievous side, and she was tall enough to lean over the half door. If she was going to snatch the hat off someone's head, Elenna wanted it to be hers.

Nina broke open the wine and poured it into the cups. She passed one to Joelle who passed it along to Elenna.

Elenna smiled and took the cup. "How can you be away from the inn tonight?"

Joelle shrugged. "No guests right now. It's too cold even for the snowshoers and cross-country skiers."

"That's too bad."

"It's okay. Means I can get the renovations finished without too much fuss."

"And the brownies?"

Joelle quirked her lips in a half smile.

"No more missing things. Maybe they're hibernating."

"Maybe." Elenna turned to Nina, their unofficial expert on all things fae. "Do brownies hibernate?"

"Who cares?" Nina said. "I want the bigger scoop. A little birdie told me there was a fancy BMW parked in your driveway last week," Nina said.

"A little birdie?"

"Well, a very large, Felix-shaped birdie. The ladies got through the fence again, and he chased them all the way to the bridge. But never mind that. Spill. It was that cute vet, wasn't it?"

"Milo drives a truck, as you know."

"Only when he's on duty. He could drive a BMW on off-hours."

"He's more of a Land Rover kind of guy," Joelle said.

Hadley nodded in agreement. "Or at least a Jeep."

Nina waved a hand. "I don't know about cars. They aren't important. So who was it?"

Should she tell them about Robert? She might as well, as soon as she cashed that alarming check at the little bank in Shawville, everyone would know about it. That was both the blessing and the curse about living in a small town.

And besides, these were her friends.

"It was my brother-in-law."

Two pairs of eyes went wide. Two mouths hung open. Only Joelle looked nonplussed. Elenna was sure the others had told her in whispered voices behind their hands about her history with Jamie, but Joelle hadn't been there to witness Elenna's utter devastation after his death. Or the frigid reception she'd received from his family. At least that was how Elenna remembered it, but maybe it was only Leah who had been cold? She couldn't actually remember Robert's reaction at the funeral.

"Jamie's brother?" Nina said in a hushed voice, as if invoking the name of a saint.

"What did he want?" Hadley was more practical. She'd held Elenna up during the funeral and had met Jamie's family. She hadn't been impressed.

"To give me the rest of Jamie's inheritance."

Now even Joelle looked surprised.

"Cool," Hadley said. "Enough to keep the farm going?"

Elenna chewed the inside of her lip and nodded. "For many years. Many, many years."

Nina shrieked and threw her arms around Elenna's neck.

"I was so worried you'd be leaving us." She pulled away and beamed. "I know this last year has been rough in a lot of ways. And I know you've struggled to keep the lights on. This is such good news."

Elenna made a noise that could have been a yes or a no.

Nina sat back, still smiling and poured more wine all around.

"Don't get too excited," Hadley said. "This might not mean what you think it does." She narrowed her eyes and looked at Elenna in a way that seemed to see right inside her thoughts. "Are you keeping the farm?"

Elenna let out a long breath. "I don't know. As Robert pointed out, I don't have to use the money to keep the animals fed. I could sell and go live somewhere else quite happily."

"You wouldn't do that?" Nina said. "Would you?"

"Sometimes people need a change." Joelle's expression was somber. "Sometimes there's no other way to get away from memories." She sounded like she spoke from experience.

All three of them stared at Elenna expectantly.

"I haven't made any decisions yet." She took a sip of wine and retreated into her camp chair. Behind her Sadie nickered and velvety lips nuzzled her ear.

She couldn't sell the farm and Sadie and Gracie and all the others. Could she?

In January of 1998, an ice storm hit Quebec and the Maritime provinces. Freezing rain fell for days, coating cities, towns and forests in ice. Everything stopped. Businesses closed. School buses wouldn't run. The great metal pylons that hold electrical lines snapped under the weight of two-inch-thick ice plating their arms. Kilometer after kilometer of these pylons simply crumpled. They lined the highways like giant metal automatons, folded at the hip with their massive arms sweeping the ground. Millions of people were without electricity. The area between Saint-Hyacinthe, Granby and Saint-Jean-sur-Richelieu lost power for over a month and became known as the Triangle of Darkness. In the cities, people died when bus-sized chunks of ice fell off roofs or when they resorted to burning kerosene to keep warm in the dark. In rural areas, animals died for lack of running water and ventilation. When the ice melted, it left behind entire forests flattened by the force of the storm.

And Quebecers never forgot it.

On a dreary March evening, Elenna stood in the open doorway of the barn and watched the freezing drizzle fall. Like anyone who'd lived through the Great Ice Storm of 1998, freezing rain always sent a little thrill of dread through her heart.

She'd been nine years old at the time, living in a duplex with her dad in the west end of Montreal. Her mom had been gone for three years and Elenna had retreated into her own world of books and art. Her dad tried his best to fill the empty space with his chatter. She remembered the days after the ice storm as one of the best times of her life. Being a child, she didn't realize that they were in any real danger of freezing, or that people were suffering and dying all over the city. She only knew that her father, who often worked long hours, was suddenly there all day and night. They made a blanket fort in the family room and pretended to camp. They ate smoked oysters on crackers for dinner and dad pretended it was a fancy meal by presenting it on their best china.

Twenty-eight years later, as the sun set, she stood in the yard between Kiso House and the barn and watched the rain fall, remembering the great storm with a mix of fear and anticipation.

While she waited for Gado to finish his evening business, she tapped the weather app on her phone and read the forecast. They were calling for rain to fall into the early hours of the morning, followed by plummeting temperatures. It was the perfect recipe for an icy disaster.

Gado shook ice pellets from his fur and sat by the door. Even with his thick Akita coat, he didn't want to be out in this weather.

The icy conditions would make walking in the pasture treacherous. Elenna didn't want anyone breaking a leg, so she'd already brought the horses and donkeys into the barn.

Since the temperatures hovered around the freezing mark,

the goats and sheep were tucked away in their stone croft with extra hay and water. Together, they would generate enough heat to keep even Newton warm. The ducks were secure in their house and Luther was keeping watch over his lemmings in their run-in shed.

She was ready for whatever Mother Nature threw at them.

So far, the electricity held. She made a small prayer to the galvanic gods that it would continue.

After letting Gado inside, she crossed the slippery trail to the barn to check on everyone before heading to bed. Sadie, Shin Mei, Jude and Missy were all contentedly munching hay in their stalls. Sassy paced. She stopped to whinny when the lights in the barn went on. Elenna shut them off and quietly retreated outside. She just hoped Sassy wouldn't kick a hole in her stall before morning.

That night, she slept fitfully, listening to the rain pound on the tin roof.

SHE OPENED HER EYES TO a strangely silent house, the kind of silence that only came when the distant hum of appliances was stifled. The electricity had gone off in the night as she'd expected. Gado had climbed onto the bed and was pressed along the length of her back to share his warmth. She sank her fingers into his thick mane. He opened one eye and his expression told her he didn't want to get up any more than she did. But the animals needed checking on. Being a farmer meant curbing her own penchant for morning laziness.

She threw on warm clothes and slipped the crampons over her boots for extra traction before she went outside to start the wood-burning boiler.

She was met by a world transformed.

Trees alongside the car park were bent under a thick sheen of ice. Fog hung between the trees, utterly still and smothering all sound. Fence rails and posts also gleamed with a coating of ice, and the ground had been turned into a treacherous skating rink. Nothing moved. There were no voices—human or animal—and no cars on the road. The silence was heart-stopping.

And then a crack resounded through the fog, so loud Elenna ducked like she was under fire. In the woods, a tree had split under the weight of ice. While she loaded wood into the firebox, she heard more branches break and tumble, and a slow irregular drip of ice melting off the eaves of the barn.

Luther bleated and the alpacas gabbled from inside their enclosure. Elenna could just make out their shuffling forms in the fog. They'd have to wait.

The horses were eager to leave their stalls. They'd have to wait too. She bribed them with grain and treats while she fired up the old Honda ATV to spread sand over the small paddock that enclosed the barn. This was an area of about forty by forty feet right outside the Dutch doors. She usually only closed the gates on farrier or vet visit days when she needed to keep the herd close. But today, the slope down to the main pasture was sheer ice. If the horses wanted outside time, they'd have to stick close to the barn.

By the time she finished spreading sand, securing the gates, and putting out hay, Sassy was kicking at her stall door.

"All right! Don't get your knickers in a twist!" Elenna grabbed a lead rope and threw it over her neck, not bothering with a halter. She led Sassy out the double doors and released the rope. The mare tore across the sandy lot until she hit the far fence, then turned, bucked and farted, and ran around the enclosure until she found the hay pile.

"Knucklehead." Elenna shook her head and went back for Shin Mei, who was much more shy about stepping into the sandy paddock. She urged him on with treats, and finally left him at the hay pile with Sassy.

Sadie didn't even need a lead rope. Elenna simply opened her stall and the old plow horse followed her to the door where she stopped to inspect the frozen world outside.

Elenna tucked her hand under Sadie's neck and rubbed her, taking the moment to steal a quick cuddle.

"Such a good girl," she murmured. "The only one who never causes trouble, aren't you?"

If she'd known then what the next hours would bring, she would have slapped herself for being a jinx.

Sadie let out a huff of breath that ruffled her lips and stepped gingerly onto the mixture of sand and ice until she was standing in the middle of the paddock. She lifted her nose and tested the air.

After releasing the donkeys, Elenna left them all grazing and made her way through the fog to check on the goats, alpacas and ducks. The alpaca pen was a mixture of muck and slush and in dire need of cleaning, but Elenna decided they could wait until the weather cleared. The ducks didn't mind their slippery enclosure and started quacking and flapping as soon as she let them out.

The trip down the hill to the goat pasture was the most hazardous as her metal cleats barely gripped the ice. She brought them more hay and water, but decided to keep them in their little shed for the morning.

When she climbed the hill to the barn again, Sassy was pacing in the paddock. Elenna thought she was just protesting her captivity, until she saw Sadie lying on the ground.

She bolted up the path. Her cold fingers were clumsy on the gate latch. Sassy whinnied in fear or irritation, but Elenna had no time to soothe her. She dashed across the paddock and skidded on a patch of ice where a large hoof had scraped away the sand and fell on her knees beside the mare.

She was breathing. Her eyes showed white all around and her sides heaved. Elenna did a quick check of her legs. Nothing was broken.

"Come on, girl. It's time to get up."

Sadie didn't move.

Elenna had been occupied with the goats and alpacas for nearly an hour. How long had Sadie been struggling to stand? There was no struggle in her now. She lay flat on her side, her head resting on the ice and her breath fogging the air. Ice crystals clung to her nostrils.

Elenna had a lead rope around her shoulders. She gently looped it under Sadie's neck. Belgians weighed nearly two-thousand pounds. There was no way Elenna could pull her up, but Sadie was well trained, and the rope should trigger a response.

Brown eyes rolled to look at her, but Sadie made no attempt to rise. Elenna skidded along the ice to examine her legs again. It was a risky move. If Sadie suddenly burst into motion she could be kicked, but the mare lay still while she felt along her knees and fetlocks, looking for heat that indicated damage to the muscle or bone.

They all felt sound, but Elenna was no expert.

She sat back on her heels and studied Sadie. She was alert and her breathing had calmed. As far as Elenna could tell, she'd simply fallen on the ice and couldn't bear her own massive weight to stand up again.

That was a big problem. Horses, especially geriatric horses, don't do well lying down for long periods of time. The sheer weight of their own bodies could put stress on internal organs, making breathing difficult and causing intestinal issues such as colic.

She needed help.

She glanced at her phone. The SOS indicator was on. She had no bars. The nearest cell tower was probably coated in ice. She stood in the middle of the paddock, turning in a circle and feeling alone.

Alone and scared.

The courtyard light was on at Kiso House. The power had come back while she was letting out the goats!

Reluctantly, she left Sadie and skidded over to the house to use the land line.

Who to call first, Max or Milo? Max was closer, but would he be able to help? Probably not. Since it was Sunday, she dialed Milo's private number instead of the vet clinic.

"Hello? Elenna?" His voice was groggy, like a normal person who'd slept in on a cold Sunday morning.

"It's Sadie. She fell and won't get up. I…" Her voice hitched and she sniffled. Damned ice storm. "I don't know what to do."

"Is she hurt? Is she breathing?" Milo was suddenly alert.

"She's breathing fine. For now. I can't find any injuries. I think she just slipped, but…" She didn't have to finish. Milo knew well enough what fate awaited a horse that couldn't stand.

"I'm leaving now," Milo said. "I'll be there in…fifty minutes."

"Okay." Her voice sounded small. "Drive safely." But it was too late. Milo had already disconnected. She held the phone to her chest as if she could hold in the dual worries of a fallen Sadie and now Milo driving on icy roads.

She called Max. He offered to come, but she didn't want him walking or driving even that short distance in this weather.

"Don't worry about me," he said, and fifteen minutes later, while she sat beside Sadie, stroking her neck, Hadley's car pulled up. Along with Hadley and Warrick, Max got out. Hadley brought her a hot coffee and Elenna gladly wrapped her frozen hands around it.

Max examined Sadie and pronounced her fit enough.

"We'll see what Milo says when he gets here, but Elenna, if she can't stand up, you'll have to make some tough decisions."

She nodded, her thoughts as numb as her toes in her wet boots.

"Best to put the others in the barn," Max said. "So Milo will have some room to work when he arrives."

"Of course." Her hands and feet worked on autopilot as she retrieved harnesses and leads from the barn.

Gilly and Shaun arrived next.

"Warrick put out the bat signal," Gilly said. "Can I help?"

"Thank you. I need to change my boots before my feet freeze. Can you get Sassy and the others back in the barn?"

"Absolutely."

Elenna left Gilly coaxing Sassy to stand still with an apple cookie so she could trap her in the harness. Inside, she took a few minutes to change her socks, boots and gloves. She threw a scoop of kibble into Gado's bowl before returning outside.

Felix arrived on a snowmobile. The General had paused on his morning walk to watch too. By the time Milo pulled up,

Nina and Joelle had also joined the somber party by the paddock fence.

Milo shot Elenna a worried smile but went right over to Sadie, knelt, and listened to her heart. He listened to her gut too, then repeated the examination of her legs, lingering over her back right knee.

He rose and came over to the fence.

"You have sad eyes," she said. "It's bad."

Milo rubbed a hand over his beard. "There's some heat in the back leg, but it's hard to say. Could be enough to bring her down, or she might have twisted it in the fall."

"Can she stand on it?"

Milo glanced at Max. Max took Elenna's hand. "That's not the problem," he said. "If she can't get up on her own, we can't lift her. And if she stays down much longer…"

She held up her hand. She knew the prognosis. They'd have to put her down.

"Why can't we lift her?" said a voice Elenna didn't recognize. Everyone turned to look at the General. Elenna had never heard him speak before.

He ignored the stunned expressions all around him and stepped into the paddock. His white mustache worked up and down as he considered the problem.

"Seems to me a good tractor and pulley system could get her standing. Can't be any worse than trying to hoist a bridge joist with nothing but a rope and a couple of oxen."

She remembered Nina mentioning Rwanda in connection to the General. He'd been head of a team of engineers who built bridges and dug wells for displaced refugees.

He rubbed the gray whiskers on his chin. "Seems a shame to put the old girl down just because she slipped on ice."

"I…My tractor doesn't start." She'd let the maintenance lag on the old 1970s Massey Ferguson because she didn't know how to drive it. Seemed simpler to use the ATV for most jobs around the farm.

"I bring my tractor," Felix said. "The 'orse should not suffer."

Hope, that double-edged dagger, stabbed Elenna's heart.

"Would it work?" She looked at the General, then at Milo.

"It's worth a try," Milo said.

Felix left to fetch his tractor. Shaun and Gilly took the General to the old barn where they stored Jamie's abandoned tractor. It also held various tools, ropes and other discarded paraphernalia. Elenna was pretty sure there were a bunch of ratchet straps in there from when Jamie used to tie his snowmobile to the trailer.

Hadley and Nina made a coffee run to Auntie Clare's. Max stayed with Sadie, while Milo pulled Elenna aside.

"Trying to lift her is a long shot," he said. His deep brown eyes were full of concern. "She could tangle up in the ropes and make things worse. If the tractor can't lift her, she could fall again, maybe break her ribs…"

Elenna put a hand on his chest to stop him.

"Are you saying we shouldn't try?"

He ran a hand through his hair. "No. We have to try. But I won't see her suffer. If things go bad, I should be ready to euthanize her."

"Yes." The word came out of her in a puff of breath. "Be ready."

Milo looked like he wanted to say more. His eyes searched hers, then he squeezed her arm and turned to his medical bag to prepare a syringe.

THE RUMBLE OF AN ENGINE and the crackle of tires on ice announced Felix's return. His tractor was a much newer Massey Ferguson model. From inside a closed cab, he navigated the treacherous driveway with a look of dire concentration. The tractor wheels wore chains and ice crackled under them. Max swung open the paddock gate. Felix wheeled in and turned the tractor so it faced the mare.

Sadie lifted her head, but tractors were nothing new to her, and she let it fall to the ice again.

The kids returned with the General. Shaun was carrying a box of straps.

It takes a village to raise a horse, and by the time they had a dozen straps wrapped around Sadie's chest, stomach and back end, Elenna looked up to find half of Mullarkey Mills standing at the fence.

She was sweating inside her winter coat from the effort to lift Sadie enough to slide straps underneath. She could see all the activity had left Sadie agitated too. Her nostrils flared and her breathing was labored again. So despite her discomfort and thirst, Elenna sat on the cold ground beside Sadie's head. She ran a hand over her soft ears and down the thick blond fur on her throat, whispering soothing nonsense—all about her beautiful mane, her soft nose and brave spirit.

A water bottle was stuck under her nose. Elenna glanced up to see Joelle's quiet concern.

"Thanks." She took the bottle and drank.

"They're almost ready." Joelle pointed to the General and Felix, who were discussing best tactics for keeping tension on the straps. This was turning out to be a lot more complicated than anyone had imagined.

Joelle's hand gripped her forearm.

"It's going to work out. You'll see. Have faith."

Elenna let out a little snort. "I'm not really one for prayer."

"I meant faith in your friends. We're all here for you. And for Sadie. We'll get this job done, you'll see."

There are moments that are easy to look back on and recognize as pivotal. The moment you fell in love. The moment your childhood ended. The moment a friendship began. It's rare to recognize that moment as it happens, but Elenna knew with sudden clarity this was one. Until today, Joelle had been the "new girl," nice enough but behind a protective barrier of aloofness. Or maybe that was Elenna? Did she put up barriers? Probably. Joelle had her secrets, her hurts and dreams. And Elenna had hers. But a gentle hand and a concerned look broke through those barriers, and Elenna knew with certainty that forty years from now, they'd be sipping tea and looking back with either sadness or fondness on this day.

"Thank you." She got the words out before her throat closed up with emotion.

Joelle smiled and squeezed her arm again. "I think they're ready."

Felix sat on the tractor's box seat and started the engine. The General finished attaching the straps to the front-loading bucket. Sadie didn't even flinch. Milo waved everyone back in case she flailed. Flying horse hooves could do a lot of damage, but he stayed on her far side, ready to monitor her breathing.

The General waved at Felix to begin, and the tractor slowly

backed up. Ice popped under its massive wheels. The ratchet straps lost their slack and tightened around Sadie.

"Stop!" called the General. He adjusted the straps. "Okay, Up!"

The bucket started to rise. Slowly. The straps strained. She saw now what the General had done. The upper straps took most of the tension, lifting Sadie at three crucial points. The lower straps were bracing her.

The tractor's hydraulics strained as the bucket inched upward.

Slowly, slowly, Sadie lifted off the ground.

An inch, then another.

*Please, please, don't let her struggle.* If she spooked at this point she could tangle herself in the straps. But Sadie was a trooper. Elenna could only wonder at the things she'd seen in her long life to make her so accepting. Her eyes rolled when the last straps snapped taut, but she didn't fight them.

The tractor strained to move its one-ton burden.

Elenna gripped Joelle's arm.

The crowd was silent.

Sadie rose enough that she could get her feet under herself.

This was the moment of truth.

She would either stand or she wouldn't.

Hooves scrabbled, kicking up sand and ice.

Sadie screamed in frustration.

And then she was standing.

"Hold!" The General's call made Felix stop. "Lower it, just a bit!" Felix complied, and the straps fell slack.

Sadie swayed and Elenna thought she'd go down again, but the old plow horse was made of stern stuff. She shook ice from her mane and took a tentative step.

A cheer went up from the watching crowd. A heavy breath whooshed from Elenna's lungs, frosting the air. She ran forward to hold onto Sadie's halter before she could begin to struggle and get herself all tangled up.

Milo and the General unhooked the straps, then Milo bent to inspect Sadie's legs.

"I think she's twisted this knee, but it's nothing serious. A few days of stall rest should do it. I'll leave you something for the pain and swelling."

Elenna nodded and led Sadie to her stall, telling her over and over what a fine, smart, brave, beautiful horse she was. She'd give her extra bran mash and apple sauce for her efforts, but first, she had an entire village to thank.

Outside, the fog was finally burning off, and the sun was a white ball behind thin clouds. Ice melted from the branches, as if admitting that this last winter storm had been a folly.

The gathered spectators had started to wander off, but a few still chatted in small groups.

"Everyone!" Elenna called out. Feet paused. Heads turned. She held a hand to her chest, to hold back the sudden emotion that overtook her.

"I just want to say," her voice croaked. She cleared her throat and tried again. "I just want to say thank you. I know Sadie would say it too if she could. You've shown us the best part of community today and well…thank you."

Her words were met with smiles and a few serious nods.

Hadley and Nina approached. "We've got to get back. Probably no one out in this weather anyway, but the stores are open."

"Of course. Thank you for coming. And for the coffee."

Joelle waved too and the three women headed to their cars with Max.

Felix followed on his tractor, and the General saluted before heading up the path toward the mill. Elenna wondered if he was going to the wind phone to tell someone about today's excitement. She would send Felix and the General an extra thank-you gift.

"We're lucky he was here." Milo nodded at the General's retreating back. "He thinks like an engineer. I would never have been able to rig those straps properly."

"He used to build bridges in Africa."

Milo's eyebrows rose. "That would explain it."

"So tell me the truth. Was this all for nothing? Will Sadie be okay?"

His lips pursed, and her eyes snagged on them. Ice clung to the bristles under his nose and around his lips.

"I won't lie. This fall took a lot out of her. She's strong for her age, but…"

She knew what he was going to say. "But we can't keep bringing in the cavalry to lift her up."

"Exactly. Whether the cause of the fall or not, that knee is weakened. She could go down again. At that point, my suggestion would be to euthanize."

She was grateful that he didn't sugarcoat it, but his words pierced the layer of false bravado she'd secured around her since finding Sadie on the ground. Her knees turned to jelly.

"Whoa!" Milo caught her arm, and she crumpled against him. He hesitated for a moment, then his arms closed around her. "It's okay. You did everything you could. You did everything right." He muttered soothing nonsense, not unlike her own words to Sadie.

And for a few brief and wonderful moments, she rested in his arms and let herself be soothed.

The ice storm of 2025 had nothing on the Great Storm of 1998. The ice melted a couple of days later, and by the following week, the sun felt positively spring-like. Elenna didn't kid herself, it was only mid-March and winter wouldn't give up without a fight. But on a beautiful Saturday morning, one week before official spring, the sun was shining, Sadie was standing in her pasture, and Elenna had just made a major life decision—she would paint the living room that sweet shade of dusty rose. She stared at the color swatches that streaked across the wall. It felt right. And just imagine all the amazing paintings she could hang on that big empty wall? In her craft room upstairs, she even had a series of acrylics on tiles that she might find a spot for. And as soon as her dad was home from his snowbird getaway, she could take a drive into Ottawa, have lunch with him and do some antiquing, visit the art galleries, and maybe the farmers' market. She would fill the wall with color.

The possibilities were endless. She felt a certain pent up energy and she knew exactly how to dispel it.

On her way to the wind phone, Elenna met Felix coming up the path from the old mill, swinging a toolbox in his hand. He'd offered to service her old tractor. She wasn't sure if she planned to sell it or learn to drive it, but either way, it needed work.

"Salut." He tipped an imaginary hat. The day was well above freezing and he'd left his floppy tuque at home.

"Prenez soin," he said. *Take care.* He must have seen her puzzled expression because he switched to English. "A coyote caught one of my sheep last night."

"Oh!" Elenna's hand went to her lips. "I'm so sorry!"

Felix doted on his ewes.

"*Oui, c'est terrible.* Keep your goats safe tonight, oui?"

Elenna nodded. "*Oui. Absolument.*" She was glad the little goat shed was working out. It kept her goats and sheep safe at night.

"*Bien.* I will let you know about your tractor."

She thanked him and continued past the old mill.

This time, when faced with the wind phone, she didn't hesitate. She dialed Jamie's number and waited impatiently for the last digit to whir away. Then she filled the empty line with her news.

She told him about Sadie falling and how the whole town came out to help her stand again.

"I know she means a lot to you, and I promise to do my best for her, whatever that turns out to be."

She told him about the ice storm and how she didn't chicken out with the wood burning boiler. She even told him about the changes she was planning for Kiso House—the new color on the walls, the craft room.

"You'd probably hate it." She exhaled with a little laugh and pulled on her ponytail.

She told him about Robert's visit and Linford's generous contribution to the farm. A thought occurred to her.

"Is that why you never worried about finances? Did you know this inheritance was coming?"

The empty line seemed to vibrate with expectant silence.

"What do you think I should do with the money? Robert thought I might sell the farm and go live somewhere warm, but I don't know. I think I'd miss winter."

She leaned against the old fence post that supported the wind phone. In the distance, she heard Jude or Missy hee-hawing—a definite sign of spring. The phone was pressed almost painfully tight to her ear.

She didn't need to hear Jamie's voice to know what he would have done with the money. He would have spent it all on his animals…and maybe a new motorbike.

Elenna smiled.

"I have to go now, I promised Joelle I'd meet her for lunch. Oh, you'd really like her. She's the one who bought the old inn. I'll…uh…come visit again soon."

She hung up the receiver and turned. The sun broke free from the clouds and right beside the path she spotted the hopeful faces of crocuses poking through the snow.

# Spring

WINTER GAVE OUT IN EARLY April. It wasn't always this way. Snow could last into May in Quebec, and the giant mountains of slush and ice pushed aside in mall parking lots could stick around until June. But this April was like the tentative kiss of a newborn kitten; it had a rough tongue, but it was trying to be sweet.

Two years ago, at this time, they'd had a record snowfall, and Jamie had been overjoyed that he could take the snowmobile out one last time for the season. It had turned out to be the last time ever.

Elenna sat in her car in the cemetery's parking lot for a full half hour, gazing at the few remaining mounds of snow on the ground mixed with patches of optimistic green shoots. Her phone rang twice. She let both calls go to voicemail, then felt guilty for not answering and listened to the messages.

The first was from her father. If he knew what day it was, he didn't say. He wanted her to know that he was home from Florida and he would be coming for a visit "after the black flies are gone," which meant she wouldn't see him before July.

The second was from Robert.

"Hi Elenna, I'm just calling to touch base." He let out an audible sigh. "That's sounds painfully formal doesn't it. Let me try again. I know this is a hard day for you. For all of us. I just wanted to say that I'm thinking of you, and if you need to talk, please call me." There was a pause on the line. "And my lawyer tells me you haven't deposited your check from Linford. I hope you won't turn down the money. I know Jamie would want you to have it. Take care Elenna."

She pressed the phone to her forehead and closed her eyes. The check was folded in her wallet. It was like carrying around a paper time bomb.

She sat in the car until the sun baking through the windshield made her uncomfortably warm.

Why was she hesitating? What was all this navel gazing going to accomplish?

Nothing.

She sighed and got out of the car.

Walking the short distance to Jamie's final resting place, she noted the difference in the weather. Two years ago, when she'd laid him to rest, the ground had been white and wet with slush. The grounds keeper had almost refused to dig Jamie's grave because the backhoe got stuck in the mud.

This April was still wet, but the snow had melted and optimistic green shoots pushed through the damp ground. Her eyes roamed up the stone that read *James Linford Nolan 1983-2023.*

He was named for his great uncle, the other Nolan who never conformed to family ideals. The same Linford whose check was still folded in her wallet.

She laid a green wreath over the headstone, stood back and tried to feel something other than the numbing cold. Two years ago, standing here, the numbness had come from overwhelming grief. Last year, she'd marked the anniversary by standing over his grave, shaking with rage for his selfish need to do everything bigger and faster.

This year? This year, the rage had ebbed, leaving sorrow in its wake, but not the all encompassing heaviness of the first months after his death. This sorrow was more wistful, a kissing cousin to regret.

And strangely, she didn't feel Jamie here, even though his bones were under her feet and the granite stone that would immortalize him for all eternity was staring her in the face. No, he was out there in the ether, not confined to a moldering casket. Maybe that's why the wind phone brought her comfort. When she spoke to it, she felt her words reach into the heavens. She'd find him there, not in this cemetery, where he'd never even set foot during his life.

She kissed her fingertips and pressed them to the cold stone, then turned and made the long trek back to her car.

On the way home, she stopped at the bank in Shawville to deposit her check.

With the warmer spring, Elenna's favorite shearer was overbooked. By the end of April, when she finally got an appointment, Luther and the alpacas were looking ragged.

Mike Lapointe was the only one who could handle Luther's antics. He was a big, sturdy guy who looked like he ate rocks for breakfast. Thick brows sat low over his eyes as he studied the alpacas huddled behind their llama commander.

"Might as well get the old bastard done first. He's gonna work himself into a right fit anyway when I start shearing the 'pacas."

That was the most words she'd ever heard Mike string together.

"Do you need me to hold him?"

"Oh, yeah. You'll have to put some muscle into it too."

"Okay, but before I get all covered in llama spit, can you come check out my new sheep? It looks like he hasn't been sheared in years."

Mike followed her to the goat pasture. Dasher stood out, partly because of his black and bronze wool that hung like the tattered cloak of the grim reaper, and partly because of his dual set of horns that framed his face like a warrior's head piece.

Mike whistled. "Is that a Hebridean?"

"I think so."

"What's wrong with his face?"

"I'm not sure. Birth defect, I guess." She felt bad that she hadn't had Milo check him out yet, but his last visit had been all about Sadie, and when a vet charged a minimum of two-hundred bucks just to come out to the farm, one only called for emergencies.

Of course, those financial policies didn't really apply to her anymore. She still had to kick herself sometimes when she realized she could afford things that had been way outside her reach only a few months before.

Mike had caught Dasher by the horns and was pulling at the matted fur under his chin. The ram didn't seem overly concerned.

"He's a pretty docile thing, isn't he?" Mike asked.

"Yeah, he's turning out to be an easy keeper. My little angel, really."

Mike smiled. He didn't need to tell her how funny that sounded. Dasher, the angel ram, who looked like the spawn of Satan.

"You'll probably need to have him dehorned, or at least blunted." Mike pushed his finger between one of Dasher's lower horns and his cheek. "This isn't normal. It's growing right into his jaw. He'll have trouble eating soon."

"I know. I'll get the vet to look at him next time he's out this way."

"Well then, let's see if he's an angel or a devil."

Mike's arms were as big around as Elenna's thighs. He easily caught the ram, locked his head under his shoulder, and started shearing. Thirty minutes later, Dasher was a new ram. He strutted away, showing off his sleek black skin with only a sheen of wool over it.

"Yep, a perfect angel." Mike rose and kicked the mass of wool into a pile.

"Don't worry, we still have Luther to contend with."

Mike grunted and gathered up his gear.

Elenna met him back at the alpaca house with halters for Luther and the alpacas.

They managed to corral Luther in the corner of the pen and get a harness on him. Elenna had set up a temporary pen inside their paddock and the alpacas twittered and fretted behind this barricade while Luther thrashed on his lead rope as she dragged him over to the shearing station.

"Best to hide his eyes," Mike said. "He won't know what's coming."

They wrapped Luther's head in a towel and Mike set to work with his no-nonsense determination. The shears glided up the front legs, then across his belly. The wool came off in undulating waves of brown and white.

Elenna hung on to the lead rope, while Mike secured Luther's legs. Unable to move, Luther resorted to spitting. And despite his blindfold, he had deadly accuracy. Elenna wore safety glasses, and they were already covered in green slime. So was her face, her neck, chest and arms. She couldn't spare a hand to wipe the muck from her cheeks without letting go of the rope, and the acidy sludge stung.

Gilly and Shaun watched from behind the fence and commented like announcers at a boxing match every time Luther landed another gob of spit.

"Ooh! That was a solid hit," Gilly said. Or, "He's battering them like shrimp," from Shaun.

"You two be quiet. Your turn is next." She licked her lips and tasted llama spit. Her stomach heaved.

Luckily, Mike was as efficient as he was strong. He was already shearing away the thick mane on Luther's neck. When he reached his chin, he stood back to admire his work.

"You want to risk doing his head? Or do we just leave him be?"

Elenna pulled off the towel. Luther's hair stuck out at all angles. With the rest of him shaved, he looked like a poofy lollipop. His crazy eyes matched the crazy do. He horked up another wad—did his supply never run dry?—that landed right on her chest.

"Oh! Direct hit," Gilly said. Elenna glared at her through the green sludge on her glasses.

"Let's leave him be," she said to Mike. "He's had enough for one day."

Mike nodded and led Luther toward the secure pen.

The alpacas were easier to handle and Elenna left them to Gilly's capable hands while she went to shower.

The green spit was drying on her cheeks and the puckered skin itched.

As she mounted the slope toward Kiso House, she saw someone coming up from the car park.

Oh, no. Not today. Not while she was basted in llama stomach acid.

But of course it was.

Milo waved. His smile was too big for even the beard to hide.

"Is this some kind of new skin care ritual?" He twirled a finger to encompass her whole, filthy ensemble. "Because I have to say, it's probably not that healthy."

"Says the guy who wears a squirrel wrapped around his face," she grumbled.

He tugged on the squirrel. "Touché."

She pulled off the safety glasses which probably didn't help her look. Milo smirked.

"Why are you here anyway?" She didn't mean to sound so grumpy, but she itched, and she couldn't stand the sour stench of herself any longer.

"I was just in the area on another call. I thought I'd come check up on Sadie."

"She's in the pasture. The alpaca shearer is here."

"Ah. That explains…this." He waved his hand in a circle by her face.

"Exactly. Can you give me a few minutes to get cleaned up?"

"Of course. I'll see if they need help." He nodded toward the sound of the shearer.

Elenna ran inside. Gado lifted his head at the intrusion and made a gagging noise when he smelled her, then went back to sleep.

"Good guard dog." She swept past him to the bathroom.

A quick look in the mirror made a tiny shriek escape her throat. Her hair was cemented into spikes by the green slime. She had reverse raccoon eyes from the glasses—pink skin surrounded by green sludge. A wet rag did nothing to clean off Luther's artwork and she jumped into the shower.

*Why did Milo have to show up today? Was it just to teach me humility? Fine. I got it. I'm thoroughly humbled.*

Then she remembered that she didn't care what Milo thought of her. They were just friends.

That didn't make her feel better.

She dressed quickly in clean jeans and a long-sleeved t-shirt. Her work boots were covered in slime so she slipped on runners.

Back at the alpaca pen, she found Mike packing away his gear. Gilly and Shaun were bundling the piles of wool into garbage bags. Later, they'd wash it and card it and sell it by the bundle to felters and spinners. One more product to help sustain the farm. Milo was nowhere in sight.

Elenna helped Mike carry his gear to his truck. "Thanks for coming out," she said. "I hope Luther didn't put you off too much. You're the only shearer who will deal with him."

"I should charge you more," he grumbled, but she knew he wouldn't. She suspected he took professional pride in being able to tame the famous mad llama of Equinox Farm. It looked good on his resume.

He waved and drove off.

Without their wool, the alpacas looked like plucked chickens running around the pen. Luther hadn't forgiven her for the recent indignities yet, but it was hard to be afraid of a naked llama with a poofy hairdo.

She opened the temporary barrier and let them into the main pen, then ducked out before Luther rekindled his spit glands.

The afternoon had turned out beautiful. Yellow sun filled the pasture like melted butter.

"Did you see where Milo went?" she asked the kids. Gilly pointed toward the low pasture. Elenna left them to finish cleaning the alpaca pen. She found Milo standing by the horse stocks, talking on his phone.

"Thank you, Jeanne. That's terrific. When do you think we'll close?" He listened for a moment and said, "Perfect. Thanks. I can't wait." He disconnected and turned to her with a grin.

"Pontiac Region just got a new vet clinic."

"What?"

"That's right. I just bought a place not far from Shawville. I close on it in three days."

"But that's…" She didn't know what to say. She frowned. Had he moved to be closer to her? Who did that? Who moved to a whole new town for someone?

Except she had done that for Jamie.

"You didn't, I mean…" She let her thought drift off, suddenly embarrassed by her assumption, but Milo picked up on it.

"You were going to ask if I made the move to be closer to you." To prove his point, he stepped into her space, not touching her, but just letting her feel the heat of his body.

"Well, did you?"

His eyes were locked on hers, forcing her to see the determination in them.

Then he shrugged. "Maybe. Or maybe I saw an underserved population and made a smart business decision."

Elenna cleared her throat. "Well, that's terrific. You're going to be very busy."

"I'm already busy. But this will mean spending less time commuting. And if I get too busy, I'll hire an assistant. I really like this area. I hope to be happy here."

The sun was setting and it lit him in a golden halo. His eyes were shadowed and as he watched her, they seemed fathomless.

"I hope you'll be happy too."

He lifted a hand to touch her face, but she turned away. When she risked a glance at him, she saw that his smile had turned wistful, and she wanted to kick herself.

"Hey, listen. While you're here, I have a new sheep with some horn problems. Think you can take a look?" That was a safe topic.

"Of course. That's what I'm here for." He stretched out his arm, indicating that she should lead the way.

MAY ARRIVED WITH A HEALTHY dose of optimism. Elenna stood by the pasture fence watching her little herd and breathed in the sweet scents of spring growth. Sadie seemed strong as she grazed in a halo of sunlight. She looked like an angel.

With the longer days and wildflowers blooming, Elenna's dark sorrow of the last two years seemed to mist away in the sunshine. Her fears for the farm's future had dwindled to nothing more than the normal worries of running a business. She had even convinced herself that her woods couldn't be inhabited by fae creatures. Hadley and Nina could believe in fairies and brownies and whatnot, but the more space Elenna put between her and those odd happenings, the more they seemed like nonsense—perfect fodder for her fiction, but nothing more. The blight was just over-active lichen. The odd noises were the sounds of trees creaking. And those glimmering fairies? Insects or a trick of the light.

Only in the dead of night, when she let her worst fears out to play, did that memory of the ghostly blue hand reaching from the black hole nearly choke her. But out here in the sunshine, watching her animals flourish? Out here, she didn't believe anything bad could touch them.

During the first week of May, she took Newton's fleece pajamas off for good as the nights lost their cold edge. He was still too skinny, but he ate and drank and played, and Milo had assured her that goats could live a long life with Cushing's Disease. She thought Jamie would be proud of how she'd managed with Newton, then thought, *Nope, I'm proud of myself.* And that was enough.

Sadie was also a source of optimism. After several rounds of meds and icing, her knee seemed fine, and with the snow gone, she was once again sure-footed in the pastures.

Elenna had mentally prepared herself for the worst. If Sadie fell again, she'd promised herself she would make that dreaded call to have her put down. The whole village had turned out to save her the first time, but Elenna couldn't count on that support again, and again. It wasn't fair to the people of Mullarkey and it wasn't fair to Sadie.

But for now, Sadie was standing. Yes, she would lose her one day, just like she'd lose Gado, and Newton and Bella. They were all getting on in years. That only made her determined to enjoy the time she had with them, and to give them all the love and dignity they deserved in their final years. That's what rescue was all about. Jamie had known it, and that knowledge was the best present he ever gave her.

Elenna turned to take in the rest of the farm. Her fingers itched for her sketchbook. New growth was springing up around every corner, painting the farm in hues of green, yellow and white.

The goats and newly shorn Dasher were grazing peacefully in the lower pasture. Excited quacking told her that Buffy, Willow and Xander were also enjoying their outside enclosure. Even Gracie Pig lay in the sun beside the barn.

They'd made it through another winter.

More good news pinged her phone. She glanced at the message. Two young women from France had answered her work-away call. Mathilde just sent a confirmation for their flight. She would arrive with her girlfriend, Théa, at the end of the month to take up residence in the farm cottage. They would get a summer of touring the Outaouais and Ottawa Valley and Elenna would get much-needed help around the farm.

The last bit of optimism was something she kept close to her chest like a warm fuzzy scarf on a cold day.

Milo was moving to the Pontiac.

She still refused to believe that his decision to open shop in Shawville had anything to do with her. But something pleasant simmered inside her, not hope exactly, but the faith that one day soon, she might be ready to let hope in.

THE SECOND WEEK OF MAY brought rain, but the days held their warmth and Elenna didn't begrudge the ground its quenching. Memories of last year's fires were still fresh, and she took the rain as it was meant to be—a gift.

On Saturday morning the rain finally fizzled out. The sky threatened another drenching, but it held off as she pushed her wheelbarrow through the mud toward the goat pasture. The ATV hadn't started that morning. She already had a call in to Felix, but until he could fix it, she was back to hauling the wheelbarrow.

After feeding the goats and sheep, she let them roam free in the pasture. Dasher had settled in nicely with the others. He was full of energy and gave Beezle someone to play with, since Newton didn't have the stamina and Bella disdained all forms of play.

His upper horns shot nearly straight back from his skull, and she'd padded them with foam swim noodles so he didn't impale the other goats in his exuberance. Milo had agreed with Mike, the shearer. The lower horns would need to be removed for his own health. She could already see how they were pressing against his jaw. Dehorning wasn't as simple as cutting off the horns. It was an invasive and traumatic procedure. She would have to do something about it soon, but not today.

Today she was going to enjoy the sweet smell of a wet spring.

She loaded up the wheelbarrow with used straw from the goat hut and was spreading it in the pasture when Ruby came bounding down the path from the forest.

"I thought you weren't supposed to play in the woods alone anymore," Elenna said. The coyote scare with Felix's sheep had finally knocked some sense into Ruby's mother, and the child had been forbidden from hiking alone.

Ruby bounced on her toes. "I'm not. I'm getting Max. He's going to show me how to hunt morals."

"You mean morels?"

"Yeah! He says they come out right after the rain. And we have to look really hard to find them. And if we're lucky the fiddlesticks will be ready to eat too."

"Fiddleheads?"

"Yeah, those!"

Delicate ferns grew in abundance along the river. If you picked them just as the leaves were budding, they were supposed to be quite tasty, though Elenna had never tried them.

Ruby was going on about wild leeks and asparagus in the fields.

"Well, don't keep Max waiting. And if you find any, I'd love to try fiddleheads."

"Sure thing." Ruby bounded through the pasture like a young colt, all legs and forward motion. Elenna watched her clamber over the gate instead of opening it and shook her head.

Had she ever had that much energy? She couldn't remember being as excited for anything as Ruby was for mushrooms.

She planted her rake in the grass and leaned on it. She was perfectly content.

That was the moment—the spark that ignited change. The cracking of ice that revealed a fork in the road she had never imagined. All kinds of possibilities suddenly opened in front of her.

When her work-away women arrived, she could take some time for herself. Hell, she could pay more farm hands to do the mucking and the feeding, leaving her to pursue other things, like drawing, writing and foraging…or even a family.

Newton, who was never far away when she worked in the goat enclosure, gently butted her arm.

"BLAAAAH!"

She scratched his head where the little horn nubs poked through the fuzz. Of course, she wouldn't give up all her farm chores. Her legs were pretty ripped from constantly tramping up and down hills. And she had to admit, there was something purely liberating about flinging poop in a pasture. And she would never want to give up Newton nuzzles. Or the gentle nickers from Sadie. Or Gracie Pig's obstinate demand for belly scratches.

No, the fork in the road was there, but it didn't mean she had to take it.

THAT AFTERNOON, AFTER FINISHING WITH the goats, she took her rake into the large pasture. As she got in her poo-flinging therapy, she noticed a flicker of light along the tree line, just past the fence. She glanced at the sky, thinking the sun was reflecting off something in the trees, but the clouds were dense and throbbing with the need to expel rain.

The light flickered again.

It was too early in the year for the fireflies that would come out on sultry July evenings.

She thought of the glowing winged creatures that had led her through the smoky forest. No way. No how. She was feeling good. The future was rosy, and she didn't need to be dragged into some fairytale.

She turned her back on the trees.

For the rest of the day, she mucked stalls, cleaned the duck pen, scratched Gracie's belly, fed the barn cats, hauled hay and water, scratched more bellies and ears, and completed the hundreds of chores that went into a regular farm day. By late afternoon, she was pleasantly exhausted. Her boots were covered in mud and water had seeped inside, leaving her feet uncomfortably cold, but the rest of her was overheated from exertion.

She decided to check on the goats one more time before heading in for a shower. Dasher and Beezle had found a new fun game called "dump the water buckets to make Elenna come running with more." She added a solid water trough to the list of much needed additions to the farm. Until she had time to install one, she checked the water in the pasture at least three times a day to be sure she wasn't leaving them dry.

For once, the mischief-makers hadn't dumped their buckets. In fact, they seemed subdued. Bella watched over her flock of miscreants with a look that said she wasn't buying it, and Newton hovered near the open door to the hut as if he might dash inside at any moment.

A glowing…something alighted on the fence. Elenna ignored it, and scratched Newton under the chin.

"Who's the best behaved goat ever," she said in baby tones.

"BLAAAAH!"

Another light appeared next to the first. Their long bodies perched on the fence with wings tucked along their backs and tails like damselflies. A third arrived. And a fourth. They were strung along the fence like Christmas lights.

Then one stood up.

The tail split and she realized it wasn't a tail at all, but outstretched legs. Arms broke away from the glowing body to hold onto the fence post, and as it stood upright, Elenna noticed distinctly human curves to the figure.

The creature let out a trilling noise that sent the goats into a frenzy. Even unflappable Bella hoofed it up to the hut. Her little herd milled around Elenna, bleating and prancing nervously.

More glowing creatures emerged.

"Go away!" She shooed them with her hands. "Go on!"

The lights zipped upward and into the trees.

"You're not yelling at me, are you?" Max's face was scrunched up. He'd come down the forest path just as the creatures took off.

"Did you see that?"

"See what?" Max looked up the path where she pointed.

"Never mind." She wasn't about to tell him she saw fairies.

Max was carrying a large basket that was half full of greens.

"I heard you were out morel hunting," she said.

"No morels today. Hard to find when the forest is so dark. Maybe the next sunny day. But the fiddleheads are out. So's the nettle. I even found some wild leeks in the field near the old gold mine. Would you like a few for supper?"

His hand shook as he lifted the precious leeks from the basket, but he wore a big smile as she reached for the gift. Then she realized her hands were filthy.

"Maybe you could just leave them by the barn on your way past the house?"

Max grunted an agreement.

"Ruby must have been disappointed not to find morels." Elenna rubbed her dirty hands on her dirtier jeans. "She was so excited. I think she thinks they're some kind of wild animal."

Max's brows scrunched together as he tucked the leeks back in the basket.

"Ruby? She didn't come out with me."

"Oh, why not?"

"Don't know. She showed up this morning before I'd even finished my coffee. Damned little eager beaver. I told her to come back after lunch but she never did. Probably found some other shiny thing to get excited about. She's like a crow, that kid." He laughed and waved as he headed up the path toward the house. Elenna watched him walk away, assessing his gait. He was still pretty sturdy on his pegs and she decided not to worry about him walking home. He wouldn't appreciate the suggestion if she offered to give him a lift anyway.

A sudden gust of wind blew through the trees and Elenna shivered. Her clothes were damp and the day had turned cooler. The sky boiled with dark clouds, making it feel later than it was.

She headed back to the house to change and let Gado out. Now in fresh jeans and dry shoes, she wrapped a thick cardigan around her and waited for him to finish his business.

He let out a deep "Woof!" and lifted his nose in the air.

"Come on, buddy. I can hear a nice cup of tea calling my name."

"Woof!"

Gado didn't get agitated. After ten years as a guard dog, he took retirement seriously. But something had caught his attention.

She peered toward the barn.

A trilling sound alerted her seconds before the little glowing body zipped past her nose.

Gado whined and pawed at the door.

"Some guard dog."

She let him inside, but didn't follow. Instead, she rounded the corner of the zen garden and looked toward the barn. The goat pasture lay beyond, and the forest was a dark stain past that.

Another light zipped around her head.

She stumbled forward. Two more criss-crossed over her back. She felt that stab like static electricity on her shoulder.

They were herding her.

The trilling changed to a sharp buzz as one flew by her ear.

"Okay, okay! I get it." They wanted her to follow. She held out her hand. "Lead the way. No, wait."

She ducked inside and grabbed her phone and her utility

knife, then headed back outside.

In one synchronized murmuration, the tiny creatures flew along the path, down the hill, over the fence, and across the goat pasture. She followed as fast as she could, but her runners didn't have the traction of her work boots, and she skidded down the slope, coming to a hard stop at the duck enclosure. The ducks gabbled and quacked in agitation. The goats were still huddled together, as if afraid to venture too far from the safety of their hut. In the far pasture, Sassy let out a raucous whinny and kicked out with her back hooves before taking off at a gallop around the fence line. The donkeys and Shin Mei were infected with her mania too. Only placid old Sadie kept her head.

What had them all riled up? Was it the fairy creatures? But they weren't anywhere near the horses.

And then she heard it too—a humming, like a swarm of bees. The sound intensified, growing in pitch and scale. It changed shape, no longer soft, but an angry, unnatural buzz, like metal scraping on metal, like claws scoring a stone wall, like giant teeth gnashing in fury, a grinding hell sound that whetted along her nerve endings to raise every hair on her body.

It blocked out even Newton's terrified bleating. Sassy was in a frenzy now and Elenna feared she'd leap the fence. She pressed her hands to her ears. The fairy lights swirled in agitated frenzy and she shut her eyes to block them out.

Then all at once, the sound died. The animals quieted.

She lowered her hands and opened her eyes.

And then a new sound came, faint and dreamlike this time… the terrified sobs of a child.

ELENNA SHOULD HAVE KNOWN THE fairy creatures were trying to tell her something. She should have opened her mind and her heart to the possibilities—no, to the realities that were right in front of her.

Later she would find time for self-recrimination. Right now, she had to find Ruby, for she was certain those were her cries echoing through the growing dark. And she was certain that the creature living under the rock in the blight was responsible. Elenna had no idea what magic Black Annis could conjure other than amplifying monstrous sounds, but she was about to find out.

Sunset was still an hour away, but underneath the forest canopy, the shadows took on new menace. Elenna ran, slid, stumbled, and ran some more. She tripped on a root and landed palms-down in the mud. The only sound in the forest was her labored breathing.

The sobs had quieted. That couldn't be a good sign.

The fairies fell back and zipped around her head. She felt a little zing on the back of her shoulder.

"I'm coming!" She rose and wiped her muddy hands on her pants, then followed the flashing fairy lights into the gloom.

She knew where they were taking her.

The blight.

With the spring rains, even the sound of the river was more violent. Instead of the gentle burble, it raged over barely submerged rocks.

By the time she skidded to a halt just outside the blight's boundary, the day was murky with gloom. Shadows stretched around the boulder with the precariously perched oak tree. They were full of veiled power and she could feel them bursting with desire to move beyond the confines of the blight, to creep into Elenna's world and swallow all the light.

The fairies melted into the forest, leaving her alone on the edge of the blight. Her toes bumped up against its boundary, and she had the irrational feeling that each thread of gray lichen turned to examine this new intrusion in their world.

"Hello?" Her voice fell like a stone on wet ground. The shadows by the boulder shifted. That eerie sound floated out of the darkness—part grumble, part laugh, part grinding of stone on stone.

Her eyes were adjusting to the deeper darkness. An object sat on the ground between her and the boulder. She squinted at the unfamiliar lines of…something. It was no taller than her knee and round. She leaned in. Was that a giant cabbage? She had a sudden vision of pod people from that old horror movie, and ominous music played in her head.

But no, it wasn't a pod.

It was a child wrapped in gray vines.

She bolted forward, no longer caring about the blight or the shadows. As soon as her foot landed on the lichen, a cackle of triumph shot from the hole like gunfire.

She ignored it. Her only thought was for the child. Ruby sat with her knees drawn up to her chest and arms folded around them. Her head was turned toward Elenna and resting on her knees, eyes closed. The vines cocooned her in an elaborate web, covering most of her face.

"Ruby! Can you hear me?"

She grabbed Ruby's shoulder and tried to shake her but the bindings held her in this stiff pose. Gray shoots bristled and squeezed tighter, like a boa constrictor strangling its prey.

Ruby's face was ashen, her lips ringed in blue.

From her pocket, Elenna pulled out the utility knife. Her fingers fumbled to open the blade, and she sucked in a deep breath before she slipped it under a vine and started sawing.

It was like cutting stone.

When she finally sheared through one vine, it snapped, scoring a welt across her cheek. Two more vines replaced it, twining tightly around the child.

"Ruby!" Her voice broke. "Wake up. You have to wake up."

She hacked at another vine, desperation making her clumsy. She felt like she worked in a vacuum and her lungs burned for enough oxygen. Stars prickled at the edge of her vision and the world spun.

The blight. It was the zone of Black Annis's power, and Tig had warned her not to step inside it.

She scrambled backward.

Laughter—dark and savage—chased her. She threw herself over the blight's boundary and heard a collective sigh as gray tendrils rustled.

Panting in the mud, she held the open blade in one hand. She'd scored her pant leg in her escape, and blood welled through the split material.

Ruby still sat in her unholy cocoon ten feet away. It might as well have been a hundred miles. Elenna couldn't reach her. Her mind raced for a solution.

Tig.

She knew about Black Annis. She was a cantankerous old bird, but surely she wouldn't let Ruby die.

Elenna stood and ran for the tiny cabin on the edge of the woods.

TIG WAS STANDING OUTSIDE HER cabin when Elenna arrived panting and weeping. The old witch didn't seem surprised to see her, and then Elenna saw that the little fairy messengers had arrived before her and were arrayed along the cabin's sloping roof.

"Yer bleedin'," Tig said in reaction to her incoherent babble about Ruby and cabbages and the Black Annis. She nodded toward Elenna's hand. The bloody pen knife was still open in her stiff grip. She looked down. The cut on her leg had soaked her jeans in blood.

"It's nothing. I cut myself. An accident." She sucked in a breath and shouted, "Why are you bothering about that? Didn't you hear me? Black Annis has Ruby!"

"Oh, I heard ye. 'Twas only a matter o' time." Tig chewed her bottom lip.

"You've got to do something!"

"Do I, now?" She squinted one eye and took a swig from the ceramic bottle that was never far away. Her medicine.

"She's bound by some unbreakable vine. I tried...I tried..." Her voice cracked and broke. She stared at the knife in her hand. "I couldn't cut through it."

"Not wi' that, ye won't. 'Tis fae magic. Ye need cold iron to break it, not that polluted metal." Tig sniffed. "Or blood. But ye need a lot more than a trickle." She nodded toward Elenna's hand that was sticky with blood.

Elenna stared, her mind numb.

Was this what shock felt like? Weren't people hospitalized for shock? She couldn't afford to be incapacitated now.

Tig leaned forward. Her breath reeked of alcohol. "I warned ye. A sheep would keep the old hag happy for weeks, but no. Didn't ye know better?"

"So, what? You're just going to let Ruby die?" Elenna shoved her face even closer to Tig's. Let her say it out loud.

Tig glared and chewed her bottom lip like a cow chewing cud, then finally she seemed to wilt as a big sigh left her lungs.

"Suppose not. Come on."

Elenna reluctantly followed her inside. All she really wanted to do was run back to Ruby. She stood on the threshold of Tig's tiny cottage, dancing from foot to foot. Pain scored her leg as the adrenaline from her run wore off and the wound began to hurt.

The cottage was windowless and stale with old smoke. The only light came from a fire that had burned down to embers in the hearth. A sleeping pallet lay against one wall. A rustic table and chair were the only furniture.

Tig muttered to herself as she rifled through several large floppy baskets that were piled in one corner. "Where did they go now? Ah, here they are."

She thrust a leather cord at Elenna. "Put that on."

It was a necklace, of sorts. A simple brown leather cord tied to a tiny metal charm shaped like a clothes iron, of all things.

Tig handed her a second charm. "For the child."

The second charm was shaped like a butterfly.

"Where did you get these?"

"On Etsy, where do ye think?" Tig grumbled something

about old hands no longer being able to work ore as she rummaged through the baskets.

"We need to go." Elenna glanced at the growing darkness outside.

"Don't be fretting, girl. I've no patience for fretters." Tig dumped a basket on the floor and began filling it with odd things—a pot of honey, a bag of grain, a wooden toy that looked like a carousel, bunches of sticks tied with string, and a black blade with a stubby handle.

She thrust the basket at Elenna and picked up a metal can with a spout.

"What's that?"

"Kerosene."

She couldn't be serious. Not when the forest fires that burned hot enough to send smoke to New York City were still a fresh memory.

Tig shooed her out the door. "Quit gawping and let's be done with this business."

Outside the sun was setting behind the clouds and the colors of the forest were muted and gray. The fairy lights zipped around their heads. Tig flailed her hands as if swatting flies.

"Damned piskays! Leave off! We're hurryin' as fast as we can."

The old bird took the lead and kept up a solid pace. Elenna's wounded leg burned, and she limped through the mud, trying to keep up with her. Not for the first time, she wondered how old Tig really was, and if the old hag posturing was just an act.

Then they were on the edge of the blight again and she had no more time to wonder.

Ruby was still as stone. Vines wrapped around her head, covering eyes and nose.

Tig held out the primitive knife. It was black with flecks

of rust, a flat triangular blade with a blunted handle all formed from one piece of iron.

"Start cutting away those vines." Tig pointed to Ruby's still form. "I'll set a ward. She'll be angry as a cat on fire when she finds out what we're doing."

"But the blight." Elenna's hand went to her throat. "It tried to suffocate me."

"But didn't ye run in all unprepared?" Tig tapped the amulet on the cord around Elenna's neck. She shoved Elenna over the blight's boundary. A cackle emanated from the boulder and ground down to a growl. Elenna crouched beside Ruby and started cutting. She waited for the dizziness to overtake her again, but her vision remained clear and steady. Tig's amulet was working. The vines snapped one after another under the iron blade, but for each tendril she cut away, two more blossomed around Ruby.

"It's not working!" She turned to find Tig walking the perimeter of the blight. With each step, she spread handfuls of grain while chanting in a language Elenna didn't recognize.

"Keep cutting!" From her basket, Tig took a bundle of sticks and planted it in the wet ground, then continued her circuit with the grain.

Elenna's hand was sore from gripping the rough blade, but she slipped it under another vine and cut. And cut. And cut. Ruby's lips were turning blue. Was she even alive? Elenna's hand trembled.

Cut. Cut. Cut.

An angry rumble came from the boulder. Vines burst forth and swallowed Ruby in a frenzy of greenery.

Elenna sat back on her heels, panting. A sob wrenched from her throat. She wiped sweat from her eyes with the back of her wrist.

"Come away now." Tig waved to her. Elenna stumbled backward, half crawling. The gray lichen felt like the skin of a giant beast under her fingers. As soon as she scrambled past the edge of the blight, Tig jammed the last bundle of sticks into the ground at her feet and shouted a word.

Later, Elenna would swear she heard that word, but she couldn't remember it. The moment it left Tig's mouth, the sound exploded. It concussed the forest, as if a meteor had slammed into the ground. The line of grain jumped into the air and Elenna saw that it encircled the entire blight.

The grains settled and the sound died. The forest was utterly silent and dark.

Tig picked up her basket and stepped over the bundle of sticks into the blight.

"Annis, let the child go. I offer ye gifts in return." Tig laid the jar of honey on the ground.

There was a deep silence, then came that grinding sound again. A figure slunk out of the hole under the boulder.

She crouched like a crab with elbows and knees jutting up from under a ragged black cloak. A hood partially hid her face, revealing only a bulbous nose and greasy hanks of soot-colored hair.

A blue arm with a gnarled and veiny hand reached from under the tattered cloth. The arm reached and reached, growing impossibly long, until it snatched the jar and in a flash, disappeared under the robe again.

"No." Black Annis's voice cracked like thunder.

Tig didn't waver. She pulled another tribute from the basket—the carousel. She wound a tiny key on the side of the toy and set it on the ground. Three wooden horses rose and fell in a parody of a gallop. Music tinkled from it—tinny like bells—and Elenna was reminded of the sound the piskays made. The jaunty music was haunting in the gloom and also magical. Simple chords strummed from a metal drum, one tine at a time. It seemed to draw the air from her lungs. It plucked at childhood memories—of laughter, and games of chase, of sunny trips to the shore and sweet, sticky cones of spun sugar.

The music died, leaving the day darker.

A single word came from the shadows.

"No."

Tig sighed. She pulled the can of kerosene from the basket.

"Ye leave me no choice. Let the child go or won't I be burning yer little camp on this earth to the ground."

Black Annis made that stone-grinding noise, then smiled, showing off yellowed teeth that were too big to be her own and sharpened to points.

The teeth weren't stone, but bone, as if the hag had fashioned dentures from spare parts of her victims. Elenna closed her eyes, not wanting to think of where she'd gotten those bones.

"I mean it." Tig held up the can of kerosene. "I'll burn it all. Ye'll have no way to go but back through the door."

"Traitor!" Black Annis hissed. "The queen will hear of your insolence."

Tig's arm was starting to shake under the weight of the can, but her voice was strong. "I'm betting yer not anymore welcome at the queen's court than I am, else ye wouldn't be here." She tipped the can, threatening to spill kerosene.

"The child will die too, if you burn us." Annis's voice was deep and sibilant.

"She'll die anyway, if ye don't let her go." The two old women glared across the gloom. It was a hag stand off. A battle of wills. Tension rippled through the shadows as palpable as static electricity. Elenna half expected them to start flinging magic missiles at each other.

Black Annis ground her bone teeth then snapped them as if snatching a bird from the air. She scuttled backward. The black cloak melted into shadows under the rock and she was gone.

The vines loosened and fell away. Gray leaves misted into nothing and the ropy stalks retreated into the ground.

Ruby collapsed sideways.

Elenna ran to her. Her fingers found a thready pulse on the child's neck.

"Put the amulet on her, before Annis changes her mind." Tig's arm had dropped but she still stared down the hole beneath the boulder.

Elenna dug into her pocket for the leather cord with the iron butterfly and draped it around Ruby's neck.

"Now get her home, sure quick," Tig said. "Ol' Annis will be wrathful now. I'll do what I can to strengthen the ward."

Elenna gathered Ruby in her arms—the child was as light as a spring lamb—and she ran.

THE NEXT DAY, ELENNA SWUNG by Auntie Clare's to pick up a couple of pies—one a savory tourtière, the other a sweet *tarte au sucre*. Hadley was busy in the kitchen and she didn't disturb her. She was still processing what had happened in the woods. Eventually, she'd ask Hadley and Nina about the fairies. But she needed to talk to Tig first.

She left the tourtière with Ruby's mother. The whole family had come down with the flu, so she hadn't been surprised when Elenna had brought the feverish and barely conscious Ruby home the night before.

Jan, Ruby's mother, accepted the gift of food with a wan smile. She looked run ragged and sick herself, but she assured Elenna that Ruby was making a full recovery. Elenna left her admonishments about letting a child roam free unsaid. What did she know about raising kids? And Jan looked like she had her hands full. She didn't need any ill-timed advice.

Elenna left, drove past her farm and turned up Rainbow Road to park at the end of the dirt track by the rusty fence that marked the boundary of the old gold mine. She skirted the fence and hiked across the open field to Tig's cottage. She'd come this way instead of taking the trail through the woods because she wasn't ready to walk past the blight again.

Tig accepted the sugar pie with a sniff. "Who'd be doing the baking now? Clare or the new girl?" Hadley had taken over the bakery nearly five years ago. She was hardly the new girl.

"I don't know."

Tig harrumphed and set the pie aside. "A tribute, is it? Like honey for old Annis?"

"It's a thank you."

"A mortal shouldn't be so careless with a 'thank you.' The fae twist such niceties. Thanks become debt, now don't they?"

"Does that mean you're fae too? Is that what the Black Annis meant when she said you weren't welcome at the Queen's court?"

Tig side-eyed her, then snorted. "It's your business, so is it?" She took a kettle off a hook over the hearth and poured hot water into a teapot. While she set out cups and plates, Elenna studied her cottage. Yesterday, she'd been too frazzled to notice much.

The one room was an eclectic mess of medieval furnishings mixed with a few modern touches. Bunches of herbs hung from the rafters. The only lights were kerosene lanterns. And yet, she spied a yellow Sony Discman sitting on a shelf beside a stack of worn paperbacks.

Tig set tea and pie for them both but didn't urge Elenna to sit. Instead, she scooped pie onto a fork and tasted it.

"Aaah, didn't Clare bake it after all, and isn't it sweet enough to ache in the teeth."

Elenna perched on the only other chair in the room, a three-legged stool, and watched her eat.

Finally, Tig sighed and put down the fork.

"Fine. Ask what ye'll ask."

The dam inside Elenna burst.

"How do you know so much about the fae? How did you know to build that ward and to barter with the Black Annis? How can you even be sure that *is* Black Annis?"

Tig took another bite and waved her fork. "It's as simple as an internet search, isn't it? " She leaned forward and pricked the back of Elenna's hand with her fork. "And aren't ye asking the wrong questions?"

What were the right questions? Her thoughts reeled and settled on the one dark truth.

"How do we stop her?"

Tig smiled. "Ah, that's a proper question, isn't it? The ward will hold her, for now. But don't be stepping inside that blight."

"Is that the source of her power?"

"Nay. 'Tis the proof of her power. 'Tis the bounds of her domain. Within the blight, she is all powerful."

"You mentioned a queen before. And a door. What does that mean?"

Tig sighed. "Ye need to do yer own research. I can't be teaching ye everything there is to know 'bout the fae, now can I? But I'll tell ye this much. There be two courts in Underhill, what ye might call Fairyland. The Seelie Court and the Unseelie Court. Black Annis, she won't be welcome in the Seelie court, sure. And hasn't she gone and opened a door to our world? Carvin' out a miserable home here, for even the dark queen o' the Unseelies won't be sharing bread with her now."

The longer she spoke, the more Tig's words became accented with that odd burr that hinted at Irish roots overlaid with some other accent Elenna couldn't place.

"So she's been banished?"

"There be a good chance."

Elenna took a bite of the sticky sweet pie.

There was a door to Fairyland under a boulder in her woods. Huh.

"As to how to stop her?" Tig's cheeks creased as she smiled, showing more gums than teeth. "Ye won't like it, sure. Some say ye drag the carcass of a poor dead cat around Annis's lair, three times, widdershins for sure. Still others be swearing that only a blood sacrifice will sate her—a goat will do. A child is better."

Elenna made a sound of protest and Tig held up her hand to forestall her. "Or couldn't ye go to the Unseelie court, sure. And petition the queen to intervene. But I'd not be suggesting that. Don't the Unseelie queen drive a hard bargain, harder than Black Annis sure, and ye'd be finding yourself enslaved for a hundred years."

"What about the police or, I don't know, a priest? Someone should do something."

Tig laughed. It was a sound like creaking wood.

"Oh, they should. Bring yer men with guns and crosses,

sure. Annis'll slink away into her hole, and won't ye be looking a fool. Or worse. The old asylums were chock full of folk who cried fairy."

"So we can't get rid of her?"

"We cannot." Tig squinted one eye. "But we can bargain."

"Bargain? You tried that. She refused everything you offered."

"So ye find something she wants more than blood, don't you?"

Tig dug out another massive piece of pie, and paired it with a swig from her flask. Elenna sighed and pushed her pie away. That first bite was sitting like a lump in her chest.

"Why does it need to be blood? And why children?"

"Children are life. Hungry for life, is old Annis. And stuck here on a few square feet of blighted ground, sure. No way of leaving. No home to go to. And yearning, she is, for home. The music, the food and dancing and frolicking. Poor wee sod. She'll be a clan of one now. And don't I know how lonesome that be?"

"Why can't you just burn her out like you threatened to?"

Tig's expression turned calm. She took a swig from her little bottle. "Could ye? Kill another. A being with a heart and a soul?"

The question made her squirm, but she held firm. "I'll debate the ethics later. I just want the facts. I need to know what we can and can't do to fight this…this monster."

"None of us are born monsters, sure."

Elenna glared at Tig, her jaw clenched so tight, it ached.

"Fine. Ye'd burn the blight, but wouldn't she only turn tail and hide in Underhill until she could return somewhere else." Tig squinted one eye. "Perhaps somewhere with no one around to watch her."

"Ah."

"Ah, indeed. And besides, the door to Underhill would stay

open. Don't we have too many unguarded doors in this valley, sure? For sooth, ol' Black Annis keeps the piskays from coming through if nought else."

"More doors?"

Tig waved the comment away, but Elenna filed it under a mental tab marked for further investigation. She left the old cottage with more questions stuffing her brain than answers, and she spent the next week learning everything she could about the fae, Underhill and the Seelie and Unseelie courts. She even learned about supposed sightings of Black Annis and her origins.

The Wiccans were particularly helpful in learning how to deal with the fae. If she hadn't just lived through an encounter, she would have laughed it all off as some delusional people who like to play at being witches. But the memory of Black Annis's grinding laughter, her pale blue face and strangely elongated arms haunted her days and nights. And so she mastered the rules of bargaining with the fae.

Don't eat anything made by their hand.

Don't follow them through any doorway, natural or unnatural.

Don't apologize or say thank you to a fae. They will consider your words and admission of a debt owed.

Do consider any bargains carefully because they will be binding, and fae are masters of twisting words to suit their dark needs.

Armed with this new knowledge along with Tig's echoing words, a plan began to gel in Elenna's mind, but she didn't have a chance to put it into play because the next day, Sadie fell.

Again.

The stories Elenna had read about fae beings and fae courts became a barrier between her and sleep—a barrier she couldn't get over. A week after her encounter with Black Annis, she spent a mostly sleepless night listening to rain batter the tin roof of Kiso House. Sometime before sunrise, she gave up and rose. Gado lifted his head from his plush bed.

"It's early. Go back to sleep."

He huffed and settled his head on his paws.

She padded barefoot to the kitchen for coffee, then drank it standing at the wall-to-wall window looking out at the zen garden. The sun was just starting to lighten the day. Fog fell like a curtain beyond the garden, blocking her view of the barn and anything beyond. The strategically placed meditation stones were stark against this white backdrop. Staring at that bleak landscape, something shifted inside her. A garden shouldn't be beds of stone. Gardens should be filled with color and life and disorder.

The world was full of wonders she could never know. Fairies, piskays, and darker creatures too. Things she might not fully understand and certainly couldn't control. There was no use pretending she could.

And that was what this house, what that garden, these blank walls and paper screens represented—an attempt to order the disordered. The un-orderable.

She had loved Jamie with all her heart—still did. But that didn't mean he wasn't flawed. Loving him meant she loved those flaws too. She recognized that now. And Jamie's biggest flaw was his need for control. It was reflected all around her. The house, the garden. Even his care for animals that had been thrown away by others. Even his need to drive every vehicle he owned faster than was safe. All that had been his way of showing the world he was in charge.

The thought made her a little sad. It hinted at fear, at a tiny boy inside him that needed to feel big and safe and never could. Maybe if he'd lived longer, he would have shown that side of himself to her.

She swallowed the last of her coffee and went to get dressed. She was exhausted from a night without sleep, but decided to get her feeding chores done early and then grab a nap.

The fog had thinned enough that she could make out the ghostly forms of the horses and donkeys in the pasture as she drove the old ATV down to them with fresh water, grain and hay. One of the ducks quacked and the sound was hollow in the fog. She parked near the lower gate, which was an easier access point for the ATV.

Opening the gate was always tricky with Sassy in the pasture. She would take any chance to escape. Not that she wanted to go anywhere in particular. She just enjoyed the challenge. From her seat on the ATV, Elenna scanned the pasture to plot out her entrance strategy. Sassy was a foggy apparition near the hay feeder. Shin Mei and the donkeys melded with the shadows inside the run-in shed.

Where was Sadie?

Elenna stood up, leaning over the handle bars to scan the terrain. A dark lump lay on the ground by the lower fence. The pasture sloped there and it was hard to see. The lump twitched.

Her heart froze in her chest.

It was Sadie. Her blond coloring was matted by mud as if she'd been thrashing in it. How long had she been down?

Elenna leaped off the ATV. Leaving it outside the pasture, she slipped through the gate and dashed down the hill. Her boots tore up the wet grass. Sassy whinnied. Elenna ignored her as she skidded to a stop by Sadie and knelt in the mud by her head. Brown eyes rolled to meet hers. Her mane was wet and muddy, and her breathing seemed labored as if she'd just given up the struggle to rise.

"Oh, my sweet girl." Elenna crooned and patted her neck. "I'm so sorry."

She knew what this meant. She'd have to make that awful call to Milo. It was time.

Sassy sensed something was wrong and galloped around the run-in shed. The muddy ground was treacherous and she slipped. That was all Elenna needed—another horse down.

Luckily, she always stashed extra harnesses and lead ropes in the ATV's small trunk. She bribed Sassy with some grain from the bucket and snapped on her harness. Shin Mei was easy to catch as always. She led the two horses through the gate and up the hill to release them in the upper paddock.

Then she called Milo.

It was still early. He was probably sleeping. The call went to voice mail.

"It's Elenna. Sadie is down again." Her voice hitched and she paused with her hand covering her mouth as if she could hold in the horror of her request. "Please call when you can."

She sucked in a gulp of breath, but it did nothing to calm her racing heart.

She dashed back to the pasture with more harnesses for the donkeys and brought them up too. Then she went to be with

Sadie. Her pasture mates didn't need to see her suffer, but Elenna didn't want the old mare to be alone either. Not now, not while she struggled to stand. Not during the last hour of her life.

She sat in the mud and braided the matted mane while she sang "You Are My Sunshine." It was foolish and her voice cracked, but she didn't care. It was Sadie's song. The one she sang to her when she wouldn't eat. It was her song because it went with her blond mane that flowed like sunshine. Her song because she'd been the sun that shone on Equinox Farm since the day she'd arrived, tired and retired from a life of pulling a plow.

Elenna's song dissolved into silent tears, and she laid her forehead beside Sadie's ear.

At some point, her phone beeped. She fumbled with cold fingers to pull it from her pocket and read the message.

*On my way.*

"Milo will be here soon," she whispered. "Don't worry. He'll make everything better."

Sadie heaved a sigh. The weight of her own body was making her breathing tortured. Her back legs flailed as if she was trying to stand, then she gave up and lay still.

Elenna patted her neck and buried her nose in the soft fur behind one ear.

"You just rest, baby. Everything's going to be all right." She continued with nonsensical babble, knowing the sound of her voice was more important than her words.

How long did she sit like that, soaking wet, muddy, with tears streaming down her face? It could have been minutes or hours. Sadie stopped struggling and Elenna's voice grew hoarse, but she kept singing and talking. She wanted Sadie to know she was loved, that she would never be alone.

It started to rain. The light patter made tiny splashes in the puddles. She didn't care. She was already soaked through from the wet ground. She wasn't leaving Sadie.

Not until Milo arrived.

It was then she noticed that Sadie was sliding. She'd fallen on the steep slope at the bottom of the pasture. While Elenna had been singing and crying, she'd slipped a good foot down the hill.

Unlike the goat pasture, which had a solid fence of wood and metal mesh, the horse pasture had only three strands of electrical wire with a one-by-six wooden board at the top. And Sadie was sliding right toward it. The flimsy wire would never slow the slide of a two-thousand pound animal. At best, she'd take down the whole fence as she slid past. At worst, the electrical wire would zap Sadie when she hit it.

The fence needed to be turned off, but the switch was inside the barn.

Sadie slipped another few inches downhill. Elenna didn't want to leave her, but she was only ten feet away from the fence now.

Oh, how she wished her new work-away women had already arrived and she had someone to call. Gilly would be on her way to school. Hadley would be elbow deep in flour as she made the morning pies. Nina…

Sadie slipped another foot down the hill. No one she could call would get here in time.

She turned and ran. Her boots slipped on the mud and she crawled up the hill, using her hands to brace herself. At the top of the pasture, she hit the gravel path at a run. She fumbled with the barn door, panting and half bent over with a stitch in her side. Ignoring the lights, she went right for the electric fence switch and shut it down.

Then she bent in two and would have vomited if there had been anything in her stomach. She wasted a precious minute to take a bottle of water from the small fridge and suck back half of it, then wiped her hands on an old towel. She could do nothing for her jeans that were covered in mud. There was no point changing now. She wanted to get back to Sadie.

*She must be so scared, lying there alone, unable to get up, unable to stop herself from sliding.*

She wiped fresh tears from her cheeks and went back outside. Sassy was rambunctious, so she threw an entire bale of hay into the paddock to keep her occupied.

The fog had lifted and the rain dried up. The clouds hadn't parted but they'd thinned enough to reveal a white sun.

Tires crunched on the gravel in the car park. It was too early for Milo to arrive from Ottawa, but she turned and saw his truck. He stepped from the cab and opened the back door to retrieve his medical bag. He met her beside the paddock. His eyes were dark and so full of empathy, she nearly crumpled.

He reached out to steady her. Her legs were trembling from cold, fear, and exhaustion.

"Are you okay?"

She sniffled and nodded. "You got here fast."

"I was at my place in Shawville. I'm renovating. It's just easier to camp out there than drive to Ottawa every day."

"Good. That's good."

His eyes drifted down the path.

"How is she?"

"She fell. I don't know when. I found her this morning. I got up early. Didn't sleep at all actually. It's a good thing, I guess…"

Her lips felt numb and she bit the lower one to stop the flow of babble.

Milo squeezed her arm. She hadn't seen him in weeks, not since shearing day. He'd promised to keep things professional and he had. Now he was here, looking at her with such heartfelt concern. He didn't seem to notice the mud on her face or her rain-plastered hair.

And suddenly, she didn't want him to keep his promise. She didn't want to stand alone anymore. She leaned her head against his shoulder. He shifted and wrapped her in a hug.

"It's okay. We'll take care of her."

"It's bad." Her words were muffled against the soft flannel of his shirt. "She's having trouble breathing."

He pushed her gently away and locked his gaze on hers. His hands gripped her shoulders and she had the irrational thought that they were the only thing holding her upright.

"We talked about this happening again, right?"

She nodded, not trusting her voice.

"We decided that if she fell again, it was time to let her go. Are you still okay with that decision?"

She bit her lip and nodded. Sadie was suffering. The falls meant she was weakening. She thought of her labored breathing and…

"Oh, she's sliding down the hill!" She grabbed his hand and pulled him down the gravel path. "I only came up to turn off the fence."

The slope meant that they couldn't see Sadie until they were right up against the pasture's upper fence. Elenna peered toward the spot of mud on the hill.

Sadie wasn't there.

"Oh, God! She's slid through the fence!" Elenna threw open

the gate and ran down the slope, expecting and dreading to find Sadie tangled in the wire fence.

But she was gone.

Elenna blinked.

She wiped rain from her eyes.

Just—*poof*—gone.

"She was right there. I swear. I'm not going crazy." She thought about the last few days, the dark fae in the woods and everything else she'd seen. Maybe she *was* going crazy.

"She fell. Right there. I sat with her in the mud for an hour. She can't get up on her own, you know that."

Milo squeezed her shoulder. "It's okay. I believe you." He pointed to the streak of mud on the hill. It stretched like a landslide down to the fence and past it.

They skidded down slope. Elenna came up hard against the fence.

"She went under," Milo crouched and tapped the electric wire hesitantly with a finger. It was dead.

"Thank God I turned it off. But how did she get up?"

"I don't know. Maybe the momentum of the slide gave her leverage?" The sun was peeking through the clouds and Milo shielded his eyes to scan the grassy area between fence and woods. Elenna followed his gaze.

Where was Sadie?

She thought of the entire village coming out to raise her the first time, the elaborate web of straps the General had constructed and the strain on Felix's tractor as it lifted the heavy mare. And she remembered the sound of Sadie's labored breathing and how her efforts had already exhausted her.

"It seems damned unlikely she got up on her own."

Milo rose and scanned the forest. "The question is, where did she go?"

If Sadie was outside the fence, she could have wandered anywhere.

Milo ducked under the wire and Elenna followed. The mud slide ended beside the creek and a few hoof prints headed off toward the duck pen. But how? They followed the tracks until they disappeared on the gravel path, then followed that.

The ducks gabbled in their pen and she could hear Beezle bleating to get out of his stone hut. They found Sadie standing in the gulley by the creek. Piskays sat on her back in a line of glowing lights. Sadie watched Elenna and Milo approach with her usual poise, then shook her golden mane. The sun broke through the clouds and glinted off piskay wings as they took flight.

"Did you see that?" Milo pointed. Elenna shook her head, but not in denial. She didn't have the energy to explain just then.

Milo took her hand and tucked it around his elbow. They watched Sadie—the miracle mare as Elenna would now call her.

"Isn't that the most beautiful thing you ever saw?" Elenna's heart was so full, she could feel it pounding in her chest.

"Almost," Milo said. She turned to find him watching her, a small smile peeking through his ruff. He cleared his throat like he was about to make a dire announcement. "I know I promised to behave, but I can't help thinking that magic happens when you're around, and I want to be a part of that, if you'll let me. That is if you can stand the beard."

Elenna's hand came up, and she ran her fingers along his jaw. He leaned down and kissed her, a soft touch, full of promise. She put a hand on his chest and looked into his eyes. Her tongue darted out to lick the taste of him from her lips.

"I like the beard." She smiled. "How do you feel about fairies?"

ELENNA ADDED A VASE FULL of spring flowers to the ledge of the *ofuro* tub. They were a wild assortment of white, pink and yellow that clashed spectacularly with the more restrained orchid. In fact, the orchid looked a little put out to be sharing its window seat with weeds. Elenna didn't care. The burst of color made her unreasonably happy.

She'd just come in from planting native perennials in the zen garden. Gone were the rocks and meditation stones. In a few weeks, the space would be transformed by color and buzzing bees.

Likewise, the inside of Kiso House had undergone a transformation. She'd finally painted the living room. The dusky pink filled it with soft light. A complimentary sage green would go on the walls in the living room. She'd already hung three paintings picked out from local artists, one was a spectacular acrylic of a fairy hanging in pollen laden air that was kissed by a yellow sunset.

Her world was full of color.

She hummed to herself as she stripped off her clothes and turned on the shower. Seven jets pummeled her with water and she decided that Kiso House had some perks that she would keep.

After she dressed, she went down to the kitchen to finish the preparations for her date. She wrapped the apple pie in a clean dish towel and stowed it in the picnic basket beside a loaf of beer bread, a simple salmon mousse, and a hunk of aged cheddar.

Other than the cheese, she'd made everything herself. Apple pies were the only pastry she could muster. Hers wasn't as pretty as Auntie Clare's or even Hadley's, but it would taste good. And for her purposes, it was more important that she made it with her own hands.

She added some old crockery plates. They had a few chips so she didn't worry about them getting smashed in a fit of fae pique. And as an afterthought, she added a bottle of sparkling cider and two ceramic mugs.

The ATV waited by the back door with the wagon already attached. She added the basket to the wagon beside a large sack of oats and four alder saplings that she'd cut earlier. Each alder was about three inches in diameter and five feet tall. Rowan would have been better, but it didn't grow well in Quebec. Alder grew in rampant thickets around the swampy patch near the lower pasture, and her research told her it could replace rowan in a pinch.

She straddled the seat, started the engine and drove around the pasture. The horses and donkeys looked up at the sound of the engine. Sadie's golden mane seemed to glow in the late afternoon light. She had no ill-effects from her recent adventure, and Milo had proclaimed her sound. They fully expected Sadie to enjoy many more years as the heart of Equinox Farm.

Elenna turned the ATV down the path at the far end of the pasture and across the little wooden bridge by the duck enclosure. Gilly, Ruby and Shaun looked up from their work and waved. Elenna could see they'd already staked out ground for Shaun's newest construction. Two bunnies had been left on her doorstep a few days ago, no doubt castoffs from another failed Easter present.

Ah, the joys of springtime at the rescue.

Shaun had graciously agreed to build them a shelter if Gilly would help. She would miss those kids when they went to college next year.

Ruby bounded over to the path and she slowed.

"Can I come with you?"

A week had gone by since Ruby's abduction by the Black Annis, and she seemed to have recovered with no ill effects. She'd said she didn't remember what had happened that day in the forest, and Elenna had decided not to fill her in on the details, but she was glad to see Ruby still wore the iron amulet.

"Not today, kiddo."

Ruby frowned. "Besides, I think Gilly and Shaun need your help. They're terrible at finding names for rabbits. But I bet you could do that job."

Her face brightened. "Really? I can name them?"

"Really, really."

Ruby ran back to the others to tell them the news. Elenna put the ATV in gear and drove into the forest.

She parked a few feet from the blight. In the silence after cutting the engine, she listened to the forest. The spring runoff had slowed and the stream's rushing roar had dimmed to a comforting burble. Birds tweeted from branches and a red squirrel scolded her for intruding into his domain.

She set to work. First, she took the mallet and alder poles from the wagon. She pounded one post into the ground by each of the bundles of rowan sticks that Tig had left. She didn't know any fancy spells or gods to invoke, but her research said that intent was more important, and words were only used to focus. As she tapped each post into place, she filled her mind with love for this forest, for this place filled with life and wonder. She thought of the delicate trilliums that were blooming right now under the tall pines and oaks; the pale purple asters that would come later; and the orange chanterelles that popped up in the fall. She thought of the beauty that came with ice storms when late crab apples became encased in ice like jewels under glass. She even included the scolding squirrels and piskays in her thoughts.

She loved it all, and she pounded that love into the ground with every strike of the mallet.

Next, she took the bag of oats and walked the perimeter of the blight, laying a trail of grain from one alder to another. By the time she finished, she felt someone watching her.

She resisted the urge to grasp the iron amulet at her throat. Turning, she spied Black Annis crouched just outside her lair.

Sun dappled through the old oak tree growing around the stone, but rather than highlighting her features the shifting light seemed to make Black Annis more insubstantial.

Music played, a tinkle of bells like from a far-away dream.

"That flimsy ward won't keep me from your world." The voice creaked like floorboards settling in an old house.

Elenna lifted her chin and didn't shy away from staring at the hideous blue face. "It's just a safety net. I have a bargain to strike with you. These alder posts will tell me if you keep that bargain."

Black Annis cackled and clacked her teeth. The music stopped.

"Go on."

Here it was. She was putting all her chips into the pot, betting on a hunch.

"I've learned a few things about you and your kind since we last met."

"You know-know-know nothing of me." She stuttered as her ill-fitting teeth clacked.

"Maybe not, but I can make some guesses."

Elenna stepped over the border of the blight, praying that the protection of her iron amulet held.

"I think this gray lichen does your bidding, and you have power only where it extends. I also believe that you're lonely, cut off from your people and your court."

Black Annis suddenly disappeared and reappeared right in front of Elenna, so close she could feel the breath puff from her flaring nostrils.

"You presume too-too-too much, human." She slid her jaw sideways and the bone teeth ground like a mortar and pestle.

Elenna straightened her back and met Black Annis's gaze. "I know that this is my land. And you're trespassing."

Black Annis stared, then her face crumpled. At first Elenna thought she was crying, but the wheezing, clacking sound was laughter.

"Shall you wave a paper deed in my face." She leaned forward until their noses touched. Elenna's vision was filled with the sight of her black irises and yellow sclera. She held her ground. "Will I recoil in the face of human laws, human words that might as well be written on sand? Hmph." She settled back and clacked her teeth in agitation or in threat, Elenna couldn't tell which.

"You may think that human laws don't apply to you. But if you push, you will find that humans don't want to know what goes bump in the night. If they find out, they will come, and not with pitchforks and torches as you might remember. They will come with guns and firebombs. If you're lucky, they will only kill you. Or they might find that door to Underhill you're hiding back there and go through it to kill everyone in your Queen's court. One thing humans are very, very good at is killing."

Black Annis hung her head, but she wasn't giving in. She was thinking.

"So what is this bargain you pro-pro-pro-pose." She clacked her teeth again.

Elenna's nails were digging painfully into her palms. Remembering the warnings about bargaining with fae, she measured her words carefully.

"I will allow you the use of this bit of land. The alder posts mark the boundary. You are free to hunt any beast that comes inside it. The fish that swim through your section of the river are yours. The birds and animals that are unwise enough to venture into the blight? They are yours. But you will not hunt children or any human, even if they stumble unknowing into your territory." She had thought about this wording for a long time, and she hoped that covered all her bases.

"And in return, what do you offer me, human?"

Elenna let out a rough sigh. "I offer you my friendship."

Black Annis's head whipped up and Elenna forged onward before she could protest. "I think you yearn for the company of your court in Underhill. I think you came here not because you wanted to, but because you were exiled."

Why else would a creature with Annis's power concede to live under a rock in a foreign land?

"You conjure music from Underhill to soothe the nostalgia and the loneliness that eat at you. So I propose a friendship. I will eat dinner with you, once a month on the new moon." She threw that bit in there because the fae took great stock on the phases of the moon.

Black Annis cocked her head. Her teeth rattled.

"You would break-break-break bread with me?"

"Yes, but with conditions."

Black Annis scoffed.

"Hear me out. We eat only food prepared by my hand. I will

not taste any food you make, nor drink any drink you pour. I won't go through any door with you, so we'll eat out here. And every visit, we alternate who gets to choose the music."

Black Annis considered her. A long whine rumbled from her chest and when she finally spoke, the words lashed from her like knife strikes.

"Twice a month. New moon and full moon or no-no-no deal."

"Deal." As soon as she said the word, Elenna felt a pulse of power burst from her. It rippled across the lichen, making the tiny tendrils jump until it reached the edge of the blight, then the power dissipated with the concussive bang.

Black Annis grinned.

"Good. Well. That's done." Elenna's heart was beating like a startled bat. "Shall we eat on this new moon day?"

Black Annis clacked her teeth and let out a raucous laugh.

"Fine, human. Bring your food. Bring your music. Annis will take-take-take them and claim this thing you call *friendship*."

She leered and Elenna imagined that in Black Annis's mind the word *friendship* had been replaced with *soul*. But she'd come this far. She'd struck the bargain.

Annis watched as she laid the gingham cloth on the ground and pulled out the food.

"Made all this, did you?" Annis sidled over to crouch at the edge of the feast.

"Everything but the cheese and the cider, but they're both locally sourced."

Annis dipped a claw into the salmon mousse and licked it. She let out a hiss, but it couldn't have been a displeased sound, because she loaded her plate with more mousse, bread and cheese.

Elenna set out the Bluetooth speaker and turned on her Quebec Folk playlist.

Annis froze with a hunk of bread halfway to her mouth.

"What is that noise?"

"Salebarbes. Too rockabilly?"

"Are they gutting a cat then?" Annis's lips twitched. Had she just made a joke?

"Fine, then tell me what kind of music you like for next time."

Annis grunted. Several minutes of silence went by while she stuffed herself with cheese, bread and pie. Elenna was starting to think that friendship was beyond reach with the odd fae.

When the plates were clean, Black Annis leaned back. "Flutes. I like flutes."

Elenna smiled. "Well, then next time I'll find a flute playlist for you."

An hour later, Elenna stopped the ATV by the old mill. The sun was low, and the shadows around the wind phone were deep, giving her privacy.

With no hesitation, she picked up the phone, dialed Jamie's number, then immediately launched into a recounting of the events of the past few days, starting with her encounter with Black Annis and ending with Sadie's miracle.

"You should have seen her, standing there in the sunshine like some kind of angel. You would have been proud of your

Sadie girl." Elenna paused with the phone wedged between her ear and shoulder. The sun was setting. She'd been talking for almost an hour.

"It's strange isn't it? How things that seemed impossible, frightening or insurmountable, just become…normal over time?" She listened to the phone line that stretched to infinity. It no longer seemed empty. It was a big sound, vast like the breadth and width of the universe, but not empty.

"Anyway, I thought you should know that I met someone special. You'd like him." She thought of Milo's calm energy and laughed. "Actually, you probably wouldn't. But *I* like him and I know you want me to be happy. And I hope…" She dragged in a deep breath and let it out. "I hope wherever you are, you're happy too. Thank you for everything you gave me, everything you taught me. You'll always be in my heart, no matter what, but it's time I stop holding myself back," she let out a ragged laugh, "in so many ways. Goodbye, Jamie. I love you."

She hung up the phone. The shadows reached deep into the forest now, but she no longer feared the things living in those shadows. She followed the path up to the old mill and stepped out from under the lush canopy to see the sky on fire.

Streaks of red and green jutted into the darkening sky like gossamer fingers, slowly waving.

Wow.

She stood rooted as the last sunlight faded and the Northern Lights grew bolder, filling the sky with their ethereal dance.

Her phone vibrated.

> *Just sent home the electrician. Want to get a bite?*

Milo was almost finished the renovations on his new building that housed his office and an apartment. Her fingers tapped out a response.

> *Go look outside.*

She waited a beat until he texted back a single mind-blown emoji.

Music lilted over the trees, the folksy strains of Émile Bilodeau telling God, *it's okay, I'll walk.* It was a perfect accompaniment to the dance in the sky.

She sent another text.

> *Meet me at Auntie Clare's. Warrick is cooking tonight. Bring wine.*

Milo sent back a thumbs-up. She headed down the road toward Auntie Clare's, pulled onward by the music and the scent of hot fries and gravy. The General waved to her from the other side of Mill Road. Instead of waving back, she crossed the road and tucked her hand around his elbow.

"The gang is mustering at Auntie Clare's," she said. "Can I treat you to poutine?"

The General's eyebrows rose, then his stern expression melted into a grin and he nodded.

# Acknowledgments

*Black Annis Year* is my heart book, the one I've been wanting to write for a long time. Many of the animal stories in it are inspired by my own adventures caring for rescues, either my own or when volunteering at rescue farms. Though I changed the names of the animals many of them actually existed, like Sadie, the old plow horse. She did fall. And a community of volunteers did come to get her standing again. And the second time she fell? Yes, I sat in the mud for her while I waited for the vet to come put her out of her misery. And yes, she got up on her own against all odds. The sight of her standing by the river is one I'll never forget. It's a memory that still makes my heart hitch in my chest.

Other animals in Black Annis Year have real life counterparts too. Shin Mei is based on my gelding, Booker, and I once described his Teeth & Sheath day in all its gory detail on my blog. Likewise, Luther is loosely based on a real llama with anger issues, and you can read about my experience with him in the blog post titled, That Time I Wrestled an Angry Llama.

For other inspirations, I want to thank Tauney Stinson of Forager Bee for help with foraging questions. Two more thank yous go to the wonderful artists who created the cover and interior art, Christian Bentulan and Anthony Smith. As always, I want to thank my editor, Elaine Jackson, for pushing me to make the book better when my energy flags. And I am also very grateful for the blessing that is my daughter, Genevieve Chatel. I so love watching her stretch her creative wings, and she helped me with several scenes in this book. Finally, thank you to my Advanced Reader team! I can't tell you how much I rely on you to make every book launch a success. Your continued support means more to me than you know.

I also want to give a big, loud, brilliant shout out to my readers, especially the ones who followed me from a post-apocalyptic Montreal to a steampunk subarctic and now to a small town in Quebec. I enjoy writing in different genres, and I am so grateful that many readers enjoy crossing these boundaries to continue reading my books. Thank you!

*Kim McDougall*

# Reviews Help Everyone

You probably know that authors love reviews, but do you know why? Reviews are important to every author, for the following reasons:

- They help other readers know what to expect from the book.
- They let me know how my books are received by readers.
- They help booksellers decide which books to show to new readers.

If you enjoyed this book I would be grateful for your honest review. It can be as short as you like. Even a few positive words will go a long way. And I'll try to make it as painless as possible. Use this link, KimMcDougall.com/Review-Black-Annis-Year to find the review site of your choice.

Be sure to sign up for the Readers' Group at KimMcDougall.com/Readers-Group to get updates on new releases. When you subscribe, you'll get two free ebooks just for subscribing.

Thank you for reading *Black Annis Year* and I hope you'll return to Mullarkey Mills for more adventures.

# WHAT TO READ NEXT?

**A royal tinker and a rogue soldier must unite to stop the monsters threatening their city—and unravel the secrets lurking within it.**

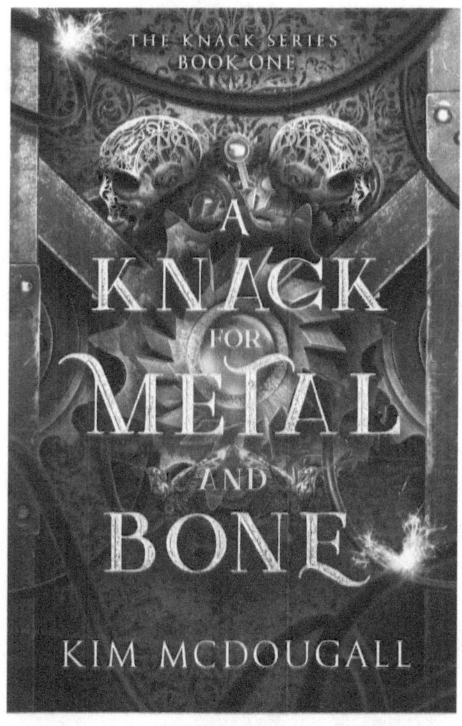



Rowan doesn't just work with machines—she hears them. The hum of engines, the whisper of gears and wires—they speak to her through the magic that flows from her mech hand. Whether she's fine-tuning the colossal automaton that protects New Torwood City or toiling in her workshop, being a mechanic is the only life she truly enjoys. But the Regent's Council wants more. They demand a princess who will embrace the pomp and ceremony of royal duty, not a tinker with oil-stained hands.

When she's unexpectedly recruited into Ranger Squad 54 for a mission deep into the wild Meadows, Rowan leaps at the chance. Finally, a way to serve her city and put her unique talents to use—far from the glittering halls of royalty.

Conall, an ex-commander, knows the dangers of the Meadows firsthand. Discharged from the Rangers when his inner wolf broke free during battle, he now makes a living running rare artifacts between New Torwood and the southern cities. But the Rangers have a new mission for him—one that could clear his tarnished record. A group of international scientists has vanished, and recovering them is critical for the future of New Torwood. Failure could push the city into a war it cannot afford.

Thrown together on a high-risk mission, Rowan, Conall, and the Rangers of Squad 54 will face unimaginable dangers in the wilderness and uncover dark secrets that could shake the foundations of the city they've sworn to protect. But the real menace might be at the heart of New Torwood itself.

Embark on a thrilling adventure with *A Knack for Metal and Bone*, the first book in an epic new fantasy-steampunk series from the author of The Valkyrie Bestiary.

Find out more at <u>KimMcDougall.com/Knack</u>

# More Books by Kim McDougall

**The Knack Series**
A Knack for Metal and Bone
Mech and Magic


**Valkyrie Bestiary Novels**
Dragons Don't Eat Meat
Dervishes Don't Dance
Hell Hounds Don't Heel
Grimalkins Don't Purr
Kelpies Don't Fly
Ghouls Don't Scamper
Devils Don't Lie
Unicorns Don't Cry
Worlds Don't Collide


**Valkyrie Bestiary Novellas**
The Last Door to Underhill
The Girl Who Cried Banshee
Three Half Goats Gruff
Oh, Come All Ye Dragons
Thorn of Vioska


**The Hidden Coven Series:**
Inborn Magic
Soothed by Magic
Trigger Magic
Bellwether Magic
Gone Magic

# About the Author

 If Kim McDougall could have one magical superpower, it would be to talk to animals. Or maybe to shift into animal form. Definitely, fantastical critters and magic often feature in her stories. So until she can change into a griffin and fly away, she writes dark paranormal action and romance tales, from her home in western Quebec. Visit Kim online at www.KimMcDougall.com.

www.ingramcontent.com/pod-product-compliance
Lightning Source LLC
Chambersburg PA
CBHW021040310726
48969CB00006B/1747